AVA MOSS

by

JOSS LANDRY

Book Beatles LLC
1201 N Orange St Suite 700 #7417
Wilmington DE 19801-1186

Copyright © 2016 by Joss Landry

Book cover design: Ida Jansson of Amygdala Design
Editing: Jill Noel of Book Beatles LLC
ISBN: 978-0-9960441-0-3
ISBN: 978-0-9960441-1-0 (ebook).

Publisher's Cataloging-In-Publication Data (Prepared by The Donohue Group, Inc.)
Names: Landry, Joss.
Title: Ava Moss / by Joss Landry.
Description: [Wilmington Delaware] : Book Beatles LLC, [2016]
Identifiers: ISBN 978-0-9960441-0-3 | ISBN 978-0-9960441-1-0 (ebook)
Subjects: LCSH: Women professional employees--New York (State)--New York--
    Fiction. | Financial institutions--New York (State)--New York—-Fiction.
    | Computer fraud--New York (State)--New York--Fiction. | Supervisors--
    Fiction. | Man-woman relationships--Fiction. | Suspense fiction. |
    LCGFT: Romance fiction.
Classification: LCC PR9199.4.A54 A93 2016 (print) | LCC PR9199.4.A54
    (ebook) | DDC 813/.6--dc23

Acknowledgments

Some days, writing a novel is like climbing a mountain.
Loose rocks underfoot can make us fumble.
Strongholds on scenes we visualize need tightening.
We focus on direction
while keeping distance to the peak short and straight.

Other days, writing a novel is like swimming in the ocean.
Vastness of choices abound fluid their motion perpetual.
Waves of emotion roll over us to draw salted tears.
We struggle to stay afloat
and risk drowning holding on to the perfect word.

Some days, we take in the affection
and encouragement of those who believe in us.
Thanks to the love of children and sweet grandchildren,
I remain grounded and anchored in reality.
Loads of gratitude to a devoted, dedicated husband
whose energy I pluck when I need to reflect on my deeds.
Last but never least, thank you Rabboni
for loving me and walking beside me.

Everyone needs a little Ava in their life.

Writing this novel, I found catharsis
in Ava Moss' unbridled innocence,
in her friends' warmth and support.
Life often rewards those who embrace
the present and all it has to offer.
Each time Ava smiles at the sweet,
small distractions, she discovers a new rainbow.
Moreover, the more courage she puts out,
the more blessings she receives.

CHAPTER 1

AVA'S FRIENDS

Ava brushed a piece of lint off her blue suede suit. Leaning against the kitchen counter, she waited in a daze for the bread to pop from the toaster. Coffee in hand went a long way to drying the weekend fog out of her brain.

Gazing at the plastic-framed mirror hanging above the toaster. a relic from the cage of a pair of doves the former tenant had cherished, Ava spotted in her eyes how much tougher on the human body were Monday mornings. In a hurry to drop the deer-caught-in-the-headlights glare, she glanced down at the toaster again her hypnotic stare willing the old shabby metal tool to work faster.

She tucked a strand of hair behind her ear uncaring the light auburn tresses Emile, the Fifth Avenue stylist, had tossed and feathered on Friday afternoon sat on her head without an inkling of chic—fluff and volume still buried deep in the pillow. At least, the shoulder-length cut gave the curve of her face more authority and cranked her nose up a notch.

She jumped when the toaster popped and juggled the hot slices while walking to the table. A little breakfast for little Ava. Of course, she appreciated being able to squeeze into a size two, but she loathed her five feet two-inch stature. How was she ever going to make a serious dent in the world of finance looking like a Kewpie doll?

A champagne flute stretched beside the strawberries blushing in a bowl next to her toasts. Graduating top of her class Ava considered well worth celebrating—studies she began when computers featured 128 MB of RAM processed by 480 MHz.

Ava gazed at the liquid tilting gold under the light and imagined the alcohol's pale reflection symbolizing her concerns over appearance—clever blindfold to mask the fact that abandoned at birth, she still lived alone twenty-seven years later.

"Here goes," she whispered. The bubbles filled the back of her mouth and spewed bitter vapors out her nose. She rose to dump the rest of her drink in the sink. Two new lessons tucked away in fat little drawers of her tiny hippocampus. Strawberries did enhance the taste of champagne or perhaps champagne enhanced the sweet berries. Secondly, more creative methods existed to celebrate her long-awaited degree in finance.

A few bites later, she plopped what remained of her breakfast in the disposal. A hand on her midsection helped soothe the knot in her belly. A meeting with top honcho Reynard Wallace would be filling enough. Reynard, Granger Wallace's eldest son and head of one of the oldest and most philanthropic families of New York City, presided over Extrade Designer Group, an investment entity catering to a demanding and wealthy clientele.

Two turns of the locks and one bolt later Ava headed for the elevator and encountered Mrs. Chapel, an eighty-year-old coiffed in blue hair and wearing a blue dress. Most mornings they'd take the trip down together as Elspeth Chapel needed help to venture to the lobby to collect day-old mail.

"Good morning, dear, you're going to be cold. Air is chilly today."

"Good morning, Mrs. Chapel." Ava looked down at her suit. "I'll be all right." She hesitated. "I'm taking a cab to work today."

"A little birthday treat I imagine. Good for you, dear."

"Thank you." Ava decided to omit the part about her birthday being the week before when an afterthought prompted, "How did you know?"

"Jeff, our smart doorman reminded me." Of course, Ava realized Jeff's tasks amounted to more than simple door attendant. He also saw to the smooth running of the building and contracted help whenever the tenants needed a plumber, an electrician or even a doctor.

The old woman dug a gnarled hand into Ava's arm, and Ava remembered to keep her bearing steady to support Mrs. Chapel. "What you need is a young man, dear." Faded blue eyes blinked up at her more from myopia than mischief, and Ava nodded to the comment she ignored at least twice a week.

When the elevator stopped, Mrs. Chapel shifted Ava's arm to get into gear and after readying her stance, she looked up and patted Ava's cheek. "You look more like her every day."

As Mrs. Chapel tottered away at the speed of a slow turtle, Ava asked, "Who do I look like?"

Without looking back, Elspeth's voice trembled as she added,

"Myriam of course."

Ava drew a blank. Aware of Mrs. Chapel's daughter, Mary-Ann, she'd met on several occasions Ava did not understand Mrs. Chapel's comment. The tall brunette looked nothing like her. She realized Elspeth Chapel, pushing eighty-five, might be forgetful. She might even be losing her mind. Refusing to allow pity to ruin her happy mindset, Ava smiled for one last greeting. "Enjoy your day, Mrs. Chapel," She stared at the octogenarian wobble away and wave without looking back.

Outside her building, a modern structure between two prewar brownstones, Ava grabbed the first cab she flagged. As always, the ride left her edgy and dizzy, and as soon as she spotted Pearl Street, she tapped on the thick pane separating her and the driver. "You can leave me here, please."

Out of the taxi, Ava ran toward the back entrance of the glass building where she needed both hands and her best dose of flexed arms to open the door, stuck from the crazy draft. Inside she shook May's breezy weather out of her hair and trotted down the corridor on six-inch heels. She spotted the green light to one of the elevators on her right and yelled, "Hold, please." After threading into the packed elevator, she stretched an arm to finger her floor button when she realized the whole panel glowed from the insurance crowd lodged on several different levels. Today's ride would come with four humps and bumps before hitting her stop.

Like most mornings, she crept off the elevator being careful to keep her purse molded to her body. Deep breaths later she straightened her jacket coming face-to-face with the big round clock—the only smiling presence to relieve the unadorned beige stretch of hallway. Plenty of time left to confer with Crystal about the meeting.

As she rounded the corner, Ava glimpsed Elaine already at her desk a cluttered little island next to hers their office a moon-shaped bay off the main corridor. Elaine beamed a broad smile as she raised her coffee cup to Ava's arrival.

"Good morning," Ava greeted her.

"Love the suit, and your hair," Elaine said. "Emile?"

Ava gave her a little wink. "Thank you so much for the birthday coupon. Would not have afforded Emile otherwise."

"You're welcome, Miss Lucky-to-be-twenty-seven." She eyed her with one brow up. "Unlike me, thirty-five and shacked up with a boyfriend who doesn't believe in marriage."

Ava turned on her computer and glanced at Elaine already engrossed with work. She encountered her coworker's expression knitted with questions and couldn't help a small grin. Elaine's petite frame appeared childlike, but when not peering out of gold-rimmed glasses, her deep black eyes betrayed a surprising amount of soul.

"What's Jerry's reason for avoiding nuptial bliss this month?"

Elaine peered over her glasses. "Let's see. Last month he blamed Middle East bedlam, as he enjoys saying. This month," she shrugged, "he found a couple of gray hairs. Says people will think he's settling."

Ava shook her head rolling her eyes. "Men." She tossed her hair. "I haven't bothered with a boyfriend in ages. I'm so much better for it—such in an great place right now."

"Right." A nod dotted Elaine's sarcastic remark.

"What's that supposed to mean?"

"Means if you partook of a little lovin' in your life, you might not be so desirous to get *a*-head," she said mutilating the sound of the *a* to a bare whisper. The grin she cast Ava spoke of how much she loved to tease.

"Elaine Duffy, you're so crude if you're not careful this will be Jerry's next reason for not getting hitched."

***

Later the same week, Ava spent the morning grinding figures with teeth clenched eyes crossed and brow moist. As usual, Crystal's promise of an interview fell through. Four days later, the cold comment caterwauling from Crystal's stout frame still bounced around in Ava's head. "Mr. Wallace is extremely busy. He can't agree to meet with every newbie who comes along." For a big-boned woman, she projected one hell of a squeaky, high-pitched voice.

The bell from the elevator caught her attention, and she stretched to catch a glimpse of the person landing on their floor. She encountered Tracy Donovan coming her way, and she smiled at her with affection. Tall, blue-eyed Tracy, who wore her corn silk hair tied in an intricate braid, at least when at work, held the Vice President position in charge of marketing their firm to other companies. Ava found her easy to befriend, and kind to the people who worked with her.

"You seem bored and in dire need of something to do." Tracy wore a broad grin.

"I'm a little bug-eyed. Sort of wish I'd taken my break earlier."

"Why not go now?"

"Can't. Elaine left. I promised her I'd hold the fort. What's up?"

Tracy plopped the files she carried on the desk and gave Ava two thumbs-up. "I enjoyed a chat with Reynard." She gave Ava a broad smile.

"About me?" Ava's heart stopped. "What did you say?"

"Well. One thing led to another, and he steered the subject to the new talent we have at the agency. Shock punched a hole in my windpipe. I needed a few seconds to recover. Who could believe? I mean, this wonderful opportunity falling right into my lap."

Ava glanced behind Tracy to make sure no one listened to their conversation. "Did he say why?"

Tracy nodded. "He's trying to reel in some hotshot guru from overseas. So he's looking to promote one of the firm's talented prospects into entry level to work with this person. I said you worked in my department, and rendered yourself indispensable proving you would be an efficient plus for the company."

"Oh, my God." Ava couldn't stop her smile from stretching.

"I also said you recently graduated and wanted to expand into analysis."

"Then what did he say?" Ava's eyes felt like flying saucers about to take off.

"He was quiet, very Reynard you know. He also asked, 'Where did Miss Moss obtain her master's in finance?'" Tracy imitated Reynard's deep voice to perfection.

"Noo!" Following the resounding no, Ava's head dropped and her eyes glued to the desk. "Imagine? I graduate with a bachelor in finance, and now I need a master's."

"Not carved in stone." Tracy coaxed her to be calm. "Understand. We're dealing with a person's most precious commodity, hard-earned cash."

"So, it's hopeless. I need to go back to school." Ava plopped her head on the desk and moaned. "This is so discouraging."

"Listen." Tracy cleared her throat. "I told Reynard about Denteck and Pharmteck."

"You didn't." A brand new avenue Ava had developed to lend a different spin on health investment packages, one which handed Tracy's department lots of money.

Tracy nodded. "I let it slip as though by accident. I didn't say how you developed the idea. But I did tell him this was a notion I would never have considered without you sharing."

"God that's generous."

"All true."

"I'm so glad you talked to him and not Crystal. Hey," Ava wondered. "Do you suppose this is what happened? Crystal spoke to him, but he didn't like my qualifications?"

"Nah. He'd never heard of you."

"So now what?"

"We wait."

"We wait," Ava echoed with huge, dramatic eyes. "What else did he say?"

"He nodded which is big for Reynard."

Grateful, though she believed Tracy's emphatic head bob was more to boost her spirits, Ava pinched her lips together and bowed her head. "Well, I owe you."

Tracy reached in her jacket's pocket. "You do. And for starters, you're going to pack up and go home."

"I can't go home in the middle of the afternoon." An eyeful of scorn followed the outburst.

"Sure you can. I'll asked Cindy to cover for you. She's sitting at reception doing nothing." Tracy reached in her pocket and handed Ava a business card. "My friend Vanessa of Mate for Life is waiting for your call. She knows all about you and says she's compiled a list of six gorgeous men, and there'll never be a better time to grab a partner than this weekend."

Ava got up to pace in front of her desk. Stashed away in one of her kitchen drawers, to avoid the risk of coming across the invitation by chance, she'd taken the time to bury Tracy's birthday gift of a speed-dating pass. She flicked the card Tracy handed her half expecting the darn thing to flick back. "You don't believe in this, do you?"

"Hey, I'm twice divorced. If I'd used some kind of dating system, I might have been able to find the man who's still out there waiting for me."

Ava's eyes narrowed as she gave her a knowing smile. "I thought you found the man of your dreams and his name is Reynard Wallace," Ava finished in a whisper.

"I thought so too. I mean the man is an absolute hunk. Tall, hazel eyes oozing with soul, full lips, I have to watch I don't drool every time I'm in his office."

"What happened?" Ava often fantasized about those two getting together.

Tracy picked up her files. "I guess he has too many choices, but enough about me. You go home and call Vanessa. And first thing Monday morning, I want to hear all about your outing."

***

Early Friday or not, Ava would never get to kick off her shoes.

After she unlocked the two bolts to her door, she ran to answer the phone. "Hello?" she inquired audibly panting.

"Is this Ava Moss?"

"Yes." She took in fast spurts of air. "I just need to catch my breath."

"My name is Vanessa Distel. Tracy said to call you at home around this time. Ava, we need to meet tonight."

"Can I call you back? I just came in. My front door is still wide open."

"No need, Ava. I am calling to set up a meeting with you at the Archives, on Adams."

"Tonight?"

"Yes, tonight. We need to go over the procedures for tomorrow night. I held our general meeting weeks ago. You weren't there. So now, I need to give you the skinny on your dates."

"How do you know? What dates?"

"I compiled a list of six men for you to meet tomorrow night. Did not do so based on any profile you needed to fill in. I relied on Tracy's impression of you, and a current picture. Don't worry, I have a degree in human relations. You will be extremely pleased. See you at six, ciao."

The sound of the dial tone brought Ava back. She stared at the phone wishing her scathing look might travel along with the phone lines, and slammed the receiver down. She thought of calling Tracy to cancel the whole thing.

Heaving a tremulous sigh, Ava eyed the open door and automatically walked over to close and lock up. She wished everyone would leave her alone. Lassitude seized her as she plopped down in the chair. This being the weekend, Ava wanted to enjoy her time off in her own way—going to her Friday night yoga class and heading to the gym in the morning for a workout and a swim. In a comfortable rut she enjoyed her time off, and lately, she couldn't seem to find enough alone time, always scrounging for more. During the week, work took precedence. During the weekend, Ava's choices prevailed.

She checked her watch and sighed for small miracles. A whole hour and a half before she needed to be at the restaurant. She wondered how much Tracy had paid for the whole shebang. She doubted any amount would be worth her trouble. The real humiliation stemmed from her friends trying to force-feed companionship down her miserable, skinny life. Ava worried they thought of her as some sort of pathetic loser.

She rose remembering a time when she went to bed every night wishing someone, anyone cared about her, and praying she might turn to someone for comfort when life's edges were too sharp. Of course, at the time, her thoughts involved a man, the love of her life somewhere in the world and MIA in a big way. Still, math principles dictated two good friends equaled more than the likes of one missing man any day.

She put the kettle on the stove and prepared a pot of tea. She stood by waiting for the water to boil wondering what to wear. The puzzler was dreaming up something decent to wear tomorrow night. She poured water in the pot and while the tea steeped, she sprinkled little flakes over Oscar's bowl the little red fish pouncing on the morsels as they hit the water. Then she put away the few dishes she'd left to dry in the sink.

With a sigh, Ava collapsed in a chair and contemplated the boredom of her life. Yet, she happened to be complacent and satisfied with her routine. Worse, she didn't believe she needed any earth-shattering change in her routine. Did she even want a man in her life?

Since leaving her last foster home in Dayton, Ohio to come to New York City, she'd attracted her share of weirdoes—full marks to Elaine for noticing this. However, Ava wondered if seeking solitude became her way to self-soothe, an instinct to protect against more heartache and disappointment.

The niggling feeling she might be going through some kind of early spinsterhood worried her—enough, she decided to go and meet the woman. She would sit with her and swallow what little pride remained while Vanessa presented her with the gift of a date—six dates to be precise.

CHAPTER 2

D-NIGHT

D-night, zero hours fell upon Ava with the bang of car doors slamming, cabs pulling up to the curb in a constant procession, and the hustle and bustle of people milling about the restaurant's entrance. All created a colorful mayhem for someone used to spending Saturday nights in front of a crossword puzzle. Ava's cheeks hurt from the smile pulled wide across her face, and she grinned and giggled like a little girl as she stared in awe at her idyllic surroundings.

Ava almost fainted when Vanessa mentioned the meeting would be held at the 21 Club. Ava never imagined she might one day enjoy the opportunity to mingle in such elegant ambiance. "Don't seem so surprised, darling. Perfect little tables for two scattered in a half-lit atmosphere, ideal for fostering intimacy."

Vanessa also reiterated she did Tracy a favor, repeated how candidates met two weeks before to hand over their bio and photo.

"How did you get my picture?"

Vanessa showed her the photo from her work-pass—worse,

the photo from her work-pass blown up to an eight-by-ten glossy. "This is a horrible picture. I can't believe Tracy gave you this."

"Let me reassure you. I showed your picture to several groups of candidates over the last few weeks, and fifteen men in our survey group of twenty-four picked you to be in their circle of six."

Ava's smile beamed back. "Wow. The outing might be worth the trouble."

"I told you so, darling. You were popular despite the picture. When you enter the 21 Club, you will be the belle of the ball."

Her only frustration lay in the fact she owned six bios, but only four pictures.

"Two of them did not submit photos—were not able to do so on time not because they are unattractive," Vanessa added waving a long ringed finger at her.

Ava's cell phone rang. Excitement radiating out of her pores, she picked up and became engrossed in her conversation.

"Not a clue. Yes, of course, Vanessa gave me the entire do's and don'ts—a giant stack of rules and regulations to bring home and study. No. Didn't read half of them—no time. Anyway, I'll tell you about the details later. I'm about to walk in."

"Did you get the sexy little red number you wanted?"

"Yes. And I found the Manolo's I showed you—on sale," she beamed animated and more alive than she'd been in a long time.

"The platinum strappy sandals?"

"Uh huh." Ava contorted right to stare at her shoes, and as she did, bumped up against the person behind her.

She tried to catch her balance but wobbled on the six-inch heels. A quick arm around her waist steadied her even as she envisioned scraping her hands and knees rather than ruin her dress.

She ignored the cell phone and stared at her benefactor.

"Are you all right?" the man asked in smooth tones not two inches from her lips. As he helped her stand on two feet again, they exchanged eye contact. Both were silent for a few timeless seconds.

Ava shuddered bowled over by the stranger's charming manner and striking looks. She backed away and glimpsed a pair of the lightest brown eyes she ever spotted on anyone, and a cute little mesh of brown hair jutting over a broad forehead. He sported a dimple on his chin and a nervous Adam's apple bobbing up and down as he continued to stare at her. His eye color might be light, but the burn from his piercing gaze oozed fire inside her.

She heard Tracy yell her name through her cell. Lost in a fog, she pondered her friend must be wondering where she'd gone.

The stranger smiled, and Ava sensed a fleeting thought of a man amused by their predicament. He appeared intent on taking in her every move, and as his eyes glided over her lips for an instant, she thought he might kiss her. Instead, he bent to stare at her shoes and raised an eyebrow at the length of the heels.

She cocked a shoulder at him. "Just trying to be up with the grown-ups," she said using her brightest smile to illuminate the moment.

His own smile stretched into a grin. "So, Ava. Lovely name—warm, unpretentious. Suits you. Are you going inside?"

Ava jumped at the use of her name. "Yes. You must be one of my Mate for Life candidates." He had to be. He knew her name which meant he'd seen her picture and happened to be one of her hopefuls.

The stranger's frown gathered for a brief moment, but his interest never waned.

"This means you're either Luke Perry or Pete Cassimere."

His frown deepened.

"You know. The only two of my dates who didn't provide pictures?"

"Ah, I see."

Ava wondered about the easy answer dotting a puzzled expression. Yet the spell he cast prodded her to babble. "I bet you're Luke. I've always loved the name, Luke. You are, aren't you?"

"You think I look like a Luke?" He laughed his expression knotted and illegible.

"I guessed right. I'm going to ask Vanessa to schedule you first." A slight hesitation had occurred before she owned up. "I put you at the back of the pile—no picture. Call me vain, but it's hard to decide when you can't tell what the other person looks like."

"Don't let me keep you from your lovely evening." As he cocked his head to the side in the guise of a salute, he took in a whiff of her hair.

She applauded her choice of cherry bark and almond shampoo hoping he didn't think her too much of a kook. When all she did was stare at him and nod, he stroked the curve of her face with the back of his hand.

"Ava. We're all waiting for you." She cursed Vanessa's call from the doorway.

"Be right there." She shook herself back to the present. "See you later."

She ran to the door and grasped the big brass handle, but

couldn't resist one last glance. She caught him dialing a number on his cell. Both their communications had certainly ended in an abrupt manner. Glancing at hers, she realized the call also ended. She listened to make sure, but Tracy was gone.

Inside Ava argued with Vanessa to obtain a quick change to her schedule. Vanessa had offered Ava the choice of which candidates she wanted to meet first, as an added favor to Tracy.

"Why do I need to choose an order?" Ava asked.

"Makes more sense to date the ones you believe might be more compatible first when you are fresh and relaxed."

Now, Vanessa argued, "I made a lot of exceptions for you, Ava. I can't alternate everyone's planner at this late hour."

"Fine," Ava muttered once she realized Vanessa would not budge. Of course, Ava couldn't expect everyone to change their plans on her account. Her fault she supposed for only glancing at the bios while staring at the pictures. Served her right for being so shallow.

Mark Simmons became the first contender on her list. Mark's dark curly hair and warm brown eyes left her with a friendly impression. The fact he measured five feet and nine inches afforded him a bonus. Thanks to her heels, they were almost the same height.

"So, you're a lawyer," she asked attempting to sound interested.

"I am." He smiled. "I want to tell you, I think you're beautiful. When Vanessa showed me your picture, I didn't think I'd encounter much competition know what I mean?" Mark caught her forehead puckering so he attempted to correct his faux pas. "I mean since I'm not so hot, I thought I might stand a better chance to convince you to go out with me, but you are hot, and I'm an idiot."

Ava laughed. She considered him charming, although a little unsure of himself. Had she not encountered her number six outside on the sidewalk, she would have found Mark's puerile and remorseful gesture delightful. So she gave Mark her phone number. Of course, she would be thrilled to meet him again.

Two more candidates filed in at her table. The last candidate before the break introduced himself as Paul, a banker. He appeared quite attentive. Ava deemed he showed potential. She gave him her number as well.

Ava checked the mural by the table once Paul left. A pastel gondola propelled down a flowing blue river crossed what she presumed the artist painted as Venice in the background. No one needed the use of imagination in this place. Even a hardcore cynic would sprout a romantic side in these settings.

Hunger pains stirred Ava. All talked-out, she decided to stretch her legs and gather something to eat.

At the buffet tables, small lanterns glowed on pristine white tablecloths casting lovely, dreamy shadows. A sigh escaped Ava. She understood why people flocked to the restaurant, and why they happily plunked down their hard-earned cash to fulfill their heart's desires. The fugue from a diet of daily grind was more than worth it. She owed Tracy big time.

She picked up a plate and surveyed the wrapped shrimps, the tossed vegetables, and mixed greens. The lavish spread, comprised of finger food, appeared fancier than any fare she'd encountered at most restaurants, all displayed on exquisite china—expensive she thought as she fingered the crystal glasses.

As she turned to leave, having stacked as much as possible on her small plate, she bumped into Luke. "Hey, I was wondering where you were. I didn't see you in line with the others." She smiled at him to hide the fact the encounter left her breathless.

"We meet again," he cooed. "Serendipity I think it's called."

Ava gave a little bow of her head. "I like the word." She frowned as she caught the fact he appeared to be in a hurry. "Just two more candidates to go," she said.

"Actually, I was just leaving." He checked his watch. "I'm late for another appointment. I saw you across the room. Thought I'd say goodnight."

What did he hope to accomplish leaving in such a hurry? "You can't. I'm not late. I'm ahead of schedule. You should've seen how fast I went through these last three just so I could get to number six—you—as quickly as I can."

He shook his head and frowned. "Something tells me your name should be Alice, not Ava."

"Alice?"

"Alice in Wonderland. Beautiful, impossible to understand, yet mesmerizing."

She sighed. The man called her beautiful. Now, Ava shook her head wearing a rueful expression. Why did he want to leave so soon?

"I'm sorry. I can't postpone my other meeting."

"At least let me give you my number." As Ava maintained her brimming plate in perfect balance with her left hand, she tugged on his sleeve with her right. "I'm sitting over there. Come," she coaxed. *You're bold*, an ear-rending clap of reason thundered through her euphoria. *So what?* A most delightful little voice argued he paid top dollar to sit with her, so did she, well Tracy did. Only fair she made sure he got his money's worth.

Luke followed her to the table and sat down in the chair she indicated. To refuse would be impolite she realized, her adamancy becoming palpable. "I'm so sorry we're not going to share fifteen minutes in the sun," she cooed as she penned her phone number on a piece of paper napkin.

He took it from her as he stood moving the chair to the side.

"May I ask for yours?"

She fidgeted as he considered her request with slight hesitancy. He fingered the piece of paper in his hand. "I'm sort of a moving target at the moment. I'm in the process of relocating to New York. So I can't give you any fixed number."

"You own a cell, don't you?" Faced with the polite inevitability she glimpsed in his eyes, Ava lost her smile. "I'm too forward. I'm sorry. I'm sure you met someone you like better in the last hour and a half." She shrugged a little sadly. Wiping the gloom off her expression, she gave him a bright smile.

He made a motion to give Ava back her phone number.

"Keep it. Next time you're in town and want to talk, call me."

"That's very generous of you. I will." A slight hand salute and he walked away. He turned once a quizzical expression marking his face as he gave her one last nod.

She sighed, the onus of this reunion once more weighing on her shoulders. Two more to go. Then she'd head home—and tell Tracy all about this. She knew she would leave out a bunch of stuff.

She got up and decided to look around to check out her competition. She wandered for a few minutes noticing most of the other women were lovely and wondered if professional models used the Service to find their unique someone? If so, what chance did she stand of winning someone's heart?

"Hope you're enjoying yourself, darling."

Ava jumped out of her reverie. She recognized the voice. "Hi, Vanessa. Listen, I don't quite know why Luke Perry needed to leave early—some emergency. Would you be able to give me his phone number? We didn't have a chance to exchange them." She crossed her fingers behind her back as she said the tiny white lie.

"Ava," Vanessa reprimanded. "Exchanging numbers on the first date is against the rules. You know that. If he likes you, he'll call the agency. If you entered his name on your follow-up sheet, we will contact you and arrange a second meeting. Only then will you be allowed to exchange numbers." Vanessa fussed a little more clucking her tongue before marching off in the opposite direction.

"Right," Ava whispered. She'd blown the rules to smithereens. No wonder Luke gave her such a puzzled look or wouldn't give her his number. She heaved a huge sigh. Now he would never call her.

CHAPTER 3

AFTERMATH

T he sun at its zenith signaled the longest day of the year to be one week away, and Ava appeared no closer to getting a promotion than to getting a date.

No one from the escapade in early June gave her a call. She made up some tacky story to keep Tracy happy her brain too riddled with shame to discuss the evening. Vanessa phoned with the report Peter Cassimere wanted a second date. Pete and Richard happened to be the only two Ava did not mark as potential follow-ups on her sheet. She even agreed to Gerald Fink, whom she found a little young for her.

"Do you want to reconsider?" Vanessa asked.

Ava debated the question for a few days. Pleasant enough, she didn't believe Peter to be her type—a science professor a mite timid and understated. Besides, he stood tall and lanky, a trait which Ava did not enjoy.

"You've been quiet these last few weeks. Anything wrong,

Ava?" Her back to Elaine as she filed yesterday's folders in their respective drawers, she sensed her friend's worry in her nonchalant tone.

"No. I'm carrying a lot on my mind. That's all." In fact, happy before the Mate for Life meeting while going about the everyday motions fared much easier than knowing what she might be missing. Now, every Saturday night when she sat at her kitchen table doing the crossword puzzle, she visualized people out in the world having fun and finding camaraderie in exotic, romantic restaurants.

So much for her being the belle of the ball, she thought with a pinch of her heart. Vanessa told her sometimes, finding a special someone necessitated two meetings. Trouble remained she never searched for anyone in particular before. Except now, finding her mystery man filled all her waking thoughts day in and day out. However, she damn well refused to go without the bare necessities to afford another rendezvous. Four hundred dollars a pop for a makeup session cost too much for her tiny budget.

Ava wondered if she owed her moodiness to Mark Simmons not returning any of her calls. Neither did Paul Dupree. Perhaps her dejection stemmed from Luke Perry's silence.

She pleaded with Vanessa, begged her to hand over Luke's number. Yet, Vanessa pronounced Luke a no-show the night of the meeting. "He postponed without even putting in an appearance," she said, and no amount of haggling swayed Vanessa's decision.

"What's on your mind? You're walking around like you're pre-menstrual most of the time," Elaine said, "with that little crease pleated on top of your nose."

Ava walked back to her desk thinking the gloves were off, and

Elaine no longer cared about hiding her concern. "My mind's not a complete blank. I'm not a dweeb. I do juggle with stuff often enough. I don't want to discuss this right now."

"Fine. You don't need to bite my head off. I'm trying to help."

Ava stopped in her tracks and turned to face her friend. "I'm sorry, Elaine. I guess I'm a little edgy of late. I'm thinking about knocking on Reynard's door to beg him to give me a chance."

"Don't do it. Not something you can take back."

Ava nodded. Elaine made a good point. If she stepped out as too aggressive at the office, she might risk losing the battle, which would be devastating, but not any worse than making a fool of herself at the 21 Club, a little voice prodded—by handing everyone her number—so eager, so pathetic. Ava closed her eyes dreading the thought even three weeks later. At least, she took solace in suffering the humiliation in silence. She certainly didn't plan on telling anyone.

"I'm going home. Catch you Monday," Ava called out.

"Hey, what are you doing this weekend?"

Ava thought of making up a lie to sound exciting, but she couldn't muster the strength. "Nothing much, why?"

"Jerry's out of town through Sunday. I thought you and I might catch a movie tomorrow night."

Ava perked up. Any other day she would find some excuse to decline. At the moment, she needed the company. "Sounds like fun."

"Super. I'll call you, and we'll pick out a movie. Hey, you can come over and spend the day at my place, stay over if you like."

Ava took a few seconds to mull over her decision. "Okay. Girl's night out!" Maybe if she unburdened some of the dark thoughts she harbored, she might get her life back.

However, getting her life back to normal appeared to be easier in theory than in actual practice. She spent the afternoon with Elaine roaming Central Park, and still couldn't shake the prevailing gloom about her future, the problem exacerbated by an attack of nerves whenever she tried to share her story.

Sitting on a park bench near the Bethesda Fountain, they scrutinized people who ambled by the vast area. Some were cutting across with heads down ignoring the sights and sounds of summer in a hurry to reach home while others lined up for ice cream or something cold to drink courtesy of concession stands wheeled in for the day.

They returned from taking a boat out on the lake—both exhausted and sunburned. Ava laughed and laughed when one of the oarlocks broke and the pin dropped to the bottom of the pond. They needed to take turns zigzagging their way back to the bridge.

"So, what movie do you want to go to?" Elaine asked.

Ava raised tired shoulders. "I can't imagine getting off this bench or walking to your apartment. That's how tired I am. And I imagined myself in such good shape." She blew a mesh of hair out of her face.

"So, are you ever going to tell me about him?"

Ava glanced at Elaine and smiled—Elaine's invitation also serving to weasel information out of her. Elaine guessed the problem, and Ava no longer hesitated to confide, tired of lugging around this lump weighing her down. "You're right, Elaine. I did meet someone. Someone who, in the literal sense, swept me off my feet. I don't think I was ever this excited by any man—not like this."

"One of your dates?"

"Don't know." Ava turned to look at Elaine. "I bumped into him on my way into the restaurant. I thought he belonged to our group. He called me by name, and since I didn't recognize his face, I figured him to be one of the men I'd scheduled for last, this Luke Perry."

"Whoa! Backup, Lolita. Who was what?"

"Vanessa gave me four pictures and six bios. Two of the men she scheduled did not submit a photo. I figured he might be one of them. I planned to meet the faceless ones last. Trying to avoid disappointment."

"Luke Perry, the actor?"

"No, no. Some biochemist or other."

"Who told you he wasn't one of your dates?"

"Vanessa said this Luke person never showed up." Ava plopped her head into her hands. "I made a complete fool of myself. Oh, God! I fawned all over him mistaking him for one of my Mate for Life dates." She shook her head remembering some of the most embarrassing moments. "I even dragged him back to my table after he told me he had to leave because of another appointment." She let out a heavy sigh.

"So? What's the problem? A case of mistaken identity is all. No biggie. These things happen, all the time."

"I went on and on. I called this guy Luke, told him I saved him for last because I didn't get his picture."

Elaine chuckled a little. "Who cares? You're never going to see this guy again."

Ava gave her friend a piercing stare. She hesitated, "Thing is, Elaine, had I not mistaken him for one of my dates, I wouldn't have rushed through all the others. I may have had a chance with one of them."

"In other words, you don't care about this guy. You're worried you ruined your evening on account of him."

"Maybe. Oh, but I wish you could have seen this man, Elaine. He's gorgeous, absolutely wonderful. Hazel eyes, dimple in his chin, and perfect for me—really perfect, the perfect height." Ava made a grimace letting out a sad little groan.

"What?"

"He looked at my heels with this little smile. I can't believe what I told him. In my defense, I don't handle self-consciousness well. I had just almost fallen off my shoes." Ava spotted Elaine's round eyes and swatted at her curiosity with the back of her hand. "Never mind. Long story."

Elaine enjoyed another little chuckle. "Life is never dull with you, Ava." She repositioned herself on the bench. "Okay, I'll buy. What's this brilliant reply you handed him, the one given the choice you would wash out of your mouth with soap rather than say?" Still, Elaine laughed.

Ava exhaled while making noise. "For the record, Vanessa is a dirty flatterer, a liar, and a flatterer. She said I would be the belle of the ball. I strutted into the 21 Club so cocky."

"Yeah, so he gives you a look about the heels. What did you say to him?"

"You should have seen my competition. I swear every model in Manhattan dined at the restaurant that night. Belle of the ball," Ava grunted. "I never stood a chance."

"Will you please answer my question." Elaine sighed to mark her frustration.

"Oh," she gave Elaine the eye. "I told him I wanted to be up there with the grownups." Even to her, the phrase sounded so ridiculous that faced with Elaine's smirk she started laughing while Elaine roared. The two laughed until hiccups and tears came to douse the mood.

"Ava, I swear you're a kook." Elaine stopped laughing to breathe and wipe her eyes with the bottom of her T-shirt. "Count your blessings all this man has is your first name."

"And my phone number." Ava gave her a sheepish smile with a goofy pair of wide eyes.

"Noo! You gave a stranger your phone number, a *perfect* stranger—your private phone number? Are you nuts? Of course, you are. What a question." Elaine shook her head from side to side between bursts of chuckles. "He might be a bloody maniac for all you know."

"I thought he was part of my group, remember?" Ava was annoyed. The nervous laughter dissipated, Ava bit her bottom lip as a sense of foolishness invaded her, the incident having left a vile aftertaste.

"I'm sorry, sweetie. I didn't mean to come down on you so hard." Elaine laughed again.

"Maybe he'll lose the darn thing. I wrote the number down on a piece of napkin, and he did offer to give the number back to me when he wouldn't give me his."

Once more, Elaine laughed while trying not to this time, which made a serious face harder to put on.

"Why," more giggles she tried to suppress. "Why would you still want to leave this man your phone number when he wouldn't give you his?"

"I already handed my number over. I couldn't take it back. I told Luke he could give me a call whenever he came to town."

Elaine got up, took a deep breath, and invited Ava to do the same. "Enough about this loser."

Elaine took another massive gulp of air still trying to shake the laughter tickling her. "We're going to a movie, and we're going to have a wonderful time. As for mysterious Mister No-name, we'll never bring him up again. Deal?"

Ava got up. "Deal."

The girls shook on it.

"Please don't tell Tracy about him."

"Sweetie, I wouldn't know where to start."

Ava nodded and pressed her hand against Elaine's stomach. "So, anything yet?"

"No—not as of yesterday morning."

"Oh! I'm sorry, Elaine." Ava stroked her arm. "You can try again next month, sweetie." Once a month, Elaine would remind her how much she and Jerry were trying to get pregnant.

"Guess so. Jerry's more upset than I am. Sometimes I think all he wants out of me is a baby, and he'll grab that baby and leave the minute I have one. Now I understand why Angelina appears so insecure," Elaine said under her breath.

"Don't be ridiculous. You'd have a baby trying to raise a child. Jerry would never be able to cope on his own." Ava asked. "Want to go see *Catch and Release*?"

"Sure. Oldie but goodie."

After they had gone to Elaine's house to change and grab a bite to eat, they reiterated their pact not to talk about the stranger and walked over to the Cinema on 59th Street.

"You're lucky to be so close to everything. I need to take a cab to go anywhere in Brooklyn."

"Jerry's apartment. His mother left him the place. I mean, eventually, we want more out of life than a one-bedroom toolbox on Lexington, but for now, the layout works. We spend most of our days elsewhere."

They walked into the theater, and Elaine began climbing the escalator two by two.

"What's your hurry?" Ava told her. "Aren't we going to the eight-thirty presentation?"

"Movie is at eight. This way we won't have to sit through news and previews."

"I don't want to miss the beginning. I've never seen this movie." Off the stairs, Ava stopped dead in her tracks her heart beating wildly. She hid behind Elaine while she held on to her sweater using her as a shield. "Please don't move. The stranger we're not supposed to talk about is standing at the ticket counter."

Elaine stared at the man who slid his credit card into the window slot. "Wow. He is a looker. Are you sure? You only met him once. Could be someone else entirely," she mouthed to her.

"Trust me. I would recognize the cute haircut and dreamy expression anywhere."

"Okay. I'm going to move right toward the vending machines. All you need to do is follow my lead." Elaine sidestepped in front of Ava and didn't need to worry about Ava following her. She mirrored her every move.

"Thanks," Ava breathed hiding behind the popcorn machine eyes riveted the stranger's way. "You saved my life."

"What would a gorgeous hunk be doing at a movie theater alone?" Elaine stopped as a woman sidled up to him. "Ah, she seems pretty chummy, Ava. Might be someone he hangs with on the serious side."

Ava's heart sank. Supposed to be a newcomer in town, he accompanied someone. Perhaps someone he met at the Mate for Life meeting.

The woman walked away but called out to him. "Scott, Emily wants popcorn, a small one. Thanks."

Out of the shadows approached young Emily. Elaine and Ava stared at her dumbfounded. She looked to be ten years old.

"This explains why he didn't want to leave his number." Elaine looked at her. "Your guy's married. Easy enough to determine why he played along. You are much too much of a temptation. I mean look at this woman. She's not close enough for a good look, but she seems ten years older than he is."

"Married," Ava breathed deflated and saddened. She couldn't explain the loss invading her spirit as though her future had upped and left. Then, Ava's eyes widened. "Emily wants popcorn," she repeated. "He's headed this way," she squeaked in a high-pitched voice. Yanking Elaine's sleeve she screamed, "Duck."

Both girls ran around the back end of the counter Ava tripping on a bump in the carpet while Elaine held her up seconds before she lunged to the floor. They ended up in the wide hall leading to the different cinemas out of breath and cramped with laughter.

"God this sighting—too close for comfort," Ava breathed.

"Good thing I got internet tickets." Elaine flashed the printed movie passes.

"Yeah. Now, what are the odds this guy will be in there?"

"Please. Do you realize how many other movies are playing? I told you. This one's an oldie. Come on. Don't let one creep spoil your evening."

"You're right, you're right. Still, let's wait a minute or two. I don't want to bump into him in the hallway," Ava whispered.

"Might miss the beginning." Elaine gave her a grimace with the singsong tone.

Sitting behind a large potted plant, they waited an extra five minutes. Then when Ava felt comfortable the coast might be clear, she got up and took a deep breath. "Let's go."

As they entered the darkened cinema, both girls took a few seconds before they realized no seats appeared available.

"I thought you said this movie was an oldie."

"Of course. You know it is. Must be some new review or something."

An attendant carrying a flashlight offered to help them find a row where they might sit together. The usher walked ahead flicking his light beams on both sides of the aisle. He stopped midway and waited for them to catch up.

Elaine went first while she thanked the attendant with a smile. Ava followed. Three pairs of feet scurried to let them squeeze by unhampered.

"Excuse me." Ava smiled at the last person of the three seated beside them. When she did, she came face to face with Luke, AKA Scott.

His face stretched into a slow smile, a smile reaching his eyes when he spotted recognition in hers. "Hello again," he whispered as Ava leaned closer not to lose her balance. "Hope you enjoy the movie."

Ava sensed her head nod too shocked to say anything. Tough to imagine, Ava Moss too dumbfounded to reply something cute, she commiserated, refusing to accept the streak of rotten luck coming her way.

She prompted Elaine to switch places with her so she wouldn't need to sit beside him. Would be too weird rubbing elbows with him for the next couple of hours.

She realized Elaine couldn't figure out the strange tic in her slanted eyes, so she bobbed her head to her left. When Elaine understood she wanted her to move, Ava knew she didn't catch the reason for the move.

Getting up, Elaine slid to sit down beside Scott looking at him as she did. When the light dawned, Ava caught her friend clamp uppers and lowers hard and squeeze her lips into one tight line—the only way possible to stop laughter from overtaking her.

Ava thanked God Elaine kept her arms to herself and her giggles under her belt, for now. Yet she suspected whatever went on in the movie she would be in stitches from start to finish.

Ava, on the other hand, would not remember a thing of *Catch and Release*—the movie—except she would need to fight to *catch* her breath and remember to *release* her sighs slowly from start to finish.

CHAPTER 4

AT THE THEATER

T hey left the theater and walked toward Elaine's apartment at a slow pace interrupted by Elaine's excited recap of hunky Scott.

A soft summer breeze whooshed by Ava. She turned her head and the laughter from strolling couples rolled toward her in muted waves. Of course, this being New York City, traffic crawled down Park Avenue while drivers delivered their best right hook to blast their horn with aggravated impatience. She even overheard the merchant at the corner of Sixtieth Street talking to himself as he packed his stall for the night. Yet every time the wind shifted, some form of adulation from Elaine about this gorgeous man floated toward her.

"Will you please stop? Two full blocks you badgered me. I mean I'm as patient as the next person, but here's where I draw the line. Bad enough I need to forget about him."

"Why? I think the way he bent over me and asked, 'Would you like something to drink? Are you hungry?' And you said no."

"I didn't need anything. We'd just had that big meal an hour earlier."

"Please! The sweet way he said, 'hungry?' A stuffed turkey would have said yes."

"So?"

"What do you mean so? He acted as though he wanted to be your date. Plus, don't forget, he introduced Liliane as his sister-in-law and Emily as his niece which doesn't sound like a man in a matrimonial noose. Since he is new to the area, he's going to be calling on family. Makes sense."

"You want the truth? I think he patronized me."

"Oh, come on. You don't believe that. I saw the way he looked at you."

"Aha! Not any differently than he did the night at the 21 Club, which explains why I made a fool of myself, and why I thought he liked me, and the reason I was so sure we connected. He oozed of come-hither-charm, his eyes worked mine, and the timing of his dreamy expression was—" Ava clumped thumb and forefingers to touch her lips. "Perfect. He even stroked my cheek with the back of his fingers."

Elaine's eyes opened wide. "What? You never told me this."

"What's the point? This is Scott's personality. The way he is period." Ava nodded faced with Elaine's rueful expression. "No, no. Believe me. I am willing to bet if a man like Scott met his dream girl, his Machu Picchu..."

Elaine laughed. "His macho what?"

"World Wonder—famous Peruvian sanctuary. Look it up," she

added to rub off the wry expression on Elaine's face. "Anyway, he'd lose the smile, be all tongue-tied—in other words, it'd be his turn to make a complete ass of himself."

"World Wonder." Elaine gave her the eye. "Men don't go gaga over women, not the smart, handsome ones. Look at Jerry. Most days he ignores me, makes me think he doesn't give a damn. And boom, just as I'm about to give up on him, he comes up with a surprise and wins me all over again. Still, nothing out of the ordinary."

"Not the same. You and Jerry have been living together for years. The gaga is gone or at least by now he's tamed the excitement. My guy has the edge, and he knows he does. I made such a fool of myself, he can afford to be kind—have pity on the crazy lady."

"Well, if you pass him up, you *are* crazy."

"What do you propose I do, torture him until he gives me his phone number? Oh, I forgot. To do this, I would need to be able to reach him." She enunciated making a face.

They'd arrived at Elaine's building.

Elaine stopped and turned toward her. "I say he's going to call you. Care to make a small wager?"

Ava eyed the twenty or so stairs they needed to climb to the top of the stoop. With renewed courage, she grabbed the handrail. Out of arguments, in silence, she took one step at a time firm about a couple of truths: she did not come prepared to wager her feelings her heart or her life. Instinct told her this man belonged to someone, too unflappable, too in control of his emotions around her to be anything other than polite.

***

Once Ava got home the next day, she checked her answering machine. No call from Scott and she didn't think she would ever receive one.

In the evening after feeding Oscar, she decided on an early night. Tired and restless, Ava considered an excellent book to read in bed would go a long way to restoring her ability to dream again. Stupid Vanessa with her crazy Mate for Life Club. She couldn't blame Vanessa, a little voice prompted. The fault lay with her. She allowed Tracy to talk her into doing something she didn't support. Romantic idylls between men and women worked best when pre-ordained, not preordered like a burger and a side of fries.

She hopped into bed with the four hundred and forty-one-page biography of Marie Curie. She sat up propping the book on her lap, and curling her knees and feet to fit snuggly under her night-gown, Ava prepared to step out of her life and into someone else's success story for a while.

The warm night entered her room and caught her attention. She couldn't spot the top of the Ash tree outside her building, but she suspected a warm wind rustled its leaves as the lace curtains trimming her window billowed lifting and rising, blowing in famil-iar aromas from the street below. The tortellini from Papa's Deli two doors down, the heady metallic musk from cars and trucks as their emissions mingled with dust swirling around the busy in-tersection. Even the native city sounds trickled in reassuringly as vivid reminders life would go on with or without her lonely heart.

She must have fallen asleep because the phone on her bedside table woke her. She jumped a tad startled and removed the book from her lap. Picking up the receiver she flinched from a pinch in her neck.

"Hello?" She rubbed the right side of her shoulder.

"Sorry, did I wake you?" Elaine asked.

Ava checked her wrist, and her watch read eight o'clock. She slept for an hour. "Fell asleep on a book."

"Ooh, the wild life we lead, Miss Moss. Turns out you could've stayed here another night. Jerry called earlier. He's not coming back until tomorrow evening."

"Just as well, I needed to do laundry, and I left dishes soaking in the sink. Oscar needed to eat." She yawned noisily, interrupted when she caught the beep of call waiting. "Someone's on the other line."

"Tracy," Elaine told her. "Said she wanted to call you. Thought I'd beat her to the punch." She laughed. "Warning you so you'll think of something to say about the movie."

"Don't remember anything about *Catch and Release.* Hold on," Ava said as she toggled to the other line. "Hey, Tracy."

"You can't seem to get my name right."

A masculine voice with a sensuous edge, one she recognized froze her to the spot. Her heart began pounding in her ears. Ava's tongue in knots, she couldn't utter the simplest greeting.

"Ava?"

"Yes. I'm with another caller. Can you wait?"

"You bet."

Ava toggled back verifying Elaine waited at the other end and not her mysterious friend. "You'll never guess who's on the other line?"

"Who?"

"Him." Her voice came out high-pitched and trembling. "Call you back."

She took a few seconds to compose herself. "Hi, Scott?"

"I love the way you say my name."

"I prefer Luke," she said. She chuckled. "Scott is okay."

"I cannot believe we ran into each other yesterday. I'd been thinking of calling you, only I thought you might not remember me. I figured you might be mated for life by now."

Only fair she thought, his turn to tease. "Not yet. It's in the works. Still, you're right about bumping into each other twice in a few weeks. A friend of mine—you met her yesterday—says the universe only interferes with the meeting of two people when circumstances make it necessary to do so."

"Does she now?"

"Uh, huh. She does."

"Why does she think the universe would want to bother with us?"

"She seems to think that it's because we're too stupid to do this ourselves."

They both laughed.

"What do you think?" he asked.

"I believe you 're much too cool a cucumber to be bothered by the universe and its fantastic plan." Ava heard him chuckle.

"I too believe in destiny. That's why I think we should meet and humor the gods so to speak. How about I pick you up tomorrow night after work and take you out to dinner?"

Ava stopped breathing laying a hand on the top of her head to stop her thoughts from spinning. She couldn't afford to put her foot in her mouth and risk losing face again. "How about I meet you for lunch in the park?"

"You're not afraid of me are you?"

"Listen, I just think we should get acquainted the way ordinary people do, with caution. If you want, we can meet in City Hall Park by the Roman numeral clock."

"Along Canyon of Heroes," he said.

"Fitting wouldn't you say? I can meet you around twelve thirty."

A long pause followed her suggestion. "Goodnight, Ava."

"Goodnight."

Ava hung up the phone dreamy eyed and smiling. In fact, she could not stop smiling even when a cursory little voice urged she be prudent. A man who took the time to please his sister in law and his niece likely had many women friends. Men like Scott—talented flirts—knew how to add a little extra sugar to make a lady feel special.

She remembered the coupons for the flirting seminar Elaine had given her for her birthday and wondered if she shouldn't take a few lessons to learn how to duck and fold.

She called Elaine back as promised. After a few minutes of giggling, after too many I-told-you-so from Elaine, Ava expressed concern. "Don't you think this guy's a little too good a flirt? I mean you took the flirting seminar with Jerry. Doesn't he seem excessively charming to you?"

Elaine hesitated. "Hard to tell. I mean, all men like to make a good impression more so when they like someone. This is usual."

"No. I can't put my finger on what's bothering me. Although, I read in a magazine how some men use charm as their weapon of choice for any sort of conquest, even work related ones. They're not called flirts, though. They are said to be charismatic."

"How to get *a*-head in the boardroom." Elaine laughed repeating her favorite joke.

"Can't you be serious for five minutes? I need your help here."

"Relax, Ava. You're still on a first-name basis. Other than having your phone number, he doesn't know who you are. Just make sure you keep one foot out of the blanket. He tugs too hard or gets too hot, you're out of there. You did the right thing meeting him in the park."

"Yeah. Now all I have to do is make sure Crystal doesn't realize I'm taking a two-hour lunch. No way can I do it under an hour."

"She won't know squat. I'll cover for you. So will Tracy. You should call her by the way. She'll get a kick out of this."

"You think so?"

"I know so. Tracy's gift got you this meeting. If it hadn't been for Mate for Life, what are the chances you would have been standing in front of the 21 Club on a Saturday night?"

"None. You're right. I waited to judge what would come out of this. I would hate for Tracy to blame herself if things didn't go right."

"What can go wrong? You're having fun, aren't you? Tell her."

"I will. Goodnight."

What could go wrong? The last sad reflection Ava's mind tossed while sleep made her eyelids heavy. On most days, Ava portrayed herself as an optimist. Moreover, she was feeling so much better now Tracy was in the loop. Except all this business with Mate for Life had worn her carapace to shreds. She could not believe how difficult securing a date in this town appeared to be. No wonder Scott's charming invitation contributed to making her worry. She wondered if he opted to string her along until he found someone better—adrift in a big city with the need to make new friends?

She turned over to her side as a nippy little thought prodded her. Scott plainly said goodnight.

She sat up in bed and wondered if she should call Elaine back and run this by her. Scott never mentioned he would meet her for lunch or stated he would not—just, goodnight.

She sighed, flopped back down on her pillow and gave up on the vicious little riddle. If he humored her, would he even show?

CHAPTER 5

MEET ME FOR LUNCH

The next morning, Ava came into the office at eight sharp. She would make up the two-hour lunch she intended taking by arriving early and leaving late—minimize the guilt of playing hooky for some boy in the park.

Her phone rang an inside line. Surprised she hurried to pick up thinking she only told Elaine she'd be in this early. "Ava Moss."

"I tried reaching you at home earlier, but you'd left already. Where's your cell?"

"Good morning, Tracy." She smiled. "Cell's charging as we speak. How come you're here so early?"

"I've been here since seven. I took a meeting with Reynard."

"What's up?" Tracy's voice sounded excited and piqued Ava's interest.

"Reynard wants to invite you to lunch with him and his new recruit."

Ava's face lit up at the rush of delight in Tracy's tone.

"He called me last night, maybe five minutes after you and I talked. He asked me to come in early today to discuss the meeting over breakfast. Both he and his brother think you would be a good fit."

Unable to articulate a single word, Ava found trouble hauling a breath.

"Ava?"

Shell-shocked Reynard even remembered her, Ava sensed a thousand questions rise in her throat and twist her tongue in every direction. He paired her with someone. "His brother?"

"I'll tell you about him later. He asked me to be discreet. And he wants me at the dinner too. The meeting's at twelve thirty, Nobu Tribeca."

"Expensive." Ava giggled.

"He's going all out on this. Nothing's too good for family, I guess."

"Oh, my God, Tracy. I'm supposed to meet the man I told you about for lunch."

"Oh, Ava I'm sorry. Wouldn't you know it?"

"I guess the saying is true. When it rains it pours—or something like a bucket of troubles. The problem is I don't know how to reach him—to cancel."

"I hope not to cancel—better to postpone," Tracy added. "Elaine met him. Why don't you send her to the park? You can't let him wait for God knows how long."

"I so had my heart set on seeing him. He's never going to call me again. He's from out of town. He never mentioned how long he'd be here."

Tracy kept silent, which made Ava regret gushing about the

date.

"Do you want me to ask Reynard if he can postpone the meeting?"

"No. Of course not. You can't reschedule now. Tell me the exact words Reynard used." She needed reassurance.

"Well, he thought since you're with the firm close to a year now which means you understand the ropes, the policies, and procedures, and since his brother is a financial expert, you two might help each other out."

"Smart," she agreed. "Smart and very Reynard. I'm out of wiggle room. I need to be at the luncheon. All I can do is hope for the best with my mystery man."

Ava hung up and blew a sigh of relief looking down at her best outfit, a slim fitting cream dress with matching waist jacket courtesy of lunch with Scott. Now, she needed to convince Elaine to go meet him.

Ava glanced at her friend's desk, forever jammed with files and folders, and a twinge of guilt inhibited her good intentions. She lost the nerve to ask Elaine to go to the park with all the work piled up on her desk.

Searching for a solution, and necessity being the forbearer of invention, Ava stumbled upon a brilliant beyond brilliant idea. She would change the outgoing message on her home voice recorder. Ava needed to keep her tone neutral while giving Scott the reason why work detained her. Once he realized she didn't show, he would call her home number, the only one she gave him.

She practiced until she got the message right. She hesitated. After changing the reference twice, she gave her cell phone number hoping no one else would call. Proud of her ingenuity, she agreed the little note addressed Scott with enough information for him to understand—or would he? After a few more trials, she decided to add Scott's name giving the particular reason for the change of plans. She would make sure to rearrange her recorder once she got back.

She spent the rest of her morning getting ready rehearsing what she would say, committing her resume to memory, and fighting nerves—mostly fighting nerves.

As the clock ticked closer to twelve, she examined the palm of her hands after she spotted little beads of sweat smudged on her folder and found them clammy and excessively moist. Ava found the opposite true when she tried to swallow—her throat dry and thick. She needed to calm down. "I can't believe Reynard picked me, Elaine."

"Why shouldn't he? Tracy complimented you to the wazoo."

"Think Tracy oversold me?"

"Relax. You're a nervous wreck."

Still, all I own is a measly bachelor's degree."

"Since boss man chose you, you're what he wants."

Ava nodded as she took a deep breath. Elaine, the voice of reason would be the mast to grab in the angst of a storm at sea. "You're right. I'll be okay. Besides, Tracy will be at the restaurant also."

Ava would never admit this to anyone, but Tracy attending the meeting made her more anxious somehow. Tracy's renowned work ethics made her a perfectionist, which weighed a ton on her mind. Branded a perfectionist herself, suggestions didn't seem to irk the same way when advice came from within. Ava preferred Elaine's no-nonsense approach next to her. At times, Elaine might be crude, and she spoke her mind more often than necessary. Nevertheless, she excelled at shrinking any crisis down to its proper size, which Ava needed about now.

"You sure you don't want me to go to the park to warn your beau?"

"All arranged, Elaine. Thanks anyway."

"What happens if he doesn't phone you? He'll never want to call back."

"Something I'll leave to chance. I waited too long for a meeting with Reynard Wallace to postpone. I can't blow the president of this company off for some guy I met outside a restaurant and don't have a clue if I'll ever see again."

"Said like this, go and prosper, my child." Elaine smiled. "And when I say go," she checked her watch. "I mean right now. Check the time?"

Ava closed her eyes and took a deep breath. "I can't feel my legs. Oh, my God. My legs are gone."

Elaine removed her glasses and gave her a scowling stare. "I swear, Ava if you blow this I will never let you live it down."

Ava grabbed her purse, turned and blew Elaine a kiss before she disappeared to take the elevators down to the garage.

The ride to Nobu managed to calm Ava down to a more natural high. She laughed as Tracy recounted her antics of the last few weeks preparing for this meeting.

"Why didn't you tell me last week this was in the mill?" Ava asked realizing Reynard's proposal did not spring on Tracy late last night.

"I told you the other day Reynard recruited someone from Europe. He considered an assistant from the office to complete this person's team."

"This brother comes with a team?" Ava showed surprise.

"Common practice in business. Good associates are hard to find. A senior prospect will travel with his entourage—colleagues he believes can help make the transition smoother."

"How long have you known Reynard would pick me—or did you twist his arm so bad he's now wearing a sling?" Ava chuckled. She'd witnessed the force Tracy exerted when pushed.

"Not at all. The one time I mentioned you did the trick, I guess. Reynard's been opening up to me lately, confiding little bits about his family."

"Ooh! Whispering in your ear. Nice."

Tracy's smile stretched from ear to ear. "Our relationship is more amicable for sure. Anyway, his brother chose you from Crystal's files. Serves her right for not introducing you."

"His brother chose me? Not Reynard?"

Tracy glanced at her and added, "There are four Wallace brothers. Reynard is the eldest. Another brother, Gareth, is busy gallivanting around Europe, traveling with the sailboat crowd." Tracy shrugged. "According to Reynard, sailing is all he ever does. He's raced twice around the world."

"Wow, that's a lot of personal freedom." Ava could well imagine what an incredible life Gareth led.

"Well, they're all independently wealthy. Old man Wallace left them tons of cash and all the secrets to making more."

"A wonder Reynard chooses to work for a living."

"He doesn't call what he does work. He calls what he does, sharing his father's blessings with others. He's quite the philanthropist."

"What about brothers three and four?"

"Bryant teaches in third world countries. He's even done T.V ads for CARE International."

"Quite the devoted family." Ava breathed out in silence trying not to make unfavorable comparisons between the Wallaces and the family who abandoned her on a church doorstep.

"The fourth one arrived from Europe where he branched off and started his own investment firm. He sold the entity last year for half a billion dollars."

"No wonder Reynard calls him the expert. Why do you think he branched out on his own?"

"No idea. He never said, and I didn't want to ask."

"Why would he pick me? I own zero experience working with a team, and I bet you I'm the oldest person to graduate at the firm, and all I hold is a bachelor's degree. Almost ludicrous he would select me."

"Don't worry. Reynard tells me he did a proper, thorough search. I happened to be in Reynard's office ten days ago when he handed his brother your file. He smiled a lot at the time insisting you were the one he wanted. He found something he liked."

"And you're telling me this now?" Ava couldn't believe her ears.

"Reynard swore me to secrecy. Besides, I didn't know when Reynard planned to hold this meeting. I told you. I found out about the luncheon this morning."

"Who called the meeting?"

"Your guess is as good as mine. For now, his brother seems to be running the show. At least, Reynard thinks the world of him."

"Reynard, Gareth, Bryant," Ava counted on her fingers. "So this one would be the youngest. What's his name?"

Tracy smiled as she drove into the restaurant parking lot. "We'll both find out when we meet him."

As they got out of the car, Ava tried again. "You happened to be in Reynard's office. Don't tell me he didn't introduce you. So, you don't want to say."

"I have no idea, I swear. I stopped by Reynard's office on my way to a meeting with a client, maybe twenty minutes, ten days ago while his brother sat at the desk going through files. Reynard introduced him as Junior, his younger brother. I doubt Junior is his Christian name."

"Well, I guess we'll both find out." They walked up to the front door of the restaurant, and Ava eyed the formal looking entrance. "Difficult to guess inside this bleak looking building one can find Matsuhisa's famous creations."

"I googled old man Wallace to try to find information on the family." Tracy gave Ava the eye, which said she spent her time searching. "Couldn't find zip. He led a very private life—oh, a lot of his business accomplishments, but nothing to quench a woman's curiosity."

Ava smiled and chuckled. Seemed to Ava Tracy researched the libraries to gouge information about Reynard, not only the Wallace family.

"Did you ever eat here?" Tracy asked opening the front door.

Ava shook her head widening her brown eyes for effect.

"It's easy. Stick with the salad and ginger dressing as an entrée, oh, and stay away from the miso soup. Delicious, but they don't bring you a spoon. You're supposed to slurp which is not the best fare when trying to impress the boss. Oh, and I love the pumpkin tempura—superb as in light and non-greasy."

"God, could this be any weirder?" Ava looked around at the people having dinner and sensed needles crawling up her legs, a real presence whenever nerves seized her.

"Don't worry. I'll pick for you. I'll say something on the menu seems delicious, and this will be your cue. Then I'll order my own dish."

Tracy no longer had her attention. In fact, Ava brought her hands to her face trying to calm the sudden burn creeping up her cheeks.

"What's wrong?" Tracy sounded concerned as she sought to follow her gaze.

Ava veered panic-stricken eyes toward her and pushed her a few feet behind one of the giant columns dressed in Japanese fare. "I can't go through with this. I can't." Ava breathed fast and could not get her whisper to come out other than in a high-pitched voice, a clear sign of hyperventilation. "The man next to Reynard is my man, the man I made an appointment with to meet in the park."

Tracy's face dropped. She stepped out from behind the column and glanced at the table they both observed on their way in. "This is ridiculous, Ava. You're mistaken. That is Reynard's brother. I recognize him."

"This is Scott, the man from the 21 Club, the one I mistook for Luke Perry." Ava closed her eyes and tried to calm herself. She realized Tracy counted on her performance. "I made such a fool of myself. I can't do this, Trace. I can't." *No wonder he never confirmed today's luncheon. He already knew I'd be here. God, the trouble I went through changing my answering machine.* "All I can say is he better not call my house—not in the next few hours. I would be mortified."

Tracy's puzzled expression showed Ava she attempted to make sense of her last remark. She saw her toss the riddle with a flick of her shoulder before she glared at her. "Listen, Ava. I don't know everything that went on between you two." She put up her hand when she noticed Ava about to spill her guts. "I'm not asking. Now's not the time."

Ava pinched her lips and felt her eyebrows so high above her eyes, she worried they'd never come down. Tears threatened to flow, and the last thing either of them needed was an epic blowout.

Tracy took a deep breath and Ava sensed a little speech brewing. A trained moderator and people specialist, she too had a lot riding on this meeting. "Remember when you say you would be an excellent actor?"

Ava bit her bottom lip, but didn't say anything.

"Because you're scrappy and resilient—huh?"

Ava bobbed quick little nods.

"Well, here's your chance to prove it, Ava. This is the fucking role of your life."

Tracy's trashy word slapped her back to reality. She never used this kind of language. Ava hauled a long breath still shaking from the sting of the comment, and decided this left her with no choice. Under duress, she would need to give her best in spite of a dismaying situation.

"When you think about this, he's the creep here. Not you."

"True," Ava stated in a breathless yet more reasonable tone. A creep, a giant leech of a creep while she would rise above his pettiness and play the role of her life. "I'll be okay." She grabbed Tracy's sleeve. "Just... just ... don't leave me."

"I won't, sweetie. I promise."

CHAPTER 6

PANIC ATTACK

Ava and Tracy walked toward the table with ready smiles on their faces, and Ava prayed she made a mistake. She would recognize her gaff, and the whole episode would blow over. They'd laugh about the mix-up at the office. Tracy would tease her in a relentless manner, but also be relieved. In all likelihood, this man might be someone who resembled Scott enough to be his twin. Many people found their double living close by in a densely populated city like New York.

As they grew closer, Ava recognized Scott—the man she quasi-assaulted at the 21 Club. The same man she gave her phone number to when he wouldn't give her his, the man who behaved like the perfect gentleman when they met at the theater and the man who proposed friendship to her during last night's call to her house.

In a few more seconds, he would glance their way and the drama would unfold. Ava gazed at him, at the familiar, attractive features wearing the garb of a dark blue suit with crisp white shirt and blue tie, and decided she found him perfect—irrevocably perfect for her. He wasn't a creep. The first night they met, she overreacted. The incident happened to be all her doing.

Both men spotted them and rose.

Too panicked to meet Scott's gaze, Ava concentrated on Reynard. She detected how squarely he stared at Tracy, and even though he didn't smile, his eyes did.

Tall and well built, Reynard wore his dark hair swept back in a wave off his forehead. He bore handsome features with his full lips almost identical to Scott's—the comparison bringing her full frontal with the man whose presence had haunted her for weeks.

Scott's eyes found their way inside hers, bold while a subtle satisfaction seemed to light up his expression. Not only a talented flirt as she said to Elaine, but he also appeared endowed with charismatic qualities he wielded with ease. He thwarted her escape as he locked her gaze in a stranglehold she deemed to be an attempt to gauge her reaction and study what might be her next move.

She managed to wrench her neck and tear her eyes away—the gesture almost painful. She blessed her lucky stars she spotted him first which explained his scrutiny—anxious, narrowing eyes branding the contour of her face. No doubt, his hazel glare betrayed surprise or perhaps frustration because she didn't seem more fazed by his presence.

For now, the decision to barricade her racing heart behind a façade of polite indifference helped salvage her dignity. She possessed excellent acting skills, she thought, smiling and eyeing Reynard.

"Hello," Reynard spoke first.

Ava noticed Tracy fought a stranglehold of her own her eyes

fastened on the man she most admired. The tall, striking blonde extended her arm to shake his hand. "Hello, Reynard. Sorry, we're late. Last minute spot checks."

Tracy turned and proceeded with the introductions. "This is Ava Moss, a rising star within our firm."

Ava flashed her brightest smile. "Pleased to meet you," she breathed as she shook his hand. "We met in the hall a few times."

Reynard reciprocated. "Nice to do it formally." He turned toward the other man she tried her best to avoid. "This is my younger brother, Junior."

"Reynard, don't you think you should drop the family moniker?" Scott smiled. He nodded toward Ava. "Hello," he said with layers of undertone. "I'm Scott Wallace."

He extended his hand as he smiled from ear to ear, brashly holding hers in a warm grip a few seconds longer than necessary. "We meet at last, Ava Moss. A distinct pleasure."

Ava maintained her smile as she mouthed. "Yes, a pleasure."

She realized her expression sent him mixed messages. She recognized her own fired miss-hits reflected in his eyes, one second coloring his air pleasant and cordial, the other hesitant and somber.

If Scott played a role using as much effort as she did, the armor of ready charm he wore served to disguise his deception well. Ava realized she put him at a loss to detect her next move. His hesitancy could not stem from ignorance of her feelings. She behaved like a giddy schoolchild around him, willing to throw decorum to the winds to own ten minutes of his undivided attention at some wobbly little table.

For now, the surprise card she sidestepped and handed back

to him served her well. No man enjoyed going into battle unprepared, she thought, and their skirmish portrayed the preface of war—a war of wits from where she would retreat with more of her plumage intact than she did after their last battle. A promise made to her bruised ego she intended to keep at all cost.

As the four sat down, the conversation dropped, each one retreating to the comfort of their own thoughts. She thanked her lucky stars Scott didn't raise the flag of their first encounter. Too proper? She didn't think so. He wasn't nervous a little voice reminded her. He had stood his ground and set her straight—refused to give her his phone number. She rolled her eyes thinking she needed to let that one go and move on instead of pouring salt on old wounds.

From this point on, she decided any sensuous, childish infatuation belonged in the bedroom, not the boardroom. She needed to hide her passion and ignore Scott's captivating charms. *Yeah, good luck with that*, practical Ava mocked.

The waiter introduced himself and asked if they requested anything special from the chef.

Reynard turned. "You can leave the menus, we'll be fine." He followed with a polite and dismissive smile.

Ava felt a slight kick in the right shin and glared at Tracy a little annoyed. Tracy showed fingers from both hands crossed behind her menu, which she made a point of showing Ava. "I'm sorry, Ava. Did I hit you? I tried to cross my feet," she said her eyes rounding as she did.

Ava bit her tongue. She would laugh at this later. Yet, Ava gathered Tracy meant the little poke to indicate solidarity, to warn her she would intercept any hard curve boss or brother might throw her way without any thought of herself. Ava gave her a head nod to show she understood.

She raised her eyes to find herself staring straight into Scott's eyes. He glanced at her and stared at Tracy, and back again showing he surmised Tracy and her were more than mere business colleagues.

Ava bit her lip as she gazed at Reynard discussing entrees with Tracy. A deep frown settled on his broad forehead, and she worried he might be sensing the tension between her and his brother. If she wasn't more careful, she might find herself out of a job before she even began.

"Ava," Scott asked matter-of-factly. "Reynard tells me you garnered some kudos in recent months when you performed a sort of coup for one of our investment partners."

Scott used the question to probe her with a hypnotic gaze and without the least bit of shame or restraint, she realized as she worked hard to remain cool under fire. She refused to show him, or anyone else, how she melted from the caramelized gaze oozing of sweet promises.

"I heard a tip. I went data mining for weeks. I believed the information held merit." She didn't smile, but sugar-coated her own gaze until she saw him flinch and turn his eyes elsewhere.

He concentrated on his menu. "I found this acute and perceptive of you, excellent analysis. I hope you can continue to do the same on my team."

Ava realized Scott revised his perception of her. He would need to adjust his opinion of her one full turn if he wanted to learn what made her tick. "I'm quite sure I can," she conceded with a smile glancing at the daily specials while unable to discern a single word.

Scott glanced at his brother. "What do you say we order? I'm famished," his light brown eyes on her as he said this.

Playing with her again, she sighed. The hard work would be to ignore his charm, remain indifferent to Scott's jabs. While her business degree had not covered boss-attraction-and-how-to-avoid, the school of hard-knocks bumping her from one foster home to the next trained her to duck and block, counterpunch when necessary.

Tracy coughed behind her menu opening a wedge to slant a peek toward Ava, to show she went ahead to pick for her.

Ava understood, willing any sparks which might fly between her and Scott to be the creative type. She didn't want the responsibility of causing her friend unnecessary grief. Ava suspected the situation happened to be just as difficult on Tracy.

"Well," Reynard ended the awkward pause. He glanced at the waiter standing at their table and conceded. "I guess we should order." He turned toward the women.

Scott nodded. Clearing his throat, he pointed narrow eyes and a dark frown at her suggesting she hurry.

Ava's smile froze—nerves. Her menu became one big blur. Why wasn't he enough of a gentleman to realize this? "Of course, we should order," she said deliberately pleasant.

"Salmon in a pepper sauce looks good with the pumpkin tempura." Tracy fudged for Ava's benefit.

"Yes, salmon seems exquisite," Ava said with a smile. She handed her waiter the menu, "with the ginger salad."

"I think I'll take the beef teriyaki with pepper sauce, a couple of sushi rolls first." Tracy smiled at Reynard and Ava while she threw Scott a cursory glance.

To Ava, struggling with all her might to fit in, Tracy's clear snub of Scott blossomed into an unexpected balm. In fact, this surprised her how much she found comfort in Tracy's show of support.

"I choose the black cod with the miso sauce, just the green salad to start," Scott ordered, handing the waiter his menu.

"I'll take the same as the young lady, the beef teriyaki." Reynard smiled at Tracy's raised eyebrows.

Ava thought, he needed to be pleasant to compensate for his brother's behavior—not because Scott was rude or overbearing. More due to the tension created by the bad mood he exuded which stirred everyone at the table.

"So," Scott addressed Ava once the waiter left. "This will be quite a new challenge for you."

"It will." She afforded a tight smile—to match his. "I want you to know that I'm very grateful for this opportunity. I'm a hard worker. You won't be disappointed."

"My brother and Miss Donovan think most highly of you." He paused as though unable to prevent his eyes from straying into hers and needing to seize the moment. "I went over your file, and I must admit I agree with them. I think you'll be an excellent addition to the team."

"Thank you." This time, the smile did reach her eyes. "How many people make up the team?"

"Including you and me, we will be five. You'll meet my team this week. They arrive from Europe Thursday afternoon. We'll have a get-together on Friday to introduce you to everyone."

"Looking forward to the meeting. In the meantime, is there anything I need to do to prepare?"

He smiled as though he wanted to say something, but seemed to hesitate while he chose to remain silent instead.

Ava waited.

"Brush up on your hedge fund knowledge." He surveyed the wine the waiter asked him to sample. "I didn't order this."

"I come here often, Scott. The sommelier knows what I like. I thought you might like to taste the wine first." Reynard spoke with quiet undertones.

Scott grunted and took a sip of the wine. With everyone looking at him, he answered. "Wine is fine, Reynard."

Ava's eyes widened. After Scott's swill, she thought she spotted a grimace on his face. She wondered why he needed to lie about the wine.

"Excellent. I knew you'd like this particular year." Reynard gave a nod to the waiter who tilted his head before he poured.

Ava considered Scott's opinion to be a mere formality. Reynard was the older brother his tone of voice relaying the fact. He was in charge.

Then she caught Scott's glance, and she glimpsed puzzlement in his eyes as he stared at her. He encountered another side to her at the 21 Club. All the crazy behavior she exuded. Now, his eyes shouted he wanted to strangle her. Well, perhaps he preferred flirty Ava to sophisticated Ava. Didn't matter because from now on, he would need to deal with the hard worker inside her, the one who studied years to be in a position of advancing her career. Adding some of her street smarts to the mix might also help—help her avoid the burn from a scorching gaze.

"Of course, you will need to move," he said deceptively soft. "We reserved space on the third floor in the right wing of the building. There's more sun in this corner, better reception for our cellular phones, and since the level owns its own elevator, getting in and out of the building is easier and faster to do."

She saw him wait for her reaction. Ava managed to keep her anger in check, which appeared easy to do. Perhaps she had no fight left in her. The meeting took its toll. More so, now Scott dictated she move out of her familiar surroundings and leave her friends behind at a time when she needed them most.

All of a sudden, uncaring of appearances, she fluttered a pair of lost doe eyes on him—unguarded and playing out the exact scene she'd struggled hard to censor. At least, she made certain no joy lurked in her eyes, no inkling of cheeriness.

CHAPTER 7

RELOCATION

Ava moved to the third floor with the help of a young man named Ralph who worked in maintenance. They packed her belongings and relocated her two floors below where she used to work.

Ava hated the arrangement. Her space, a little corner located off the main elevator cosseted her this past year like a warm fuzzy blanket, and she would miss her friends especially Elaine. Worse, perhaps she imagined this, but Scott seemed to relish her disappointment and confusion at being uprooted, as though her reluctance to move entitled him to dictate how and where she would spend her time from now on.

Ava didn't peg him for an alpha male. But then again, neither had she gauged as control freaks all the other bozos she dated, not until they took their toll. At least, this time, she realized beforehand how Scott liked to play the dominant man, more proof she should not consider him dating material.

Ava leaned against the window looking at the street sprawled at her feet. Resentment prompting her to play hooky, she spent the better part of an hour daydreaming. She pondered her time might be better spent going over the notes gathered from her recent textbooks.

Yet, the joy of speculating and beating the system by picking the safest, smartest ways to make money came in last on her list of priorities, drowned under the rolling waves of a rough tide brought on by a storm named Scott.

"The newness is making you crazy," Elaine mentioned. "We can still eat lunch together. Spend time with each other outside the office. He doesn't decide who you hang out with or how you live."

Ava blessed Elaine's rational thinking. Ava loved her career. Yet, the wind flew out of her sails for a reason. To puff them up, she thought, would only create massive rifts between her and Scott. For now, she needed to remain low-key and stay pat. Once better acquainted, she would find a way to chart her own course.

Ava sensed Scott also traipsed in unknown territory. He appeared different from the man she met—twice. No rational explanation for this transformation, but something she did got his back up. The presentiment, though tenuous, led to guilt-lined sensations, which dulled the joy of her new promotion. The strange culpability she shouldered became harder to support than being alone on the new floor without any of her friends.

The intercom buzzer rang twice. An internal call for sure. "Ava."

"Are you free for lunch?"

Why would Scott want to ask her out? "I made plans, why?" She expected to eat with Elaine and Tracy, pour out tidbits of her soul, heed office gossip and welcome a reprieve from her self-esteem trampled underfoot.

"I thought we might go over our new client roster over lunch, take the time to peruse some of the targets."

Ava hesitated. Scott's menu involved extensive information to digest during a meal. Whatever happened to us taking a lunch break? "Can we do this when I get back?"

Ava heard Scott's long sigh. She bit her tongue not to jump in and countermand her plans. She asked him a question, only fair she wait for an answer.

"I scheduled back to back appointments this afternoon. In fact, I would like you to come with me. I want to introduce you to two important clients. I believe a first meeting is crucial so these people can meet who they deal with when they call the office."

Ava perked up. Scott reaching out to her and wanting to add to her responsibilities got her excited. "Sure, I'll cancel my plans. Where do you want to eat?"

"I thought we might order in, save some time. Cindy said there's an assortment of good restaurants in the area, and they deliver."

"Yes. Makes sense." Ava smiled loving her job again. They could work together. She needed to keep their rapport professional.

"Whatever you order will be satisfactory. In my office in an hour?"

"You bet." She looked at her desk—an L-shaped teak piece cornered by three half-sized movable walls—and decided her little island could use some arranging. When she yanked on her desk drawers, their emptiness reminded her of the boxes containing all her personal effects still stacked against the back wall near the window. Time to unpack and decorate a little, she thought, hands on hips as she surveyed the place.

First, she would call Cindy and ask her to order the Chinese food she liked. She made sure to choose enough variety to allow Scott to pick his own assortment of goodies.

She looked at her suit relieved she appeared professional in a light olive skirt with a beige silk blouse, tan sandals, and bag to match. She decided she needed other attractive ensembles should today's impromptu visits unveil a sign of times to come.

An hour later, sitting across the desk from Scott eating moo goo gai pan and chicken chow mein, Ava relaxed at last. She smiled as she caught the image of Scott hustling with his chopsticks.

"Hold them like this," she indicated the best way to hold the chopsticks. "Here, let me help you." Ava placed her right hand on his to manipulate his fingers to the correct position. Their eyes met and held.

When Ava spotted his Adam's apple contract, she retreated to her side of the desk. "Only takes a little practice," she whispered back in her chair with her own chopsticks in hand.

"All right, here goes."

He tried to be a good sport, she realized. Nevertheless, she laughed when a big shrimp he stabbed went flying across the desk.

He excused himself grinning as though he won first prize. "I never learned how to use these sticks." He tossed them and opted for the plastic fork. "Good thing I'm not Chinese. I would starve to death."

She agreed, pleased he had a vulnerable side and the fact Mr.

Perfect had room to grow meant she could help him in small ways. He wiped the grease off his fingers and slipped her a folder. "I made you a duplicate of the list and the forecast. What should we tackle first?"

"You want my opinion?" Surprise rendered her eyes wide as she stared at him.

"Of course, Ava." Scott's grunt sounded louder than necessary. "Cooperation is why I want you on my team. You'll understand when the others arrive. Their input is also valuable. To juggle with today's market trends five heads are better than one."

"I agree." She bobbed her head unhappy she let her inexperience tucked out of her skirt. "I'm thrilled you thought of me."

He kept on eating as he waited for her to scan the inventory.

She did as she ate, studying the content while taking stock of the big names at the top of the list. She thought Scott might be wiser to start with smaller players if only to become better acquainted with the mechanics of the place or at least until they were accustomed to working as a team. "Quite a relevant directory," she breathed unwilling to look his way for fear she would say the wrong thing. Ava compared treading around Scott to stepping through a minefield. She never understood when or where she might trigger his anger or worse, his disdain.

"Meaning?"

She hesitated. Staring at Scott, she added. "Do you want me to be truthful? Am I free to say what I think?" A sentence she regretted uttering as soon as she saw the smokestack spewing out of eyes at once dark.

"What the hell does that mean?" He sat back in his chair as though she'd punched him in the gut. "The last thing I want is for you to humor me. You tell me the truth or nothing at all."

"Fine." She got up and crossed her arms about herself. "You, you're," she sputtered unable to get the words out. She designated him with the flick of her hand. "This explosion is exactly what I mean. I can't ever tell if you're going to smile, jump in my face, or wring my neck."

"I beg your pardon?" His voice sounded dark and menacing. "I never threatened you. I'm not a scary person. I'm never impolite."

She paused and took a deep breath. "Scott, if you're not happy about having chosen me for your team, if you want me out, just say so. I'd rather be sent back to the research pool than be walking on hot coals for God knows how long."

He rose from his chair and walked around the desk. He stopped two feet away. "So, what this hissy fit boils down to is you don't have the nerve to see this through."

"That's a rotten thing to say." She interrupted him.

He put up his hand. "I'm not finished. You had your turn."

He waited until she closed her mouth and clamped her lips shut. He shook his head avoiding to stare into her eyes. "You're all talk about wanting to advance your career, but you don't have the guts to do what needs to be done."

Ava considered how triumph glazed his smirk in spite of her narrowed eyes and flared nostrils.

"I'm right. You're ready to run back to your comfortable life with your office friends, your office gossip, and your weekend soirees at the 21 Club looking for a mate—for life. Not very career minded if you ask me."

"Why you awful person." Her face flushed as she stomped toward him Ava hurried to cover the few feet separating them. Taking a big swing, she aimed for his face, but he blocked her wrist. Ava swung her left arm, but he blocked that too. She hauled gobs of air through parted lips dreaming up something hurtful to hurl at him. "Seems like you're used to getting your face slapped," she hissed.

"Is this the best you can throw at me," he snickered.

"Let go of me." She panted in her effort to pull her wrists out of his grasp. "How dare you talk to me like this? You don't know the first thing about me."

As he watched her struggle, his eyes took on a strange glazed quality. "Maybe it's time I found out," Scott groaned. Dropping her wrists, he strapped an arm around her waist and closed the gap between them kissing her on the lips hard while maintaining his grip even as she fussed.

Scott clamped his right hand to the back of her neck as he drove his tongue inside her mouth, and what started as punishment soon became a pure pleasure for her as he relaxed his hold driving his kiss deeper.

Soon even his arms became sensuous. Caressing her back in what seemed to be a hunger to get close to her, Scott uttered between two breaths, "Nothing but sweetness here."

Ava gave up the struggle. Her loins on fire and her legs getting weaker she would soon need to pick herself up off the ground, but she no longer cared. She moaned as she complied with his kiss, giving back as much as she got.

Scott must have realized they were both so aroused if he didn't stop, he'd be having Ava for lunch because he pulled away without warning even tugged on her arms still hooked at the back of his neck.

She peered at him through the haze of steamy urges. She noticed his eyes were still closed, and he breathed in short, unsteady gulps. His parted lips trembled, and his arousal dug into her hip affording proof positive of how much he wanted her.

"I'm sorry," he whispered. "I'm sorry I've been so irascible. I never meant to hurt you." He looked at her. "I don't know what this is." He designated the both of them still locked up in each other's arms. "Let's not make anything of this, please."

Ava caught the supplication in Scott's eyes. She stepped back when she realized how hard he struggled to recover. If she kissed his lips again or licked them with the tip of her tongue, she realized he might come undone. "It's not your fault," she spoke with hesitancy searching for the right words.

Wrapping her arms around herself, she added. "It's because of the way we met. I want you to know I never blamed you." She smiled. "You were the perfect gentleman. You can blame the whole misunderstanding on me. The first thing I wanted to say to you had we met in the park for lunch, well, perhaps the second thing." She tried to brighten her smile, but her spiked eyebrows refused to come down.

Scott walked away and turned his back to her. "It's nobody's fault, Ava. Immutable circumstances—life." He rubbed a hand along the back of his neck. A few minutes passed and after taking a deep breath, he faced her.

Ava recognized the kind, handsome face she first encountered. She didn't recognize the sensation or the spell Scott cast upon her—this hot and cold feverish need of another human being. Lost and zapped, Ava realized she'd never encountered such a strong reaction. Twice in a couple of minutes, Scott punched the wind out of her. No wonder she remained shell-shocked around him.

"I felt like a heel because I didn't give you my number—such a simple thing to do. I just worried I guess, complications. When I saw your face in the personnel files."

"Is this why you wanted me on your team, guilt because you didn't think you acted correctly?"

"No, no. I considered all aspects before giving you the job trust me—if anything I was more demanding." He hesitated. "I can't face any romantic involvement in my life right now, Ava."

"Romance? Between the two of us? No way," she fudged. "We don't even know each other."

He smiled his pleasant mood restored, she thought. "Good. Glad you think so. The day after tomorrow the team is arriving from Switzerland and one of the members, Sylvia Danes, is my fiancée."

He stared at her—to gauge her reaction, she thought. "Sylvia was the reason I needed to leave in such a hurry. She'd booked a flight to Geneva for that evening, and we wanted to spend a couple of hours together. She's in Europe now renting out our apartment and taking care of last-minute details."

Ava called on all the acting skills she mastered in her young life. They couldn't fail her now. She didn't want Scott to discover the room spun round and round or realize he packed her with a jab so powerful she thought she might faint. Scott scored three for three, and she found no means to defend herself. She smiled from ear to ear adding quick head bobs as she said, "This way is better. Now we can concentrate on work."

"Honestly?"

Ava wondered why her utter capitulation seemed to throw him

for a loop. She read disappointment in his eyes. What did he want from her? "Of course," she whispered her smile widening. "I'm sorry too. I made a mistake jumping down your throat. You're in a new city with a new company, and new people. I'll be more patient. I promise."

He breathed out. "I got to tell you. A giant weight's been lifted off my shoulders. Thank you."

"Oh?" How was she ever going to carry this off? "Because of the way I accosted you?" She smirked. "Did you worry I might put the moves on you?" She added.

"No. Oh, but you mesmerized me the night we first met. Sassy, bold, with those huge brown eyes staring right into my soul. Well, Ava, I wanted to follow you everywhere." He smiled. "I'm relieved the situation is out in the open."

She pinched her lips and gave him a crooked smile. "Yep. Now, we can get to work."

CHAPTER 8

WORKING TOGETHER

C omfortable in the soft leather seat of Scott's Aston Martin, Ava rejoiced in her newfound talent for pretense. Pleased to bury the hatchet and show Scott the more amenable side of Ava Moss, she took pride in being pleasant and cooperative. Truth be told, grateful to be spending time with him, Ava needed to watch her body language—and her eyes often responsible for giving her away in any situation.

On their way to meet investor number two, Ava found the traffic more vicious than usual, and she realized Scott didn't relish driving in a city like New York where obeying signals veered to nothing more than common courtesy. "You bowled them over with your smarts," Ava said as she smiled at him.

He reciprocated while negotiating a turn. "For the record Abir displayed those wide grins for show. I thought his brother might develop apoplexy from staring at me. He meant the glare in those dark beady eyes to intimidate us."

She glanced at his profile with the warm smile and realized she might never get a better opportunity to ask him about his personal choices. Their proximity, the success of their first meeting, and the truce they struck earlier in the office gave her added courage. "I don't want to pry, and please tell me if you think I should mind my own business, but what made you decide to work with your brother?"

He chuckled. "How long did this question burn at the back of those lovely doe eyes I wonder?" He nudged her with a smile. "I guess my decision stemmed from a combination of factors. By now, I suppose you 're aware from the gossip mill I owned my own firm in Europe."

He paused to negotiate the busy intersection of Broadway and West 33rd Street.

"I think I heard something about a company in Europe," she said in a teasing tone.

"At first, my need to be independent, which my father called an act of treason, I performed to prove to him—and to myself, I guess—that I could stand on my own two feet. In a sense, he found me out. My departure did stem from rebellion on my part. Although at the time, I put an ocean between us because I didn't want to become him. I dreaded turning into this cold man everyone feared—even his loved ones."

Ava always thought life difficult growing up without parents. "I suppose being part of a family doesn't guarantee you love. I mean no one can ever be assured they'll be surrounded by caring siblings or even kind parents, I guess."

"Of course, at times, we tend to take our families for granted which doesn't help. However, being the baby, you could say I became weary of walking in the shadow of not one famous man but four, although I found Reynard never anything other than supportive—a superb big brother. No, the competition ran more between my father and me. We didn't always agree on well, everything."

They stopped at the light, and he glanced at her a little hesitant. "As I mentioned, I'm engaged to Sylvia—over two years now. We never formalized our agreement because we've always had too much on our plate, too many responsibilities."

He put the car in gear and continued down the street in search of parking. "Six months ago, she gives me an ultimatum. Find a partner to lessen the workload, set the date or she leaves and moves back to the States. Her family is all here." He sighed. "I figured the timing might be right. I tried to find a partner to run the European operation. I eyed California for an American version of my overseas layout. But instead of finding a partner, I found a buyer."

He rolled down his window to talk to the attendant. "We're going to be here a couple of hours at the most." He took the stub and entered the underground garage.

"Little while later, Reynard made his proposal."

"Yes. Reynard heard through the grapevine I sold my company, so he called me. Father passed away, gone three years now, and Reynard needs help. He wants to put in fewer hours and doesn't trust anyone else with the reins of the family business."

Ava searched the area gone dark all of a sudden. So engrossed in the conversation, she didn't realize they'd arrived at their destination. "Where are we?" she chuckled.

"We're in the underground parking of the Empire State Building."

"God, we got here fast. I didn't even realize. Of course," she darted curious eyes around her as she stepped out of the car. "I've only ever been here once, would you believe?"

"I hear this a lot from New Yorkers—the fact they run around with blinders. Then again, I'm guilty of the same sin. Lived and worked in Geneva, but almost never took the time to appreciate the sights."

They walked into the elevator, and Scott pressed the button indicating the fifty-fifth floor. Once the doors closed, in the confines of the quiet elevator chamber, Ava asked, "So, your fiancée wanted you to work less, Reynard wanted you back in the US, what do you want?"

The elevator stopped to let someone in. Scott didn't even glance at the person so intrigued did he seem by her query. She noticed his tightly knitted brows bounce the question as though at a loss for an answer. Gazing into her eyes, his expression even more perplexed, he breathed, "I guess, no one ever asked me this question, Ava." He flicked her nose. "You're the first."

Down the corridor upon entering the office, a soft chime resonated. A few seconds later, a young woman came to the reception desk and greeted them with a polite smile. "May I help you?"

"We are here to meet with Maxwell Saunders. I'm Scott Wallace, and this is my colleague, Ava Moss. Mr. Saunders is expecting us."

"Please make yourselves comfortable, I'll tell Mr. Saunders you're here."

The young woman returned and led them to a door she opened after a discreet knock. She smiled as she allowed them in.

A tall, slim man rose to greet them. "Well, hello." He took giant steps removed his glasses and extended his right arm to shake Scott's hand. "Please to meet you, Mr. Wallace."

"Call me Scott, please." He turned toward Ava. "This is a colleague and a valuable collaborator, Ava Moss."

"Miss Moss," Maxwell bent as he extended his hand toward her. "You are indeed the prettiest investment analyst I ever laid eyes on."

Ava smiled her eyes narrowing unsure of Maxwell's greeting. She wondered about the hint of discrimination behind the comment.

"Please don't take offense. In my mind, beauty and intelligence go hand in hand."

Ava gave in and nodded, flashing her brightest smile. "I like your way of thinking."

Maxwell laughed and kept Ava's hand in his longer than seemed necessary relinquishing his hold to walk back to his chair.

Scott broke the ice with ease. "I believe the package we offer will be of immense value to your upscale buyers."

"Please take a seat," he said as he poured water from a large pitcher sitting on his desk. "Well, when Reynard called me and said he enlisted the partnership of a hotshot broker from Europe, I hired a team of experts to investigate your credentials, Mr. Wallace—Scott. I didn't care that you were Reynard's brother or that you were raised by a famous daddy. I needed to be comfortable with the sort of experience you are liable to bring to my firm."

"Of course, this is normal. I would not expect any less."

Maxwell smiled outright as he rubbed his hands together. "My team and I are impressed with your work, with the results you gathered in such a short time period." He pushed two glasses of water in their direction. "Help yourself to refreshments. The beverage is a favorite of mine, good old H2O with a twist of lemon and a zest of lime, quite refreshing."

"Thank you." Scott gave Ava the first glass.

Slapping the edge of his desk, startling them both, Maxwell grabbed their attention. He chuckled. "What have you got?"

"Well, we've got several possibilities for you, some daring, some a little riskier."

"Hell, we live for risk. Nothing like mangled nights rattling your cage." He smiled and winked toward Ava. "Bring it on."

"One of our most lucrative projects in Europe involved keeping an eye on weather patterns. As you can well imagine, fuel and electricity are commodities in which prices fluctuate a great deal. When violent weather is involved, big governments play with the outcome—and are successful, I might add."

"Weather?" Maxwell's face cringed. "How the hell is a damn thing like weather going to make us any money?"

"For starters, many huge corporations' cash flow and profit margins depend on weather, and all of its derivatives. Take the new trend in hurricane research established by some of the leading atmospheric scientists. They say the Atlantic basin floor has changed, become active, and will likely be prone to hurricanes and violent storms for the next twenty to thirty years."

Maxwell shook his head demonstrating a little impatience. "Let's go over to my boardroom. You can show me on the viewer."

The three walked next door through a pair of communicating doors. While Maxwell's well equipped and vast, audio-visual room impressed Ava, she stood by as Scott removed his laptop from his case and reached for the DVD he carried in his briefcase. All business, he proceeded to show Maxwell his weather-pattern presentation.

An hour later, after the litany of a precise technical show and tell, Maxwell smiled, his eyes staring into the distance.

"I'm sure you understand how the flow of potential gains increases and decreases in direct proportion to weather patterns. Rightly predicted, they can make a corporation a lot of money."

A slight smirk flitted over Maxwell's face. The meaning of Scott's words did not escape him. He toyed with the idea aloud. "What you're saying is, by knowing in advance when temperatures are going to soar in the heart of Philadelphia, Hydro will send extra energy to cool the area and charge a bundle for the privilege. If you speculated the right way, you earned an easy profit."

"That's one way to look at this situation. Of course, the examples I offered are only one small wedge of the fund. The reverse is true for being able to pull out on time from ventures we discover are going to fail because of inclement weather. I'll give you the scenario of a major ski lodge we helped in the Pyrenees. The owners depend, during a particular year, on an abundant amount of snow by the time tourist season arrives, before December if all goes well."

"Of course," Maxwell agreed.

"Last year, we prompted the owner to speculate on the lack of the amount of snow they needed to make a profit at the end of their fiscal year. They did. Hardly snowed the whole winter. The sum of money they earned from their speculation more than offset the loss they sustained from a slow season."

"Which also means had they lost the speculation, they would

still pocket a ton of money because of their earnings from the ski lodge—not a loss, but win, win?" Maxwell chuckled rubbing his hands with satisfaction.

"One slice of the many speculations we can extrapolate."

"Almost sounds too easy. Are you doing this with inside information?"

"Nothing illegal about this. Knowledge is out there for anyone to graze and collect. The trick is in the data's interpretation. We employ a dedicated team of successful meteorologists. They're experts in their field and have worked with me for years. Weather speculation pays more than fluctuating currency, and as I mentioned to my other investors, profits are much easier to predict."

"I like this," Maxwell smiled. "What's the scale? Where do we launch?"

"We're thinking the million-dollar portfolio to start. We can let other players in as soon we agree on the models we want to use. Might take us six to ten months to streamline the procedure to fit your comfort level. A question of adapting the material to your type of investor." He glanced Ava's way, and she smiled to demonstrate her approval. "Whatever we decide, we never want to go below the quarter of a million-dollar mark. Otherwise, wouldn't be worth the effort."

"Hell, Reynard was right about you. I like the way you think." Maxwell pushed the chair away from his desk.

"Good," Scott said as he rounded up his presentation. "And we've got a lot more cats we will parade in front of you. Ava is working on a presentation of her own. She came up with a model covering health trends which are hard to shake."

Ava nodded putting away the laptop and CD.

"Like the way this sounds. When can we buckle down to work? I'll need advance notice to get my analysts in here."

"My team is coming in from Geneva tomorrow. We'll be operational as of the beginning of next week. Let me know how much time you'll need, and we'll try to comply."

Maxwell got up with a jerk sending his chair to hit the window wall behind him. Maxwell seemed wound up, and Ava wondered if the project they offered cause Maxwell's excitement or if this attitude happened to be in the man's nature. "Thank you." Walking around the desk, he extended his hand to shake theirs. "I appreciate the information. Making us tons of money is the best compliance." He laughed in a boisterous manner as he walked with Scott and Ava to the door.

Out in the hall, Scott smiled at Ava. "Now this presentation went well, don't you think?"

"Yes, I found so too." She smiled from ear to ear. She was proud of him and pleased he mentioned her in such glowing terms.

Scott pressed the elevator button. "I tell you, Ava. Much different dealing with Americans than it is working with Europeans. In Europe, we wine and dine heads of corporations who as a rule need to like you before they can trust you." He put his briefcase down and little side steps brought him closer to her. "In this country, our ideas hold all the merit. If they fly, you're on board."

"Two very different cultures I imagine."

Scott stared at her. She realized by the subdued smile, the heat in his eyes, he remembered the kiss they shared. He seemed poised to rekindle this kiss, bent to recapture the mighty grip he held on her.

She caught him shaking his head in what might well be an effort to dislodge the thought and Ava figured he didn't crave her in particular. The tender way he spoke of Sylvia meant he missed her, and he needed her company.

The bell indicated the elevator's arrival. Once they entered the gilded cage, Scott picked up his briefcase and slid the valise between the doors to stop them from closing again—perhaps keeping his little bird from flying the coop? "How about I take you out to dinner tonight to celebrate our productive afternoon?" He beamed a bright smile while staring into her eyes.

Ava hesitated. She still relived the sweet torture of his tongue kissing the breath out of her, the warmth of his hands caressing her body. "Do you think this is such a good idea? I mean."

Scott interrupted her. "Listen, Ava." He jammed his left hand against the doors to stop them from jostling. "I'm sorry for my behavior earlier in the office. I'm not sure why I kissed you." He gave her a sheepish look. "I guess I don't do well as a loner. I understand, using the loneliness excuse is lame, but please say you'll help me celebrate. I promise no kiss, no pawing of any kind. I vow to be a gentleman." He bowed from the waist. "I give you my word. We can start planning next week's schedule."

She bit her bottom lip in a hurry to nod her consent least she changed her mind. She was going to hurt in the morning. For now, she planned to enjoy being with the man. "Sure, dinner will be fun."

CHAPTER 9

DINING OUT

S cott parked at the foot of Ava's building. He got out of the car and glanced at the splayed orange light bouncing over the red brick as a glorious sun tipped its crown through the many trees lining the narrow avenue. He took in the quaint neighborhood heartbeats from Manhattan and thought the picture beguiling, right out of a storybook of the New York he always imagined.

He wanted to visit Ava's apartment and how she lived. She had the good fortune to reside in an enchanting area of the city where a chalk outline of the Brooklyn Bridge, one of the oldest suspension bridges in the country, stood tall in the distance championing a modern world as the proud erection humped the East River.

On his way inside Scott found himself questioned by Jeff, the door attendant, "May I ask where you are going, sir?"

"Ava Moss' apartment," Scott answered with a smile. "She's

expecting me."

Jeff tilted his head seeming eager to please. "She phoned a few minutes ago, and she is on her way down."

Elspeth crossing the lobby stopped to take a breath while leaning on Jeff's console. "Do you need help to go upstairs, Mrs. Chapel?" Jeff replied polite as usual.

"In a minute, once I catch my breath, dear. Thank you."

Alerted by the bell Jeff glanced toward the elevators. "Here she is now," he told Scott.

Scott acknowledged albeit a little disappointed. He looked forward to gathering Ava at the door, perhaps even peeking inside her apartment. Nevertheless, when he glanced at the bright smile on her face at the smart navy slacks and white top she wore, he smiled appeased in an instant. For a petite woman, she packed a lot of class.

"Hello," she greeted him a little out of breath.

"You are lovely, quite chic," Scott responded by taking her by the hand. He bent to peek at her shoes. "Still trying to be up with the grownups I see." He chuckled.

"Ava, dearest," Mrs. Chapel chimed in. "Is this gentleman your young man?"

Ava spun around, surprised by the comment. "Oh, hello, Mrs. Chapel." She stared at Scott an apologetic frown creasing her brow, at a loss for words.

Scott stared at the blue-haired Mrs. Chapel dressed in the same color. "I'm Ava's co-worker, Mrs. Chapel," Scott said executing a slight head bow as he did. "And yes, tonight, I am her young man." Scott stared into Ava's eyes wide with surprise.

Elspeth Chapel did not appear impressed. "Too bad, Ava." Mrs. Chapel nodded while grabbing Jeff's arm. "Here's hoping, dear."

"Enjoy your evening, Mrs. Chapel," Ava told the old woman hobbling down the hall her right hand grasping Jeff's arm. Unable to turn, Elspeth gave her a left-handed backward wave.

As Scott opened the passenger door for her, Ava cornered him with an eyeful. "About the shoes, not allowed bringing up any of the stupid things I said before our truce, deal?"

He didn't say anything but waved a crooked smile her way as he waited for her to take her seat in the car. He closed the door with a gentle hand.

"Deal." He laughed while taking his place behind the wheel. "You might want to relax and wear flats sometimes, give me the advantage of being the tall one."

"How tall are you? Five nine?"

"And a half. Five ten when I wear proper shoes."

"Well I'm only five two—and a half. But I'll remember to wear shorter heels on our next date."

A strange silence followed Ava's words. She regretted them dearly. She bit her bottom lip as she glanced at Scott. By the stern frown on his brow she suspected he caught the comment, and in his silence stewed some dire warning. He would be gentle enough she thought, as gentle as a man telling one woman he is in love with another. "By date, I meant work-date, of course."

"Of course." His features eased somewhat, but his smile did not return, not the way he first dispensed it.

"I think you're going to enjoy the One Green," Ava added. "I remembered you liked Japanese the other day. They serve excellent sushi, and the yellowtail sashimi is quite good."

He glanced at her with a suspicious smile. "Are you nervous?"

"Me! Nervous? Not at all. Not when I go out with friends—if you consider us friends. Maybe you think of us more as business colleagues?"

He chuckled as he drove into the restaurant's circular drive. "Relax, Ava. Meeting is not going to be all business. Let's call the dinner a get-acquainted round table," he said with a teasing edge as he turned off the ignition.

He allowed the valet to take his car and led Ava inside the oriental establishment. Though a decorated lantern's bright light adorned each table, they muted the bent heads of entwined couples in soft shades of amber, creating little islands of intimate shadows.

"Exotic, quiet," he commented as he led her toward the seating host after which he turned as though a thought struck him. "Did you make reservations?"

A slight grimace on her face, she added, "Didn't think the place might be busy on a weeknight."

"We can offer you a table soon," the host supplied with a mechanical smile. "You can wait on the terrace or start with a drink at the bar."

"The terrace sounds fun," Ava suggested.

"At the bar," Scott said at the same time.

They laughed, and Ava opted to follow Scott to the tall stool she needed to mount with caution not to let her heels hook around the foot's scalloped base. Scott catching her once again was more than enough she ruled.

Scott ordered a scotch on rocks and turned to Ava.

She didn't care for alcohol but refrained from mentioning the fact. Some men frowned on the gesture. "I'll take a club soda." She smiled. "With a twist," she added.

The waiter went to prepare their drinks.

"What are you? Recovering alcoholic?" Scott asked, pretending to be concerned.

"You're funny." Her chin forward she slipped him a casual glance. "Don't like to drink, don't like the taste." Her nose creased. "Effect is worse on an empty stomach. With my weight half a glass of wine well, let me tell you, I can become quite uninhibited."

"I think I wouldn't mind seeing this side of you."

"You did, the other night at the 21 Club."

"Is this what happened? You were inebriated?"

"Not on alcohol. High on life. Evening showed so much promise. Besides," she threw him a daring glare. "You wouldn't want me to start chasing you around the place again now, would you?"

"I get your point," he said wearing a crooked smile. He grabbed the soda the waiter plopped on the counter and slid the drink to her. Scott raised his scotch. "Here's to us, to me for taking the foot out of my mouth, to your beauty for putting it there."

"I'm not so sure I should drink to your lovely, yet misguided tribute," she shot back soda in hand. "Your toast implies, whatever happens is always my fault."

"So like a woman to possess the exceptional skill of turning a compliment into an accusation."

She laughed. "Well, since you're admitting, in broad daylight, you're handing me real praise I will drink to your attempt at a compliment."

"Seriously," he added his eyes probing her upturned face. "Why does a beautiful woman use an organization like Mate for Life to find a boyfriend?"

"Your question suggests I do this on a regular basis." Ava showed him the index finger of her right hand. "First time—a birthday gift from Tracy I didn't have the heart to turn down."

"Your first time which means you're going to do this again?"

Ava's turn to search his expression and she read in his eyes the hope she would deny the comment. Why would he care whether she copped an interest in finding a soul mate? The escapade took place in her personal life something she indulged in her own time. "Maybe," she fudged. "Got to love what the organization has brought me so far," she said with a tease in her tone.

"Ah, beginner's luck. Doesn't mean you're going to score again."

She turned to gaze at her reflection in the mirror behind the bar's counter. She wondered about the safety of continuing down the slippery trail of insinuations. His attitude portrayed a playful mood. However, Ava could not afford to expose her weakened heart. His handsome face would wear down her mettle in no time.

She took a long time considering her reply. In the mirror, she caught him staring at her as he waited for an answer. She wanted to give him something. "I wasn't under the impression I did," she whispered almost to herself. Staring straight at him, she continued, "Scored, I mean."

She read Scott's cringe under the direct glare of her fierce stare. He took a long breath while their host's arrival saved him from giving an explanation.

A hand invitation and a smile from the well-dressed woman signaled she would lead them to the right place.

Walking to their table, set behind a couple of columns at the back of the restaurant, Ava noticed Scott's shoulders rounding.

Either she pricked his ego or he realized she caught him flirting again.

She bit her bottom lip watching him precede her to the table. She didn't mean to chastise him. Neither did she intend shaming him with the sting of her reprimand. In no position to judge or understand the sort of thoughts racing through his mind, Ava regretted her comment. Scott stood alone, separated from the woman he loved by an ocean, logging hours of overtime in a desperate attempt to fit in. No wonder he traipsed all over her feelings with nonchalance. She needed to grow up and not be so quick to judge.

He turned as if all of a sudden realizing she trailed a few steps behind him. He extended his arm for her to go first, and she smiled as she passed him.

Two right turns later, Ava sat down and eyed him with an earnest expression. "I'm sorry about the last remark. Not a clue why I find it necessary to appear clever sometimes."

"No. Don't apologize, Ava. Don't ever be sorry about anything you say to me. I like when you call me out on my mistakes. I guess I need to release all this pent up energy and don't know how to vent. But that's no excuse. I'm the one who should apologize. No more innuendos I promise."

Once they ordered, and Ava replaced her soda water with a glass of warm sake, more for show than form, she eyed Scott squarely. "So, how do you enjoy being a part of such a powerful family?"

He chuckled. "Dying to jump inside my head, aren't you?" He laughed at her worried expression.

"I'm so sorry. Not my place to ask you such personal questions."

"No. I enjoy your curiosity. My team and I have worked together a long time, and we are familiar with each other, which makes working together easier. So you and I getting better acquainted is not such a bad idea, and we need time to catch up." He laughed, and she guessed her shy expression might be causing her trouble again.

After a few minutes of silence, Scott admitted. "Don't get me wrong, growing up with my family did offer a lot of advantages, except for the usual downsides I mentioned this afternoon. Being the baby, you feel you need to prove yourself always." He shrugged. "It's all been done. First step, first word, first extravagant demand you need to work hard to carve your place among the others."

"The good part?"

"Well," he smiled as though giving her question some thought. "I guess owning the biggest share of my mother's undivided attention. She's wonderful—and still around. Lives most of the year in Palm Beach with a couple of her sisters."

"You were her favorite?" Ava didn't quite understand family synergy, but she knew about favorites never having been anything other than an outcast in most of the foster homes.

He shook his head. "Nah. More because she and my father became estranged by the time I came around—nothing nasty. Usual story. Forty-year-old man sweeps twenty-five-year-old beauty off her feet and they get married. However, he preferred work as his lady. After a while absence took a toll. So they lived together but apart."

"This may be the reason you and your father never got along." She raised a shoulder, her comment tentative.

"You think my father envied my relationship with my mother?" Scott gave the suggestion a brief pause. He parked his eyes into Ava's concerned ones and nodded. "Might be. I guess I never thought about this side of things—never cared enough I suppose. A lot of the arguments happened because my father and I were too different—or too much alike as Reynard would argue."

Scott made some room for the plates the waiter balanced on two trays. Once the waiter left, he continued. "Reynard's argument got my blood boiling as I imagined becoming like my father."

"That's why you moved three thousand miles away." She winked at him. "I'm sure there are worse things than being similar to a man who succeeded in business beyond everyone's expectations—not to mention he took the time to share his secrets with the world. After all, he did sire four boys, and took excellent care of them."

"He did. No one can reproach him on this." They ordered the yellow tail sashimi for two, and he distributed the fare equally.

"This is way too much for me, Scott. I want to save room for the sushi."

"What about you? How is your family?"

"Oh, you know." She moved the food around in her plate with her fork "The usual." For once, a lie became less complicated than the truth.

"Where are you from? Couldn't find anything in your personnel file."

Ava dreaded the question. When asked, she made up some enhanced story concerning her family, their whereabouts, and their occupation. No one suspected the truth, except for Elaine aware she had flown solo for a long time, and Tracy acquainted with some version of the truth. Yet, no one understood Ava Moss or who she portrayed—perhaps because she wasn't quite sure of her own identity. "I'm going to need more sake to talk about my family." Instead, she took a big gulp of water, laughing her remark away.

"That bad, huh?"

She glanced at Scott, at the warm light in his eyes, at the sensuous lips parting as if he clung to her every word, and all at once she wanted to confess the lot to him, all the sordid details, at least, the ones revealed by the State's meager records.

"Well, here's more courage brew in your tank." He refilled her water tumbler and cheered with his. "To families."

"Wherever they may be," she added with deliberate prudence. She downed her water and eyed him with sadness. "I don't have a family."

He cocked his head, a puzzled frown on his brow. "Adopted?"

She nodded but didn't elaborate. She dug into her food with gusto. This saved her from adding anything else.

"You sure you don't want more of this yellow tail? So delicious."

"I know it is." Ava agreed.

"Were you raised by an aunt a friend?" He asked.

An innocent question, she thought as Ava gave him a negative nod.

"Adoptive parents." He nodded. "I hope they were good to you."

She shook her head. "No adoptive parents." She tried concentrating on her food, but all she did was take more gulps of her water to try to swallow the knot lodged in her throat.

"You weren't raised by wolves," he added with a snort, mocking her answer. "And I doubt you came down to Earth aboard an alien craft."

Ava considered Scott attempted to make light of a strange situation, his playful mood engineered to help him cope and for her to lighten up. Only, his mood didn't inspire to confide. "Foster parents—a bunch of them," she answered quickly before her nerve disappeared.

He sat back in his chair. "You're serious."

Oh, oh. Her head recognized before her heart did how she'd woken the beast. The curiosity present in all fellow humans whenever a measure of pity reared its head. Ava hated pity. The last thing she wanted: Scott's commiseration of her troubled youth. She smiled. "I found trying to adapt to a foster home difficult. Always new rules, new demands, and sometimes diametrically opposed to the last ones I'd learned." She raised a shoulder. "I discovered over the years, no one respects a child abandoned on a church doorstep."

"Is this what happened?"

She nodded while the smile gelled on her face.

"Why wouldn't anyone respect you? Doesn't matter where you're born."

"No roots, no past accomplishments, no name, no formidable clan," she concluded under her breath. "The nuns said the initials of A.M. were penned on the blanket my mother used to wrap me. Since I had pneumonia when they brought me in, their primary concern dealt with nursing me back to health, not discovering my origins. My identity or the name of the character who dropped me on their doorstep became immaterial after a while."

"I'm sorry," he whispered.

"Don't be. Being alone allowed me to be independent early in life. When I turned sixteen, I thumbed a ride from Dayton to New York City. The nuns found me in the nave of St Patrick's Cathedral, in Manhattan."

"Not a small church." He mouthed.

Ava acquiesced with a smile, appreciating his support. "The reason I came back here is because I figured I should have grown up in New York City. Anyway, I legalized my name and my date of birth."

"Your date of birth?"

"Nuns thought I appeared to be a few months old when they found me, late August. I picked May to be my birth month. I always thought May to be the prettiest month of the year, and I chose the nineteenth—my favorite number."

"How did you live, go to school?"

"You mean when I arrived in New York?"

He nodded.

"I worked in a flower shop for a while, hooked up with two other girls who needed a renter, and I finished high school at night."

"Hard road to take," he said without looking at her. "Here I am complaining about my family, and you possessed next to nothing," he mumbled.

"No. Don't say that. In fact, I personify luck." She laughed. "Eight years ago, I met Penelope Arden. A kind, grand old woman, the sort of person I imagined whenever loneliness struck or I became upset or when I needed a shoulder to cry on. Much like the grandmother I always hoped I'd find."

"Another version of Mrs. Chapel?"

Ava couldn't help a chuckle. "Much more lucid, with a warmer personality—oh, Elspeth is also charming, but her memory is failing."

"How did you meet Penelope?"

"She collapsed in the subway one morning."

"Collapsed, as in fainted?"

"Yes, on the platform just outside the door to the train. We sat facing each other for a few stations. I remember because she kept staring at me. When the train stopped, I bolted for the door. Can't remember why I looked back, but when I did, the old woman was lying on the floor, a few feet outside the doors. People stepped over her and went on their merry way. I almost did too. Then I paralyzed, like in the parable of Sodom and Gomorrah—my head racing to get to work on time while my heart refused to let go of my legs."

He laughed at her choice of words. "They must have thrown the Good Book at you more than once."

"You know the story?"

He smiled. "Lucky for me, you didn't turn into a salt statue."

"Lucky for me, because Penny and I became friends, and I got the bigger share of our friendship, by far."

She waited until he finished laughing. "I did odd jobs for her, kept her company. Penny became family, a real family. When she passed away I was alone again." Meeting with the sad look in his eyes, she cheered up in a hurry. "But she left me her condominium and a little money I used to put myself through college. I changed my job to something more related to the field I studied, and here I am."

"You're lucky she owned no family to leave her belongings to. The condo is an expensive one."

"Yes, of course." Her eyes lit up. "I mean, I inherited lovely brocade furniture, all with flowered patterns." She smiled, happy he was laughing. "Chipped dishes I haven't had time to replace. Tons of candles I don't have the heart to throw away, and despite the fact I'm the only person under sixty living in the building, I, Ava Moss, own a piece of real estate on a street named after a fruit, three stones' throw from the Brooklyn Bridge."

He continued to laugh at her words. Still chuckling, Scott raised his glass. "Here's to quiet neighbors—and the brief summary of what I suspect to be a rather bumpy beginning to your life. To your courage, Ava Moss, and to all the success you deserve."

"Thank you," she said wetting her lips to his toast. A furtive glance told Ava his eyes lost their subtle gleam—the hungry curiosity borne since the day they bumped into each other. Was he hosting a pity party in her honor?

Ava's heart lurched in her chest. She'd encountered men like Scott—handsome well-to-dos who demanded the whole package with regards to close friends. Fringes like wealth, good looks, smarts, and most of all, pedigree. Scratch wealth and pedigree and leftover scores meant two out of four. Not much to offer the man she so admired, the sum amounting to a failing grade at best.

CHAPTER 10

MEETING THE TEAM

F riday morning, Ava prepared her presentation at the office for Scott to examine before she paraded the finished product in front of Maxwell Saunders the following week.

Despite his promises of being in the office as early as Thursday afternoon, Scott called to say he would be in on Friday, after lunch.

Her last memory of him went back the dinner they shared on Wednesday evening. In the aftermath of her confession, Scott steered the conversation away from families and friends and kept the topic of business on his sleeve.

Of course, they shared a good laugh at her expense about the Mate for Life incident more so when she dusted off her comedic talents to mimic Vanessa Distel.

The phone rang. Ava resented her daydreaming and pressed the flashing green light indicating an inside line. "Ava Moss."

"Ava, Scott."

Ava hurried to pick up the receiver.

"I'm introducing everyone to Reynard. I'll be down in an hour or so.

"Okay, I'll be ready. By the way," she didn't finish. He hung up. She made a face at the receiver slamming the piece down a little harder than she intended. His voice sounded edgy and brooked no amity whatsoever.

Why in the world would he be angry now? Unable to answer this question, a thought occurred to Ava. Perhaps she should be upstairs with him as he introduced everyone to Reynard.

***

In the conference room on the fifth floor, Scott applauded his earlier decision not to bring Ava to their get-acquainted meeting— the inequity of a lamb in a den of wolves struck his fancy.

In fact, sitting around Reynard's roundtable to discuss the strategy of new beginnings, he tried not to compare the two women in his life after which he wondered why he even considered Ava as a woman in his life.

Flipping the question on its belly, Scott couldn't understand why Ava had made such an impression on him—young, inexperienced, a baby in the adult world of finance. Yet for all her immaturity, Ava became the first woman in a long time able to whip him good. She whirred through his world like a newfangled beverage shaker with the powerful little motor able to blend his common sense and raw emotions into a heap of mush.

He hadn't experienced such intense passion for a woman in as long as he could remember, not even in the two years of his engagement to Sylvia. He'd hoped Sylvia's return might dissolve the burning need to gather Ava Moss in his arms. Yet embracing Sylvia only enhanced his longing for Ava, to the point where his desire to sense her heartbeat against him deepened. He grew hungry for the sweet breath he tasted—the pleasure a few days old.

"Scott?" Sylvia asked him. "What do you think?"

Jerked free of his thoughts, he turned toward Sylvia while he groped at the bits and pieces he'd overheard before drifting off. "What do you mean?"

"I don't want to put you on the spot," Reynard added. "I thought you ought to rein in a few specialists here at the office instead of contracting out."

Scott acquiesced. "I gave the matter some thought." He glanced at Sylvia. "Well, Sylvia and I discussed the pros and cons in length. I'm going to stay with the firm we hired in Europe for now, at least where the weather model is concerned. Later we might train someone new. Experience has taught us, Reynard, capable forecasters are hard to find."

"I understand. Still, the less our information is out in the open, the more confidentiality we can hope to maintain." Reynard smiled. "Remember what father used to say? 'Leaky lips sink ships.'"

Scott caught Trevor's eyes on him as a slight malaise ran through the small group. "Of course, I remember what father used to say," Scott said teeth clenched. "Fact is, with today's technology, computers are an even bigger security risk than people are," he added.

Reynard stared from one to the other a silent question in his raised eyebrows.

Exactly like Father. Expects everyone to understand what he wants. "Trevor discovered a small discrepancy when we closed shop in Europe—possibly a breach in our midst. No way to verify now."

"Well," Reynard breathed as he raised his chin. "Here's hoping the breach did not follow you here. All in all, technology, computers—operated by people. I think you should direct your efforts to hire the staff you'll need to work on these task forces—keep a closer eye on potential violations."

"Don't worry," Trevor intervened in Scott's defense. "We're monitoring the situation. I'm also digging into the legal ramifications of accomplishing what you're proposing. I'm mere weeks away from tying all loose ends."

"Good, good." Reynard rose. "I'll let you get to work, Scott. Thank you for the brief. We should meet again in a couple of days and lay out a functioning agenda. In the meantime, I'll see you all tomorrow night."

At once, facing Sylvia became inevitable. Rising, Scott turned toward her. "My brother is having a small get-together in our honor." He glanced at Mathilda and Trevor. "For all of us." Eyeing Sylvia again, he said. "I'm sorry, sweetheart. The invite slipped my mind."

Sylvia leered at him before turning to glance at Reynard. "Thank you for the invitation, though belated. We are all looking forward to it, of course." She included Mathilda and Trevor in her statement."

Reynard acknowledged. "Good. I'll expect you around seven."

Tracy went down to the third floor in search of Ava. "Sweetie, what are you doing?"

Sitting on the floor rifling through stacks of papers and thumbing through dusty textbooks, Ava smiled at Tracy.

She rose while shaking some of the carpet lint from her skirt. "I'm trying to find an equation I came across when I wrote my paper. I made the annotation on the page. Now, I can't locate the trail—to back up my findings should I need to." She paused for a second. "What are you doing here?"

"I came to ask you what you are wearing to the soirée tomorrow night?"

"Soirée? What soirée? No one told me."

"Reynard invited the team to his home for a little welcoming party. Informal, business attire." She smiled. "Asked me to be the hostess."

"Lucky you. I'm not invited. I'm the new kid, pretty much the Cinderella in this story—for now."

"Of course, you're invited."

Shoving her books closer to the desk with her foot, her back to Tracy, she added. "Don't think I am. Scott would have said something."

"I suspect Scott doesn't know if he's coming or going just about now. Anyway, he doesn't extend the invitation his brother does, and Reynard asked me if you needed transportation. Do is in the Hamptons."

Ava turned toward Tracy. Taking a deep breath, she blew a mesh away from her face. Speechless, Ava didn't need new drama in her life. Working with Scott happened to be quite different from socializing with him. "The Hamptons?"

"Family's New York two-story penthouse is being remodeled."

"What am I going to wear? No time to go shopping my presentation is this afternoon."

"Wear what you did at your Mate-for-Life gala. Perfect city chic for the type of evening."

Ava nodded. "Scott admired the outfit. Won't he think I'm lame wearing the same dress twice?"

Tracy laughed. "Ava, men never remember what we wear. He gawked at you what ... the whole of ten minutes while you wore the outfit?"

"True," she breathed. "Wow! Well, what do you know?" As the excitement dawned on her, she exclaimed. "Cinderella is invited to the ball." She shook Tracy's arm with enthusiasm. "Will you turn your pumpkin into my horse-drawn carriage—horsepower drawn?" She laughed at Tracy's sarcastic expression.

Tracy admonished with a raised eyebrow. "Yes. I will take you. Oh, and I know my car's small, but if you call it a pumpkin one more time, deal's off."

Ava laughed excited by this new prospect. Then, the elevator bell signified to Ava she should hurry Tracy along. "You better leave. Don't want the team to catch you here—not on day one."

Soon they squared the hall and approached her little island, and Ava thought the incoming four displaced a lot of air. She chided herself not to stand on guard for their arrival.

Wearing flats to complete a blue pinstriped business suit, Sylvia was not what Ava had imagined, not at all. The same height as Scott and clinging to him like a tether, she wore her light brown hair cropped short, sporting blond streaks stringing down her neck and across her forehead. Her face appeared slender, but her jaw was square and strong, and though her lips seemed puffed up, they did not draw attention from trendy blue-rimmed glasses dressing up keen eyes of a cool, indiscriminate gray.

Ava felt more than she noticed Scott wait for her and Sylvia to connect with underlying nerve, the tension between them palpable. In fact, her own will to fight the shakes aside, Scott's unctuous behavior somehow managed to deepen everyone's malaise. She had never seen him this smooth, this purposely collected not even during their meeting with Maxwell Saunders.

Sylvia made the first move. "A pleasure to finally meet you, Ava." She stretched out a hard hand and took a firm grip of Ava's little grasp. "Scott has told me so much about you." She threw Ava a tight smile and a knowing look.

Ava wondered how much she knew about them—whether they enjoyed a good laugh about her and Scott's first meeting. She smiled attempting to keep the hurt in her eyes from showing.

Scott cleared his throat. "Sylvia is talking about all your good work ideas you've implemented. I told her you're sharp and well aware of the game."

Ava smiled. *So glad you cleared that up.* Breathing again she whispered, "Thank you."

He turned toward the other two in his entourage. "This is Trevor Hardy, the law consultant in our group. An important part of our team."

Without leaving Ava the chance to greet Trevor as though realizing he made a blunder, he faced the last person in the group who remained off to the side. "Last but not least, another valuable cog in our machine, Mathilda Redding. Mathilda is Sylvia's cousin. She's a pistol with public relations."

"Pleased to meet you both," Ava shook Mathilda's hand and

realized the woman would not be an ally. Although at first, Mathilda seemed more pleasant than Sylvia did—almond-colored curls crowning a Botticelli face oozing with charm—the penetrating dark eyes she posed on her ran shivers up her spine. They demonstrated how formidable an adversary Mathilda might be.

She glanced at Trevor Hardy who displayed a round, ruddy face with a warm smile. He appeared young despite his stout and tall frame because of his eyes Ava thought—big, blue, unguarded and seemingly oblivious to everyone and everything around him.

"You ready, Ava?" Scott asked when he spotted the files piled on her desk.

"Absolutely." She gathered her slides and folders and wondered what Scott found interesting in a woman like Sylvia. She didn't think her beautiful—not homely, though—in fact quite slender and stylish. Yet Scott's fiancée was not the gorgeous woman Ava thought would be on his arm, and even though Ava tried to picture them together without resentment clouding her judgment, she didn't understand the fit.

Then Ava remembered her scale. Sylvia 's wealth, smarts, and pedigree made up a desirable combo, and Ava recognized the woman was attractive so four out of four created an excellent grade. No wonder Scott and Sylvia belonged together.

CHAPTER 11

PRACTICE MAKES PERFECT

Thirty minutes later, shelving all thoughts of Scott to the bottom drawer, focused and attentive, Ava began her presentation.

"The health industry has been a steady source of income over the years, and with baby boomers reaching the critical age factor, investment experts are calling health the next big bubble." She met with Sylvia's pinched expression, but Trevor's smile motivated her to continue.

"As we witnessed in the past most investment groups tend to lunge or reach on the surface when building a portfolio for their clients by picking nothing but blue chip earners. They like to skim well-known companies with proven track records like someone might scrape off the icing on top of the cake. For investors, this tends to mean long-term possibilities with small immediate gains and slow cash growth over the years."

She rounded her next two slides.

"The health industry," Sylvia sighed with a tone laced with annoyance. "Scott, I thought you said we would be envisioning a fresh new idea—something exciting. This is another hard sell."

"I agree," Ava smiled. "You're right, Sylvia. However, I geared my presentation to cover new angles."

She flipped to her next slide. "I propose we dig deep rather than lunge across the surface—go vertical as in search all the way down to the smaller entities. Along the way, we will find a variety of valuable stock from different sized companies."

Scott nodded his eyes mere slits as he thought aloud. "By digging to the bottom of the barrel, we might even pocket the biotech fledglings." He glanced at Sylvia and the group. "I always thought biotech showed promise."

"Scott, with FDA approval needing to be stamped on every outcome, with the government's slow rate of response and its puny funding, not much to go on with this." Sylvia raised her hands far from convinced. "You witnessed what we were up against in Europe a few years ago."

"A lot has changed in the last five years, Sylvia." Ava countered. "For instance, United States' health bill is now a two trillion dollar industry representing close to eighteen percent of the gross domestic product." Ava flicked to the slide illustrating her figures. "Financial advisors expect the budget to double in the next ten years."

Sylvia sat back ready to listen.

Scott smiled.

"In the past ten years, costs soared in all health domains. Until now, insurance companies have endorsed the biggest part of the medical crunch. Yet by providing coverage for an aging and unsuspecting population—baby boomers who are dangerously reaching the limit to where these benefits will be cut off—we risk beleaguering our industrialized nations with medical upheaval in the years to come when we need health benefits the most."

"Why does this concern us?" Sylvia asked.

"Biotechnology, Sylvia," Scott said. Turning toward Ava, he asked. "May I?"

She nodded. "Please."

"Over the last decade, the National Institutes of Health have dumped $140 billion in grants to fund new frontiers in the development of products, devices, and any significant patent that lies in wait to alleviate the emergency healthcare everyone realizes is imminent."

Ava smiled, as she added. "This has left the market open for any smart biochemist or group of young scientists to develop the next great tools of our future health care."

Scott added, "They even posted all they can about the Human Genome Project and its findings in the public domain to encourage project leaders and researchers to develop new vaccines, new products, and new technology as it relates to the human body."

"Yes," Ava reinforced happy to count him on her side. "Now, many small companies that don't look like they're going anywhere are on the verge of significant breakthroughs. All we need to do is identify them which I did here." She clicked on the last few pages of her data. "These are names of some of the potentials who are on the verge of announcing their work plan or have released new technology a few short months ago—some as recently as last week."

"You didn't happen to find Xfinite in there by any chance?" Trevor asked. They had not heard a peep out of him. Busy taking notes, he stayed out of the discussion.

Ava shook her head. "I don't understand."

Scott rolled his eyes. "Trevor, this is not the time."

"Sorry, Scott. Pathetic attempt at humor."

Ava looked from one to the other to get answers.

With a heavy sigh, Scott satisfied her curiosity. "The name belongs to a fraudulent online investment shadow—fraudulent because they've been dipping into our confidential data and helping themselves to our files."

"This is terrible," Ava whispered unable to hide the surprise in her eyes.

"Trevor came across them a few weeks after our last audit, months before we sold the company. Every time we thought we tapped their source, they disappeared, eluded us."

"How is this possible?" Ava said. This wasn't her fight, and the mood around the room implied she mind her own business, but she found their calm about a potential leak shocking. "To be a ghost in your system means they would need a handle on your secret codes your encrypted formulas."

"We don't know," Trevor added.

"They are discreet. We didn't notice a single wrong move out of the jokers. They don't steal money out of our accounts or pilfer anything they believe might be too visible," Scott delivered his explanation with a perfunctory tone.

"Wow. How did you obtain the crook's name? Or is this only a name you gave them?"

"One of our investors came back inadvertently alerting us to the problem. They stopped short of giving us details." Trevor answered.

"I'm thinking of asking the SFO to investigate." Scott supplied.

Sylvia shook her head. "Daddy said alerting the Serious Fraud Office would be bad for business, dreadful—for our side. Investors would read about the investigation in the news and pull out in a panic."

Trevor agreed. "I take no pleasure in saying this, but in our business, victims are too often linked to the victimizers. Investors don't care who does what to whom, so long as their information is not blasted on any front page."

Scott put a stop to the discussion. "Back to the presentation. Your proposal shows merit, Ava. I'm willing to work on the timing, streamline the offer to suit the savvier investor and perhaps add a few specialists to work on deployment." He eyed Trevor. "Possibly the same setup we established in the weather sector? What do you think—legal point of view—keeping in mind the angle we discussed with Reynard earlier?"

"Doable. I'll need to do some research. But all in all, doable."

Scott turned toward Mathilda. "You're awfully quiet. What's your take on this?"

Mathilda's shrewd brown eyes veered from Sylvia to Ava. "You know me, Scott. I go with the flow. I can invite takers on both sides of the ocean, regardless of whether we lunge—or dig." She addressed Ava with a cavity-sweet smile.

"Then it's settled. We'll use the next couple of weeks to study the pros and cons and get our act ready by the end of the month."

"What about our promise to Maxwell Saunders—to present

him with a new project by the beginning of next week." Ava smiled.

"You met with clients?" Sylvia's delicate tones expressed shock. She glared from Scott to Ava, eyebrows raised and forehead puckered.

Envy churned in the mix Ava realized when she caught Sylvia's glare.

"Of course. Why not? You know I like to jump in as soon as I can. Plus, I found this the perfect time to introduce Ava to our new group of investors." He smiled at Ava. "They were impressed with her work."

Ava noticed the others' expression revert to calm professionalism. She pondered Scott could be quite formidable.

"As for Saunders, he'll understand. We still need to streamline the weather model with him next week."

Trevor rose first. "Well, now you showed me my office, Scott, that's where you'll find me. I've got more than enough to get started."

As he got to the door, he turned and addressed Ava. "Can I call you, Ava, should I need your expertise on the subject?"

Startled Ava could not detect any sarcasm in Trevor's smile. He displayed everyday kindness. "Sure, my pleasure," she said enthused.

He raised his right thumb in the guise of a salute and left.

"I think we should all get to work, Scott finished. Ava, can I talk to you?"

She nodded and stayed behind as Sylvia and Mathilda left.

She bobbed a polite nod their way without glancing at their faces. Sylvia seemed angry. Could be her natural disposition or fatigue might be the factor. They had landed the day before. Scott took pleasure in driving them, she realized.

"Sit down, Ava." Scott sat in the lounger next to his desk inviting Ava to take the straight back chair facing him. "I enjoyed your presentation."

"Please," she gushed a little embarrassed. "This is not the way I intend presenting to the client. This happened to be more shop talk than a sales pitch." She stopped when she did not draw his attention. He fidgeted with the round copper handle affixed to the drawer of the small table beside him. "You didn't like my presentation—you're just saying you did out of professional courtesy," she whispered.

He stared at her.

Ava stared back at the eyes always capable of making her legs weak.

Without looking away, Scott explained. "The tricky part of show and tell is to know how much to divulge, and what is best left unsaid."

"Of course." She shook her head. "Didn't I say this is not the way I would present the package to the client?"

"Listen, Ava." He leaned forward. "Here's what I want. I want you to work with Trevor and Sylvia on this. They're your ideas, and both need to understand how best to implement them. By the end of the month, if all goes well, Sylvia will present the material to our better clients."

"Sylvia!" Out of stupor, she rose and towered over him. "You would ask Sylvia to present my ideas to Maxwell Saunders?"

"She is more experienced. This is teamwork, Ava. It's not about yours or mine."

"Oh, I understand." She began pacing in front of her chair.

"You think because I seem so young, and because I collected so little experience, the client will believe the project is all child's play and if a child can do it, anyone can, right?"

She checked his eyes, and they probed her in a strange way. Did Scott care this happened to be her baby, the one project she dreamed of using to launch her professional debut? "Darn it, Scott. I worked too hard on this plan to let someone else collect the laurels. You heard Sylvia. She doesn't even believe in this project's merit. She shot me down a few lines in which did not help my delivery, by the way."

He rose and came around to meet her. It was his turn to appear menacing as he sat on the edge of his desk. "Why you need to make her realize how good this is. Combining our strengths will allow us to double our success. Your smarts and her proficiency."

This was bull, and she didn't need any of his screwed up advice. Ava remained adamant and kept shaking her head pinching her lips in a tight and mutinous line her arms flung about her to stop the shakes, to prevent her from resembling an angry teenager.

"How long have you been in the game, Ava? Two—three weeks? How much experience have you garnered at convincing a group of hard-nosed investors to see things your way? Yesterday, you were in a pool of research technicians looking for your first big break."

Ava fought to keep her pout, but his logic left her empty and exhausted while her face reflected the doubt and inadequacy she'd kept hidden for weeks. No longer mutinous, she paid attention to what Scott tried to tell her.

"I picked you because I knew you were smart, smart enough to realize, Ava, boardroom dancing is best learned while observing an experienced artist going through the moves—and practicing.

There's a lot of practice involved."

Ava released a long sigh and sat on the edge of her chair. He was right of course, she thought as she stared at the tip of her fingers. Vain of her to think she might come in and trigger everyone's imagination.

"Ava, look at me," he told her in a soft manner.

She looked up her heart lurching in her chest. Scott's eyes were so kind. Staying angry became difficult to muster.

"You think Sylvia was hard to you just now? Let me tell you, she was polite and proper. An angry investor can be much more direct."

"So, what you're saying is," she added needing to clarify his words. "When I've studied performances,"

"And practiced," he added interrupting her.

"Of course." She bobbed her head with quick little nods. "And practiced, then you'll give me the green light?"

"You bet. Might not be with one of your ideas. Doesn't need to be. As long as you present a project as though you believe in the content."

"I guess this means I've got my work cut out with Sylvia." She didn't intend spitting out the woman's name.

Scott agreed, eyeing her strangely. "I would say you do."

CHAPTER 12

HAMPTONS SOIRÉE

Tracy had been driving for over an hour while Ava navigated their trajectory in a road Atlas. "I thought he'd be closer to Westbury or somewhere in the area. We've been heading toward the Hamptons all this time," Ava told Tracy.

"I realized as much. In fact, the mansion is quite a ways from Manhattan though I didn't expect the drive to be this long."

"I guess this explains why Scott and the others chose to stay in the city even if this means living in a hotel room."

"A hotel room!" Tracy exclaimed. "You can't call a penthouse apartment at The London, a hotel room. The penthouse offers two floors of luxurious living with wrap-around views of Manhattan, royal furnishings, cleaning staff, and one of the top Michelin Guide chefs to prepare meals."

"Hum," Ava attempted to form a picture in her mind. She gave up when beige images of her dowdy furniture and chipped dishes began to multiply while the stack rose higher and higher to cover a second floor she did not own.

"How much farther?" Tracy tried to peek at Ava's map.

"Well, we're on Noyac Road—finally." She twisted the map to read the small print by the waning light of a blinking sun. "The turn off doesn't show a name, just an X you drew to mark the spot, maybe a mile—no, more like half a mile—east, northeast of here."

"Good thing you're not Ned." Tracy glanced at Ava. "My second husband would be swearing at me about now—tearing me to shreds. Yelling things like, 'You're lost again, you, bleep, bleep.'" Tracy laughed. "Well, I'll spare you the colorful labels. He was right about one thing. I should have taken the GPS option on this car."

"Why didn't you?" Ava smiled rubbing Tracy's arm.

"You pick your battles. I don't like to drive. I almost never take this thing out. And, at the time, I needed to choose between a GPS and bikes for my kids'." She shrugged. "I receive no alimony from either of them. Private schools, nanny, the cost of living all add up."

"I'm sure the cost of raising three daughters can be formidable. I'm sorry."

"Nah, don't be. On the bright side, I enjoy peace and time away from both these jerks. No one bothers me about visitation rights." She rolled her eyes. "They wouldn't dare."

"Do the children miss their—them?" Ava remembered two exes Tracy mentioning to her once.

"No. This is the beauty of having three girls. My youngest is so cute—Brittany. Three years old and she's a real feminist. She's Ned's daughter, but he never comes around. Kevin takes her with his two whenever I need time to myself. Brit calls him daddy."

Ava hesitated. She didn't want to pry, but curiosity got the better of her. "Kevin sounds devoted. What's his story?"

Tracy flung her right shoulder at her. "Too sensitive, too." She paused. A huge sigh later she said, "Eight years of marriage and he tells me, too many women in the house." A quick glance at Ava with a pleat of her nose she added, "Gay—late bloomer."

"Really?"

Tracy gave Ava an emphatic nod.

"Well, different. I guess this explains why you went the other way, with Ned I mean—more macho."

Tracy rolled her eyes. "Ned isn't macho—more like a macho windbag."

Ava couldn't save the chuckle. "What's the name Ned short for anyway?"

"Neanderthal—though he would say the name is Edward."

Ava laughed unrestrained. Tracy made light of her situation, and she knew laughter fostered the best encouragement.

"Oh, up ahead," Tracy jumped. "Those brick pillars and the large plaque extending from the bushes. Can you read the name?" Tracy slowed down but kept her eyes on the bend in the road.

"Yes. Reads, Cedar Lane—is this the place?" Ava smiled at Tracy trying to conceal the plea in her eyes.

Tracy checked the rearview mirror and slammed on the breaks. She breathed out a long sigh of relief.

"You got us here, Trace."

"I thought they'd need to send a search party out for us." She veered down the well-manicured lane. "I think I'll cave and sign up for GPS on my cell."

They arrived forty-five minutes late after having gotten lost more than once. Still, when they drove up the pebble lane meandering toward the house, Ava forgot her frustration when she stared at immaculate lawns spread each side of the drive. Oases of floating islands bloated with pink azaleas and blushing rhododendrons ran intermixed with yews and juniper shrubs. Weeping willows and Russian olive trees in bloom drew Ava's breath away.

Nearer to the mansion, Ava spotted jutting sprays of spiraea and old-fashioned weigela, groveling at the feet of tall Japanese snowbell trees their white blooms hued a soft pink from the western sun. "Did you ever see anything as wondrous as this?" Ava found the gardens so natural their beauty appeared as though all the plants grew unattended, their splendor untouched and born long before people populated the area.

"Take a look at the set of lights—over to your right, tennis courts."

Ava turned questioning eyes toward Tracy.

"And on the other side, closer to the house's patio, huge pool. Always wanted to see the 20,000 square-foot mansion up close and personal."

"You've been here before?"

Tracy shook her head. "Reynard has a picture of the grounds in his office. I'm taking a stab at the size."

"So, this is how the other half lives," Ava said as they pulled up the circular drive.

Tracy parked her late-model red Mazda next to a silver Bentley. "I think half is a stretch. Only a small fraction of people live like this, sweetie."

"I know," Ava said a tad on the defensive. "Guess I shouldn't complain. My life is good and all. Yet, seems to be a whole world I can't reach—not saying I would ever want to," she said rolling her eyes. "Still, you wonder. How did these people ever reach the other side? Does this make any sense?"

Stepping out of the car, Ava acknowledged Tracy's emphatic nod as her friend's glance veered from a Mercedes coupe on her right to a gray Rolls Royce Phantom parked in front while she stared at a silver Bentley gleaming in the setting sun. She caught Tracy's downward glance coming to rest full circle on her own little roadster and realized Tracy's sad eyes and droopy mouth no longer concerned the cars. Ava thought Tracy might consider herself out of place like she did.

"Come on. We're on." Tracy led the way walking the quarter mile to the front door. "I'm the hostess and the last one to arrive," she said her tone edged with irony. Tiptoeing not to catch her heels between the stones in the walkway, she admitted, "I'm not used to wearing heels. Can you tell?"

Ava stared at her friend's tallness enhanced by an ankle-length skirt. Gray and slit on one side, she paired the sarong with a blue lamé top while the matching waistcoat dangled on her arm. "Well, you are the hostess with the mostest. That's for sure."

Tracy's eyes ran up and down Ava's red dress. "First time I gaze upon your Mate for Life outfit. Quite the teaser with the tiny waist and the swooping neckline." She winked at Ava. "No wonder heads turned at the Club."

"You think I'm overdressed?"

"Of course not. You're terrific. Give Miss Dane something to gawk at."

Ava chuckled. She wished for Scott's gaze, not Sylvia's. Still, nothing prepared Ava for the picture about to loom before them.

After an effaced young man greeted them with a polite bow, the bright, airy foyer with the skylight pouring pink sky in their midst did not stop Ava in her tracks. She couldn't be bowled over by paintings on walls or sculptures adorning floors and mantles, as she knew nothing about art.

In the distance, through wide double doors, she spotted Sylvia and Mathilda dressed in casual pants and short-sleeve blouses. Reynard, flanked with two male guests dressed in business attire, came toward them with a bright smile on his face. He sported a plain t-shirt and summer slacks.

"Not overdressed?" Ava tugged on Tracy's skirt to show irritation.

"Smile," Tracy said through clenched teeth readying for the round of greetings.

"Sorry, we're late, Reynard."

"Don't apologize. I spoke to Carole. She faxed you directions to a lot I own in Long Island. She sent you instructions supposed to go to a realtor who wants to rent it out."

"Ah," Tracy breathed out. "After I called here and your valet pointed me to the right spot on the map, I must admit, I could not figure how I got the two sets of instructions so confused."

Everyone laughed.

"I would like you to meet Richard Hallowell, of Hallowell Securities—and his partner Bruce Cob."

"Gentlemen," Tracy shook their hands. Richard was taller than her with broad shoulders and a friendly face. "I hear your company just made the 500 list. Congratulations."

"And this is Ava Moss, the new cog in our machine," Reynard

smiled nodding for Ava to come forward.

She did catching Bruce's eyes assessing her up and down. A whole head shorter than Richard he sported dirty blond hair combed to the side. A firm grip squeezed her hand when she shook his. She bit back an apology for her outfit thinking this would serve to draw attention to her dress.

Mathilda, Sylvia, and Scott joined them. The three appeared relaxed each with a different glass in hand, and while Scott locked eyes with hers in a warm and flattering squeeze, Sylvia's smile curled mocking and mean—or perhaps she imagined the meanness.

"You look beautiful, Ava," Scott said with subtle undertones.

She tried to keep a poker face, but when she thanked him, a slight blush invaded her cheeks.

With an arm around the newcomers, Reynard invited them to step forward across the hallway. "We are the ones who are late. We all need to change for dinner," he told Tracy and Ava. "If you don't mind catching up on cocktails and crudities in the small salon, I'll leave you in Richard and Bruce's company."

As he left, followed by Sylvia and Mathilda, Scott intervened. "I'll stay behind too, Reynard. I brought a jacket over there on the chair."

Reynard directed raised eyebrows at Scott's open shirt.

"And a tie." He glanced at Sylvia. "The one you brought for me. Noose is in my jacket pocket."

Sylvia gave Scott a cursory look and continued up the round staircase.

An awkward silence followed the three's departure. Richard recovered first. "Well, I'm glad I came prepared. Early bird gets the prize." He looped Tracy's arm to enter the salon. "What would you like to drink?"

Bruce approached to do the same with Ava, but Scott placed a delicate hand on her back to lead her inside. "After you, Bruce."

He waited for the other man to be out of range to whisper in Ava's ear, "You look beautiful, just as you did at the 21 Club. How I remember this dress."

So much for Tracy's theory she thought. Now, Ava's chief concern was to prevent Scott from hearing the fast knocks of her heart. To sense the light strum of his fingers on her bare back pricked her with a delightful slew of goose bumps—a sensation which faded in a hurry as she juggled with the torture of pretending indifference.

"I don't think Sylvia is too pleased you didn't follow her upstairs—neither is your brother." She didn't want her first words to him to be reproachful. Her only defense, the useless words were uttered in frustration. Didn't he realize teasing her while she felt overdressed or underdressed, and tiptoeing on six-inch heels across fairy tale surroundings fringed on cruelty?

"Sylvia's a big girl. She can dress herself. And Reynard puts too much onus on wearing formal attire for dinner. More of my father's mannerisms."

To keep her mind occupied and Scott-free, Ava focused on what Reynard referred to as the small salon—not small, although still cozy and snug the room's warmth likely conjured from the magic wand of a sound designer. A Persian rug swept the dark pink slats the rug's center a bright salmon matching the softer pink and beige settees. An ornate wood mantle painted white dressed the far corner, and she could imagine soaking up the fire's warmth on cold winter nights sitting on the plush rug next to the stone structure, wrapped in Scott's arms.

Shaking her head to ditch the thought, a blue spec caught her eye beyond the windows. "Is that a pool?" Flowers and trees surrounded the body of water. "Pool can't be indoors?" White curtains pulled back along the wall of floor-to-ceiling windows, rendered a superb view of the gardens and a huge tent which covered what resembled an outdoor arboretum.

"Indoor and an outdoor pool. We keep the place open during summer. Glass walls encase it during winter."

"So lovely."

He led her toward an island of silk rosebud love seats facing a glass table and overlooking the windows, but Bruce called out to him.

"So, Scott, how long have you been with the firm?"

Ava stared at the alteration on Scott's face while his eyes veered from charming warmth to business cool. She caught their light hazel darkening in an ominous way and thought he might throw some facetious remark Bruce's way, but she realized Scott knew his brother earmarked the meeting for work. She considered the part with the pleasure pure bonus.

The long breath Scott exhaled tickled the back of her neck as he led her toward the middle of the room. Tracy and Richard sat on one sofa, Bruce on another with room for one more person to wiggle in beside him. Two chairs completed the semicircle.

Ava realized Scott would be considered unchivalrous to sit her in a chair alone while he occupied the place on the sofa. He had no choice but to seat her next to Bruce—which he did.

Bruce's gleaming eyes and crooked smile greeted her as she sat down. "Well, Miss Moss," he strapped an arm on the sofa behind her. "If your financial wizardry matches your," dark eyes swept her up and down. "Poise, we're all going to be very wealthy."

Ava understood—big business, big ego—except this full version of confidence brought out her skinny version of social graces. With all the nervous electricity of a debutante ignoring the need to calm down, to call on diplomacy not to bruise the man's ego, she straightened and said a tad too loudly, "Not at all, Mr. Cob. Should you let your," here she stared at him up and down. "Business sense be influenced by mere looks, none of us will get very far now, will we?"

Stunned silence followed Ava's words. Casting a quick peek at her friend, she caught Tracy's reproving eyes and Richard's raised eyebrows. But the proud smirk on Scott's face convinced her she'd put her foot in her mouth this time. Wanting to redeem herself, she added, "What I meant to say is I'm just one cog in a sophisticated machine. Scott and Reynard are the real wizards here. Oh, and please, call me Ava." She smiled sweetly her eyes attempting to bat away their panic-stricken color.

The tight balls of her fists began to relax when she spotted Bruce's eyes drop while his eyelids moved in a constant flutter. He pondered her evident retraction she thought, and as she smoothed her dress, she offered up a little prayer he wasn't offended.

Scott moved to be closer sitting at the edge of his chair, and elbows on knees, he asked. "Bruce, did you read the proposal Reynard sent you and Richard?"

Ava tossed Scott a grateful glance.

Rubbing his hands together a little twitch still tugging the corners of his mouth Scott ignored her, waiting instead for Bruce's answer.

Bruce sat up reaching for his drink. "Perused the document. Richard has questions. I know he and your brother scheduled some time together to go over our concerns." Then he turned toward Ava. "I hope you will grace the project with your presence." Saying this, he toasted with his glass. "To one of the finest cogs I ever encountered." He smiled showing no hurt feelings. Realizing she didn't hold a drink of her own, he offered. "Can I get you a glass, some wine perhaps?"

"Of course, Ava." Scott stood ready to comply. "I'm sorry. I should have offered you refreshments. How about a Perrier with a twist?"

"Yes, thank you." Ava worked hard to contain her smile. Time to send Street Ava packing she thought and leave the room to Ava Moss, financial expert.

Scott turned toward Tracy. "Tracy, how are you set with your drink? I'm going to the bar. Would you like me to freshen that for you?"

"Thanks, Scott. I'm going to nurse the drink for a while." Tracy tilted her head toward Ava with eyebrows raised in caution.

Ava signaled with a surreptitious nod. Mouthing off would not endear her to her friends and colleagues—except perhaps to Scott, who appeared to enjoy toying with her nerves tonight. No matter how much he detested his father's old rules or Reynard's extravagant protocol, she would not play the rebel to placate him.

"I hope I didn't ruffle your feathers earlier with my foot-in-mouth approach."

Bruce's apology sounded sincere. She gushed to accept it. "Oh, of course not."

"People tell me I'm a klutz when it's time for social affairs.

In business, I can find my way fast enough. When I can't, I plow through." He made a dynamic motion by flexing his arms his expression a grimace that made Ava chuckle. "I also tend to plow through with the ladies when their beauty intimidates me."

"Well, don't worry about me," she breathed hard as a means to ignore the sudden heart bump brought on by Bruce's candor. She wasn't sophisticated enough to read his expression, but she did notice the blue eyes searching her face were kind. "I don't think I deserve all this fuss for working on the project—any project. I mean, I prefer to give credit when credit is well deserved."

Scott came back with her drink. "This is perfect, thank you."

He mumbled something his eyes somber barely acknowledging her.

Ava wondered how she offended him now when she caught Scott's attention veer toward the room's entrance.

CHAPTER 13

HOBNOBBING

S ylvia and Mathilda walked into the salon in regal style their grand entrance drawing everyone's attention to their lithe and graceful movements.

Sylvia wore hip-hugging harem pants that fluttered around her long legs like soft wings. A fitted pink-wool bustier left her shapely midriff bare.

Mathilda, her hair tied up in French braids, wore a few ribbons woven through the tresses, and the long white dress flowing from an empire waist gave the impression of a woman out of time.

Scott stared at his fiancée more pleased with her than he'd been in a long time, at least since her return from Europe. Still, the butterflies were quiet—or absent. His only jitters came from the big brown eyes he knew were parked on him a few feet behind.

Reynard entered the room in a dark three-piece suit, caught

up with the women and encircled them both. The women leaned against him in unison the snapshot in an instant embellished.

Richard rose—his male interest shaken and stirred and Scott sensed the envy of one man for another holding a beautiful woman on each arm. He hoped Tracy's fondness for Richard served only good business sense. Richard Hallowell's reputation with the ladies preceded him. He read about some of his exploits on the Internet when doing research on him and his company for this meeting. Surely, Tracy did the same.

He hesitated, took a deep breath and walked over to claim his fiancée. After all, the best way to douse the burning need of one woman involved filling his mind's eye with another. Ava seemed content to sit on the sofa with Bruce.

Shrugging off the dire jealousy warning, Scott smiled as he held out his arm for Sylvia. "You are fetching, my dear."

She'd relegated her glasses to the jewelry box and donned contacts. Sylvia's gray eyes sparkled as they dipped into his. "So glad you're back, Scotty," she whispered. "You haven't been my knight in shining armor in a while."

"Work, resettling—you understand." He squeezed her against him leading her toward the seating area. Sylvia's name of Scotty for him reflected their undergraduate days at Wharton. They'd been on opposite teams back then debating like cats and dogs. Years later they needed a second meeting to even like each other. Still, he realized the name of Scotty became her I-knew-you-when card each time she wanted to lay claim to him. Most times, the shift would bring back memories followed by nostalgia which would breathe intimacy between them. Tonight, the name sounded hollow as though she spoke to someone else. "Martini?"

Ava doubted her own eyes. Richard stood as though prodded by an electric stick, used a brief nod to take his leave of Tracy, and sprinted over to Mathilda still dangling on Reynard's arm.

"Reynard, shame on you for monopolizing this lovely lady." He smiled at Mathilda's upturned face. She slipped her hand from Reynard's arm to curl her fingers around Richard's bicep. "I am part of the team," she glanced at Reynard. "This is teamwork, right?"

Both men laughed as Richard steered her away. Ava realized Reynard seemed pleased. Perhaps Mathilda's people skills consisted foremost in her powers to delight.

She shook her head trying to catch up to what Bruce said while ignoring Sylvia's gray looks pointed at her as she snuggled up to Scott.

Tracy and Scott were right she thought dejectedly. She happened to be an ingénue of colossal proportions—her words not theirs. Ava considered her learning curve steep. Not only did she need to practice the right moves to glide through the boardroom, but she also needed to rehearse dancing in general as in stepping through life. A long way from her little apartment and her thick, musty tomes on financing, Ava considered even an MBA would not better prepare her for moments like these when everyone played the art of seduction, and she traipsed yards away from understanding the strokes.

At least Tracy didn't seem to bear animosity. She exuded the perfect smile as she sat inches away from Reynard, lost in their conversation.

Mathilda poised in one of the chairs, tugged on Richard's arm as he stood beside her his hand resting on her shoulder.

In the distance, a soft bell rang. Reynard bent next to Tracy's ear and whispered something that drew a smile from her. Then he announced. "Dinner is served." He stood offering his arm toTracy.

As they walked to the dining room Bruce firmly fastened to her hip, she realized the lot of them formed couples. She cast a glance at Reynard's broad shoulders leading the procession his arm assisting Tracy, his head bobbed her way to catch what she said. She underestimated Reynard. Ava always thought him to be a shy, gentle giant who didn't have a significant other because he had no other life than the one his father carved for him.

Turned out Reynard might be golden—one to whom only good things ever happened— or a brilliant schemer. He managed everything and everyone around him to file in with his wishes. After all, the evening placed Tracy by his side and beautiful Mathilda in the arms of the client. The fact he finagled Scott from Europe to lessen his workload depicted him as a shrewd architect in the process of redesigning his life.

As they entered the dining room, Ava wondered where the natural light came from. She looked up and spotted a glass dome for a roof. Ava gazed at the indigo colored sky and a slight cluster of stars promising to shine even brighter come the stroke of the next hour. Somewhere the gong from an old-fashioned clock ricocheted in dark muted tones, and unable to stop herself she tiptoed in the rest of the way.

A small card with her name stood high on a little decorative pitchfork rising from a heart shaped pedestal made of wax. Right next to hers she spotted Bruce's nametag peeking from behind a water goblet.

Ava's seat located at the second place setting right of Reynard meant she sat next to Tracy. Chatting with Tracy evoked pleasant thoughts although this arrangement deemed she face Scott, Sylvia, and Mathilda. Richard became the other head of the table. Same arrangement as Reynard enjoyed, flanked with his partner on his left and his new damsel on his right. Well done Reynard, she thought.

Ava considered someone seemed to be missing. "Isn't Trevor joining us this evening?"

Scott answered standing over Sylvia he helped tuck in. "He made plans to visit family." His eyes bore into hers, and she couldn't look away.

As a uniformed attendant began serving the first course, soft music drifted throughout the room from concealed speakers. As though evoked by magic, the lights dimmed allowing the diffused candlelight chandelier to cast a romantic glow over their table. Gazing above, Ava realized the stars held their bargain in the affair. They shone with a brightness that drew her breath away.

Soon the conversation grew from being a side dish to the main entrée. As it often happens during a lavish meal laden with wine and delicious morsels, inhibitions disappeared, and feelings of seclusion paired with the delicious sense of being one with the world prevailed as all clamored to be heard, words pouring out about everything and nothing.

Funny anecdotes of Scott and Sylvia's adventures in Europe peppered the duck confit. Laughter and admiration rose with the clink of glasses toasting their group's accomplishments in Geneva in such a short period. Ava's heart swelled with pride as another side of Scott began to emerge. She found him nurturing and willing to be charming to the woman he loved. She caught him cooing to Sylvia as he filled her plate with what he knew she might like. Typical. They had a history together, a long one—a history holding more cachet than any infatuation he might have for her.

She nodded to herself satisfied with her resolve to be reasonable.

"Great," Bruce said.

She stared at him trying to understand why he seemed so pleased.

"I'll call you next week, and we can set up a meeting—brainstorm on the proposal."

She'd agreed without realizing what he asked. "No, no. I can't." Seeing how thrown back he appeared to be, she explained. "I'm new to the team, Bruce. I don't know anything about your project."

"All the more reason we should hold a meeting."

"I should run this by Reynard first." She smiled and patted his hand to alleviate the disappointment in his eyes.

"I understand." He turned to ask. "Can I still call you?"

"Of course." She wondered whatever for but didn't care enough to argue the matter.

Yet over the process of the evening, she began to appreciate Bruce's thoughtful charm which served as a big boost to her ego each time her eyes strayed toward Scott and Sylvia.

With the last of their vanilla meringue and compote de figues whisked away, Reynard proposed they all move to the drawing room. "If you will follow me next door, a selection of fine liqueurs is decked out on trolleys—and please help yourselves. Ladies, to work off this rich food, you'll find a small area floor for dancing—

tonight is big band night. Also, the French doors are open. Please feel free to stroll through the gardens at will."

Cheers welcomed his proposal, and they rose to walk to the communicating doors on the far sidewall.

Ava found the room bigger, more imposing. The impression of drifting through space disappeared as a dark, and woodsy ceiling held them captive. Moroccan wall sconces fired the ambiance spewing jagged blazes and streaking the walls with smoky, exotic shadows. French doors, wide open with their curtains billowing in the warm night air, allowed Glen Miller's big band song, In the Mood, to waft beyond their threshold and spill throughout the evening.

The room, in fact, the whole estate lay congenial to holding meetings and private parties and romantic rendezvous Ava thought as her eyes glued themselves to Scott. She gave in to the ecstasy of staring at him. After all, in the muted atmosphere what might be the harm? She sighed content to treasure the moment. Until she met with Scott's willful, inscrutable eyes—a bold glance holding the power to liquefy all her good intentions. In a matter of seconds, her legs weakened, and her body singed from the fire in the fierce hazel glare.

Ava found difficult to haul a breath, so she turned to Bruce to ask him if he wanted to accompany her outside to stroll through the gardens. Not waiting for an answer, she grabbed him by the arm and led him toward the doors to freedom. Ava deemed this sumptuous mansion to be the last place where she wanted to make a fool of herself—not in front of Sylvia, not with so much depending on this meeting.

Before crossing the threshold, Bruce held her back with a gentle nudge. "Would you like a crème de menthe or a cognac?"

"No, thank you. I drank too much wine with dinner."

"Do you mind if I get one for myself?"

"Of course not."

"You go ahead, I'll catch up."

She walked through the doors and on the cobblestone path meandering through the trees and bushes. She strolled waiting for Bruce to catch up. The night air, warm, inviting and filled with the heady aroma of violets and roses, filled the lingering breeze with the spicy scent of summer.

She walked to the feral beat of In the Mood with itchy feet her hips swaying to the lilt of saxophones and clarinets wishing she could dance the Swing. She took pleasure in the wild rhythm, the jumps and the spins she'd caught in old movies. She waited for the crescendo, but it landed in a soft sound amidst the little gusts of wind as the breeze wrestled with the lilac bushes. Silence enveloped her. Ava detected only the beat of her heart echoing in the night's stillness.

Soon another song rose to cheer the evening. She listened while nostalgia tugged at her heartstrings when she thought she recognized Stardust's melody amongst the horns. The enchanting sound became fainter as she walked farther and farther from the house. She wondered what kept Bruce when she caught the muted sound of ocean waves beyond the property, and Ava imagined the salt spray cooling her face and limbs. Urgent footsteps on the flagstone trail alerted her to Bruce's proximity. She smiled grateful that his gait prevented him from startling her.

She turned to greet him, and the sound of her own scream startled her. Not Bruce, but Scott, the man she was running from, the very reason she wanted to escape to the garden. Unable to stop her motion fast enough, she bumped up against him.

CHAPTER 14

THE LAST DANCE

I n the garden under the moonlight, Ava screamed. "My God, Scott you scared me." Ava backed up a few steps. "What are you doing here?"

"Nice to be appreciated," he said in a sarcastic tone, eyes dark and face taut.

"You surprised me. I expected Bruce." She spotted his Adam's apple move and his jaw tense.

"Reynard called a meeting. Richard, Bruce, and I will be attending."

She nodded looking forward to spending a little time with Tracy. She wondered why he seemed so distant, so proper, or why Bruce didn't come to tell her himself. She didn't dare formulate her last query out loud.

She stared up at him more transparent than she realized because his next words gave her the answer she sought.

"Bruce doesn't know his way around the house now, does he? And Reynard waits for no one." A brief salute and he left.

Ava witnessed Scott turn as though struck with the need to add something. "Oh, and Tracy is attending the meeting."

"Tracy?" She looked at her watch and remembered the hour-long drive they shared on the way up—in broad daylight. "This is going to put us back in the city kind of late."

"The meeting's thirty to forty minutes tops." He hesitated then said, "Sylvia and Mathilda are still in the drawing room. Be a good time to become acquainted."

She watched him turn and leave without another word. He didn't need to speak. His eyes communicated in eloquent fashion how she needed to tend to her duties and he would tend to his. Ava found Scott's expression dipped in business and a bit derisive. When her thoughts strayed to Sylvia and Mathilda, she wondered if there might ever be an appropriate time to approach those two. She realized attempting to work with Sylvia and Mathilda would be difficult enough, but to socialize with them—on purpose—appeared an impossible task to surmount.

When she strode into the room, she saw a valet taking the glasses and trays in preparation to wheel them away. Her eyes scanned the room but detected no one else in sight. She ran up to the man heading away and asked him to direct her toward the nearest powder room.

She thanked him and followed his instructions leading down the corridor as large as her own living quarters.

When she returned, she stood alone. No doubt, about the room since the music still blared and the open doors bayed to her to explore the grounds.

Ava resisted the temptation to venture out alone and risk getting lost even though she knew beyond the gardens flowed the ocean—the salt air invigorating and softly scented. Walking through the rest of the mansion might result in the same fate. She decided to stay put and search the area's nooks and crannies. She spotted many books on the west wall of the room, all bound with intriguing covers. The recessed partition, a little alcove behind the sound system and home theater display, fashioned a little island of tranquility for her.

She fingered the books and settled on a biography of Benny Goodman, the clarinet Swing King, and considered the size of the tome would be more than sufficient to see her through the next 40 minutes.

She found a comfortable loveseat where she curled up while resting her feet on the matching ottoman. As though in tuned with her mood, the music calmed down to a much slower tempo.

Time went by fast since the first thing Ava noticed happened to be Scott standing over her trying to nudge her awake. In a soft tone, he called her name, and she opened her eyes stretching to move the thick book off her lap. She fumbled, but spotted the tome on the coffee table. Scott removed the book, she thought still a little sleepy.

She yawned and rubbed her eyes. She tried to rise, but her right leg weak with pins and needles gave out.

"Whoa," Scott exclaimed as he tried to catch her before she dropped back into the sofa's pillows. "Someone needs to find her legs." He helped her up by slipping an arm under hers. "Are you okay?"

He acted solicitous and kind, nothing like the business hound she encountered earlier. "I will be. What time is it?" She looked at her watch but couldn't see the needles her eyes still blurry.

"The meeting ran twenty minutes longer than planned. Richard and Bruce left. They asked me to convey their wishes. I had the devil of a time finding you."

"Where are the others?" By now, she'd gathered her wits. She remembered to hold her feelings in check and not stretch against him like a lost kitten needing to bask in warm caresses.

"Mathilda and Sylvia opted for an early night—right after we left. This is why you found yourself alone down here."

"I stayed put—didn't want to get lost."

"Come on. I know how we can salvage the evening—work the kinks out of your leg." An arm around her waist, he walked her to the drawing room. The music stopped so he used the remote to request a song.

"Where's Tracy?" she asked. As Scott brought her around to face him, she studied his expression as he picked up her right hand and held her mere inches away. "What are you doing?"

"Saving the last dance for you, Ava Moss."

She stared at his face and his beaming smile drew stars in her eyes. In a daze, she allowed him to twirl her around the room. Scott happened to be a terrific dancer because even though she never learned the steps, she needed only to follow his movement to glide across the floor. After a few spins and whirls, her leg was back. "I love the music. What is this piece?"

"*Moonlight Serenade*, Glenn Miller. My father once told me this happened to be the last piece the band would play at the end of the party before musicians folded their music and stowed their instruments. The slow piece became a sign for a fella to grab his best girl and share the last dance—so he could go home with her."

His words brought an army of butterflies fluttering inside her stomach, and she made sure to follow his steps and stay glued to his every move—both her legs weak now. They glided in a smooth lilt, and she would have followed him to the ends of the earth not skipping a beat so charmed by the light in his eyes, the ease of his pace, and the brush of his hand on her back.

When he dipped her, she laughed. When he brought her back up so close, she hung on the hope he might kiss her. He did, but only with his eyes staring at her lips for such a long time, Ava imagined the two of them frozen in time, and when time resumed, they would be only for each other.

She heard footsteps in the hallway coming closer their quick tempo shattering the magic of her romantic image into millions of little pieces.

Scott dropped his arms and slowly backed away. Smiling, he performed a formal salute from the waist. "Thank you for the dance, Ava, lovely."

She acquiesced with a smile while swallowing the disappointment welling up inside her. Scott grabbed her for the last dance all right and in the convenience of his own home. Yet they would not spend the night in each other's arms. Slowly she turned to see Reynard and Tracy coming toward them.

"There you are, Ava. We were looking for you," Tracy said with a big smile.

"I fell asleep—in the alcove," she pointed toward the shelves. Glancing at her watch, she mentioned. "How will we ever find the courage to drive home at this hour?"

"I invite you both to stay the night," Reynard said. "This house offers more than enough rooms, and don't worry about clothes. They can be provided."

"My mother and her sisters keep a stash handy," Scott added. "They spend time up here, but they won't be back again until late August."

Ava stared at Tracy, Scott, and Reynard and realized this new twist troubled no one but her, and this did not bode well. She wanted to go home. To spend the night under the same roof as Scott while not owning the luxury of spending time in his arms would not be conducive to sleep. "You don't understand. I brought no toiletries of any kind, and I need to feed Oscar. I can't stay, I just can't." She wanted to ask Tracy about her daughters, but she hesitated not knowing if she confided in Reynard.

"You don't need to feed your fish every day, do you?" Tracy asked.

"No. But he likes the company," Ava finished with hesitation afraid they might think her a kook.

Tracy moved closer to put an arm around her shoulders. "Well, his loss is our gain. I'm sure Oscar can spare you for one night. Besides, leaving in the morning will be so much easier to navigate my way back when I can see where I'm going."

"All set then," Reynard said his tone brooking no argument. He looked at his watch. "Lila will be sleeping by now." He looked up. "She's our devoted caretaker."

"That's okay, Reynard. I can show Tracy and Ava to their rooms." Scott put up his hand. "I remember the ones—with the ensuite—on the East side."

"Lovely." Reynard's eyes poured into Tracy's, and Ava wondered why he wasn't the one showing them to their rooms. Did he not consider the action proper—because of emotions he might harbor for Tracy? She found Reynard to be quite the mystery or an old-world charmer. Ava tossed her interpretations aside when she caught the long stare Reynard afforded Tracy—a stare well worth a good night kiss. She figured the eldest Wallace might be shy.

Scott showed no such sentiment. In fact, he led them to the rooms in a polite, proper, and almost abrupt manner. He showed Ava and Tracy the communicating bedrooms, the two bathrooms on each side, and the clothes hung in the walk-in closets. "You should find something here that fits. Oh, and you'll find a refrigerator behind the plant. Small but capable of holding a few tidbits."

Ava found a sink and a few cupboards next to the refrigerator. She opened the fridge door and discovered bottled water, fresh fruits, and tins of pâté. "Wow, all you need for a midnight snack."

"Sheets are stored in the linen cupboard in the next room. Sorry about this. I thought the beds would be made."

"Don't worry about the sheets, Scott. We're capable of making a couple of beds, trust me," Tracy said. She smiled and reinforced her affirmation with a nod when Scott's frown wouldn't budge.

After a swift nod, he left—almost running away Ava thought. She and Tracy glanced at each other and laughed.

"God, Scott and Reynard are different." Tracy turned to rummage through the closet as she continued. "One is sophisticated and charming, the other is modern and edgy. Could Scott have left here in more of a hurry?"

Ava agreed while sitting on the bed still dazed from Scott's sideswipe—a close dance, an almost kiss, and now this quick dismissal. The last hour amounted to one big train wreck—at least that's the impression he left her with, lost, hurt, and in need of something.

"Are you all right, sweetie?" Tracy picked out a pair of jeans and a blouse for the trip back, a nightie and a bathrobe.

"Sure. I guess Scott is in a hurry to get back to his fiancée."

Putting down the stack of clothes she chose on the divan next to the dresser, Tracy walked over to the bed to comfort Ava. Tracy wrapped an arm around her shoulders. "Listen, the right man will come along, Ava. Scott's not the one. He's so wrong for you. I mean after what you've told me? Obviously, he's an emotional straddler."

"A what?"

"A man who stokes the fire with one woman while he keeps an eye on another. Just a way of saying, sweetie Scott can't commit."

Ava nodded. This made sense.

"Straddlers are forever looking for the angle, Ava."

Ava cocked her head puzzlement in her eyes.

"The next big thrill around the corner the best prospect or any girl who will make them shine like a million bucks. You deserve better, Ava. You need to be with someone kind and considerate—someone like Reynard. Now he's a catch."

Ava didn't want to say she found Reynard a little starchy around the edges. "Do you think Reynard's still a virgin?"

"God, no! Whatever made you think that?" Tracy sat back on the bed bouncing a little as she did. She leaned back on her arms propped behind her to steady herself.

Ava hadn't meant to induce such a forceful reaction in Tracy. She hoisted her shoulders in an attempt to make light of her remark. "His conventional ways around women—he didn't even want to walk us to our rooms." Her words painted Scott to her, and this featured another area where he and his brother differed. Scott appeared to hold no qualms about expressing how he felt—or showing her.

"Well, he's not some hot-shot playboy, and he is shy I suppose, but he's not inexperienced." Tracy hesitated as she sat up smoothing her skirt seeming as though she wanted to reveal something important. "He lived with a woman a couple of years ago—almost against his will to please his mother."

"Really." Shock rounded Ava's eyes.

"Hum. Reynard's mother tried to match him with some hot Latina model she brought home from Florida." She eyed Ava as though to impart some forbidden truth. "When his mother left to go back to Palm Beach, she stayed. Hung around Reynard's neck and played house."

"Huh." Ava gave the picture some thought. "So maybe he is shy—gun-shy."

Tracy nodded. "Had the devil of a time breaking off with her."

"How did he finally do this?"

"Gareth's wife intervened—sent Miss Big-boobs packing."

"Liliane, the woman I met? Emily's mother?"

"Yeah."

"How do you know all this?"

"Gloria is her name. She came to the office once or twice searching for him. Before your time. Very intimidating—a real knockout." Tracy rolled her eyes.

"And who filled you in on the details?" Ava tilted her head and motioned with her hand.

Tracy tripped on a big smile lighting up her face. "Reynard did, a couple of weeks ago." She nodded vigorously.

"Did you tell him about your daughters?"

"Yep. Told him." She let go a huge breath. "He said he likes little girls."

Lying in bed staring up at the ceiling Ava pictured Tracy holding up crossed fingers with both hands as she uttered that last sentence. She figured although Reynard and Tracy were poles apart, after the rough patch Tracy survived, being with an easy going man who wanted nothing other than to give her the reins to his heart might be the right orientation.

Her ramblings became fanciful and her eyelids heavy, although she doubted she would get any sleep in a stranger's nightgown, in a stranger's bed, next door to Scott sleeping in a stranger's arms. She rolled to her side trying to get comfortable. She remembered Scott turned left at the first corridor on top of the stairs. Only one door stood at the end of the hallway—Scott and Sylvia's room.

A mischievous smile floated on her lips. *This is crazy* she thought, but unable to soothe the itch, she kicked the blankets aside and jumped out of bed.

She opened the door. Looking both ways, she slipped out of the room and tiptoed barefoot down the hall. At the top of the landing, she turned left and walked toward the door she thought led to Scott's room. Her little escapade made her believe she'd lost her mind. What did she hope to accomplish? Knock on his door and ask him to sleep with her instead?

Eighty-sixing all logic liable to douse her Ava urges—code for longings responsible for getting her into trouble—she continued down the corridor eyes peeled for any movement indicating someone else's presence. She stopped in front of the door and stroked it with the palm of her hand. To be so close yet so far she thought as she applied her cheek to the wood, as though mere desire might draw him out of bed and into her arms.

Ava found this bigger-than-life hunger for another person so unlike her. Under most circumstances, she sported a firm head on her shoulders. The sound of voices inside the room piqued her attention.

Surprised she jumped back realizing they might discover her— standing in the hallway in front of their room, barefoot and in her nightie, hugging the door.

Small seconds ticked away before curiosity won the day. She stuck an ear against the door and sensed a brazen desire seize her.

She tried to listen to the voices. A man's voice and a woman's— Sylvia she presumed, and she had to be enraged considering the shriek she caught. She couldn't make out why they argued, only a whole bunch of jumbled words.

Scott's menacing words stood out. "You calm down, or I'm sleeping somewhere else."

Another scream and something thumped against the door— some heavy object flung her way Ava supposed.

"You better be in a friendlier mood when I return."

A few seconds elapsed before she got the implication of Scott's threat to Sylvia. When she did, she grabbed bunches of her night-gown and started running down the hall until she caught the click of the door.

Best to walk slowly, she thought. She didn't want Scott to think she needed to run.

CHAPTER 15

IN THE HEAT OF THE NIGHT

A long the hallway of a Hampton Mansion, Ava froze unable to say a word.

"Ava? What are you doing here?" Scott said.

Ava fidgeted with what to say when she turned to face him. She bit her bottom lip at a loss for words—more so when she spotted him in pajama bottoms with a bathrobe draped over his shoulders leaving his torso bare. He appeared tanned and muscular.

Smoothing the creases out of her nightgown, she worried the lightweight material might be transparent.

"Are you lost?" He asked a frown marring his handsome features.

Shame washed over her when she sensed her head bobbing up and down. He supplied her with the only way out, and she grabbed the out with both hands.

He glanced behind him, and then stared past her. Questions ignited in his eyes as he came toward her. "Where did you want to go?"

She heaved a deep breath as he moved closer. She inhaled the faint aroma of his aftershave lingering on his clean face and gasped at the moisture in his hair. She could tell he stepped out of the shower. "I wanted something to drink," she said. She wrinkled her nose at him hoping he would not judge her with too much severity and allow the little lie to slide.

His eyes darkened as he stroked strands of her hair. "I mentioned the refrigerator in your room stocked with refreshments, including bottled water. What are you doing here?"

He went the other way she thought. He dangled her desire for him in front of her daring her to deny the sentiment. She didn't—more because she lost her tongue and Ava lost her courage to fudge an excuse. She wanted so much to protest, yet she became unable to utter a single word. Instead, she stared into his eyes mesmerized by their own glowing message. He wanted her too, evident in the burning trail his hands left on her bareback, in the hardness of his body pressed against her.

She tried to push him away wondering why his hands traveled all over her bare back only to realize he rummaged underneath her nightgown. "Stop this, Scott. What are you doing?" She didn't recognize her voice, husky and sensuous. She wondered if this wanton woman might be her—uncaring of usurping another woman's property without the least bit of shame?

"Don't you know to go wandering about the corridors alone at night is dangerous? In a strange house," he finished in a throaty whisper.

His hands began moving over her body caressing, and fondling in an all-out effort to possess her, and she moaned with delight while stretching against him wishing he would remove the damn nightgown so they might be closer.

She moved her kisses from his neck to his lips. Maybe if she plunged her tongue into his mouth with all the hunger she saved up over the weeks, he might oblige her and take her right here in this hallway. She didn't much care where, as long as he burrowed his way inside her this exact moment.

"Scott! What the hell do you think you're doing?"

Both of them needed to heed the warning. Through a bewildered haze, Ava became aware of Sylvia standing in Scott's back fuming at them. She spotted tears hovering in her eyes, and in normal circumstances, tears in another would be sufficient to engender remorse into her actions. Only, Ava no longer controlled her actions. Scott propped her against the wall, shed his bathrobe and bottoms, and prepared to execute the bold, hungry pleas she begged of him while in his arms—what seemed like hours.

"Leave, Sylvia. Go back to the room," he muttered half-crazed which Ava thought only served to add insult to injury. He took Ava while he continued to ignore the fact Sylvia stood behind them, as though his fiancée filed in with both their urges so intense were their needs.

Too late, Ava spotted the glimmer of a shiny object in Sylvia's right hand. As she raised the knife high, the edge caught the light and took the shape of a long serrated blade. She wanted to yell at Scott to move to protect himself, but no words came out the pleasure of having him inside her too intense.

Afterward, blood splattered everywhere, and Scott's expression became marred with pain. He stared at her, regret carved into his lined forehead, sadness in the turned-down mouth for the love which would never find release. As the life in his eyes receded fast she screamed, yelled out his name as loud as possible to make all of this disappear.

It worked. The scream catapulted Ava to a sitting position in a strange bed inside a strange room while her panic-stricken eyes searched the dark for familiarity. Echoing in her ears beat the loud claps of a fibrillating heart constricted in her chest like a caged bird wild with fear and some other exotic, delicious impression she didn't recognize—an awareness that tickled her loins yet chilled her to the bone.

Memory resurfaced adding to the mix of strange sensations. She slept at the Wallace mansion in the Hamptons. "Scott," she whispered as the dream returned all too real.

The tension eased from her limbs. She plopped back into the pillows. A vivid dream—there could be no other explanation for what happened.

Lying down helped release some of the tension and shed some of the anxiety still restricting her breathing. However, a horizontal position helped crystallized the dream's haze into the identical shapes formed a few short moments ago. Scott's moans and caresses, his lovemaking, all inflicted awareness of how she never experienced this burning need for any man. Uncharacteristic of her to ignore another woman's tears or anger, the dream seemed so real she worried she might conduct herself in a similar manner should Scott decide to have his way with her.

She wouldn't care if a horde of people stood by and watched. Ava wouldn't care if he took her roughly against a wall or on a cold, hard floor. She still smoldered with the ache of wanting him, of almost being his—but not really—only a dream.

Now, all the previous misgivings Ava harbored about working with him, and Sylvia began to mount a fear fest inside her. She would never be able to look at him again without trembling, without walking up to kiss him on the mouth so their breath mingled, so she might swallow and feed on the hungry groans she had sensed him muffle.

She shook her head. She didn't want to go through another dream like this one again. In fact, another such nightmare and she'd need to quit her job. What Sylvia did to Scott in the dream was horrid, but their actions didn't score much higher her conscience reminded her.

About to fall asleep, she heard voices in the next room, muffled laughter. She got up her legs still shaky and wobbled over to the communicating door. Tracy and a male companion laughed and exchanged words. She figured Reynard's old-world charm took a step back to embrace his newly discovered emotions for Tracy. First, he found his way to Tracy's heart and now, the way to her room.

On the way back to bed, she turned on the little lamp on her nightstand to make sure this wasn't another dream. She eyed the time scrolled on the alarm clock—a little past one. No wonder Tracy wanted to stay so much—certainly not to get a good night's sleep since she might be exhausted in the morning.

Moreover, Ava considered Tracy had to be aware of Reynard's intentions. As discreet as he might be, she didn't believe the elder Wallace would ever show up at a woman's door without first asking her permission to do so.

Lights off and cuddling in bed, she smiled up at the ceiling. Her friend's luck managed to bring a smile to her face and a dose of serenity. Hope prevailed if even one of them spent the night in a lover's arms.

She heard two more bouts of laughter and crumpled over to one side jamming a pillow over her head. "No more dreams," she whispered to herself unconvincingly. "No more dreams."

The next morning washed dressed, and holding onto her evening clothes hanging in a slipcover, with her fancy shoes and purse in the bottom of the bag, Ava waited to leave.

She opened her room door, and the full-bodied aroma of freshly brewed coffee tickled her senses. Wow, this morning she would hand over her shoes for a concoction like this.

She began walking toward the stairs thinking they were fixing breakfast in the kitchen, but as she did, the scent all but disappeared.

Curious she walked back toward the room next to hers. She could see movement in the beam of light under the door when the door flung open, and Scott walked out. He wore bottoms and a bathrobe draped over his shoulders showing a tanned and lean torso above a hard abdomen.

She heaved a deep breath as he came closer and froze midway. She sniffed and got a whiff of the faint aroma of his aftershave lingering on his clean face. She came close to fingering the moisture in his hair. He just stepped out of the shower. This whole scene appeared so familiar dizziness struck her with a bolt of nausea.

She tightened her hold on the bag draped over her arm to shield how much her hands trembled and pinched her arm to make sure this was not another dream.

"Good morning," he said a cup of coffee in one hand. Then he raked what seemed like a weary hand through his hair.

He tilted his head assessing her with a crooked smile.

She gathered he was eyeing her T-shirt, jeans, and jean jacket, and she garnered mixed feelings about not wearing a sheer nightgown anymore—the burn of his eyes roving over her curves pure enjoyment.

"The perfect Cinderella transformation," he said with a tight smile.

She nodded still too uncomfortable from her nightly visit to look him in the eye. She wanted to tell him she moseyed over there for coffee but could not get one word out.

"Would you like a cup of coffee?"

Again, she nodded. She called herself an idiot for not being able to speak or even mumble anything with coherence.

He came closer cup in hand and slipped a finger under her chin to look into her eyes. He held her gaze for what seemed to Ava like a long time. "Rough night?" he asked in a low, raspy voice.

She swallowed as she gave her ascent letting go a long breath that came out in trembling little spurts.

His hand dropped by his side. "You too," he mouthed softly. He fingered the tips of her hair.

At the moment, she wanted to niche in his arms where she knew the steady beat of his heart would soothe her aching need. She would rub her cheek against his chest and enjoy a good, long cry, the lonely sobs pent up from years of living alone with chin first to avoid bumping up against the odds.

As the healing process began to soothe, he backed away. "Sylvia and I had an argument—more like a fight. I slept in my office. At least the office I use when I'm here."

Her eyebrows rose even as she fought not to let her face betray surprise. What might be the odds of her having a lucid dream of that type? "Your office is right next door." She turned to look at where she spent the night. She bit her lip not to finish the sentence. She berated her choice of words finding the thought childish.

For a long time, he stared at her until he gave her a sly nod. "A wall," he whispered. "A few coats of plaster standing resolute between two people."

If they let it. She didn't dare whisper the thought.

He tied the belt to his robe and walked passed her heading toward his room. "Help yourself to coffee and croissants—they're in the office. Laura brought enough for an army."

"I will. Thank you."

"Oh," he stopped, turned, and snapped his fingers as if only now remembering, "and I'll drive you into town. Just give me ten minutes to get dressed."

"Please don't bother, Scott. I'll wait for Tracy."

He chuckled. "Funny thing happened. Reynard bunked in with her last night. They might be getting up late."

"I know. I woke up at one point, and I picked up on what sounded like a man's voice," she trailed when she realized he cracked a smile at her naiveté. She hated her lack of poise and blamed the slip on her lack of sleep. "I can take a cab. A long ride there and back."

He shook his head. "No need. I scheduled a meeting in a couple of hours. I'm staying in town."

"What about Sylvia and Mathilda?" At least, Tracy came with her car.

"Georges will bring them in—if Reynard doesn't—chauffeur."

"Why don't I hitch a ride with Georges?"

He frowned and cocked his head. "Afraid to be in the same car with me?"

"No, of course not."

"I told you I am going into town, Ava. Now grab some coffee, have croissants, and meet me downstairs in ten."

She nodded her assent ogling him as he left. She waited for him to turn the corner before reaching to clasp the balustrade. She couldn't let him know how weak her legs were, or how fast her heart pounded. To dream about Scott and Sylvia's argument when he admitted they shared one. How odd?

All at once, she longed to talk to Elaine about all this. She would understand in her own peculiar way, perhaps even help sort through the mess.

More to the point, the Scott of her dreams, the man who pinned her against the wall while pressing his naked body up and down her own with an urgency she could not forget, appeared identical to the version of Scott she encountered this morning—lean, healthy, and just as vibrant. Did this mean wallowing in his arms would be as mind-melding hot as in her dream?

CHAPTER 16

THE MORNING AFTER

S cott opened the passenger door to the bright red Mercedes Benz convertible the chauffeur drove up to the door. "Do you mind if we drive with the top down?"

She shook her head as she settled into the tan leather bucket seat. She had no inkling of what riding without a roof meant, and she didn't want to say anything. Her bag in the trunk she squeezed in, stretched her legs and made herself comfortable.

She caught Scott's jump over the side and into his seat. She realized by the grin on his face he took pleasure in emulating a little boy with a shiny new toy.

"This car's so tiny the model reminds me of one of those kiddy cars," she said.

He laughed. "This is without a doubt what I like about the B551 coupe: small, sporty, and the little roadster packs a big punch." He stared at her with a point to make. "Like Ava Moss."

Surprised she said, "Never been compared to a car before." As she watched him flip his sunglasses off his nose to tickle her with a pointed gleam, the breath poured out of her in a chuckle as she added, "Definitely a first."

Glasses back in place, he spotted the croissant wrapped in a napkin and sitting on her lap, about the same time he eyed the coffee cup she held. "This won't do, Ava. You won't be able to eat on the run, not when the wind takes over. Tell you what. Leave your coffee and croissant with Georges, and I'll buy you a proper breakfast along the way."

"I guess." She took one last sip of her coffee hating to part with the delicious brew and handed both the croissant and the cup to Georges who waited for final instructions before they left. "Thank you, Georges." She smiled at him.

"Good. Now, we're off." Scott tipped his cap at Georges. "Thanks, man. Tell my brother he can take the Aston."

Scott fired the engine and barreled down the drive slowing to an unscheduled stop. "Almost forgot." He lunged for the glove compartment. "I keep an extra cap in here—this one's denim. It'll match your outfit." He appeared to be having fun at her expense.

She grabbed the brim out of his hands and twirled the hat around on her fist in a show of protest.

"Trust me. You'll be glad you wore the damn thing. The purpose is to prevent your hair from collecting our entire fair city's much-touted pollution."

Ava rolled her eyes as she gathered her hair to slip the strands under the cap, posing for him afterward.

"Fetching, Ava Moss. Quite fetching."

The top down became an adventure for her. The sun beat on their heads from a sky-blue roof, yet a brisk breeze whizzed past her cheeks to cool the invading heat—or did Scott's presence mere inches away quicken her pulse? "Why aren't you taking the Aston?"

"I enjoy trying new cars. Get bored with the ones I've driven too many times."

She turned her head to gaze at the countryside flowing by. Familiar with the expression fast cars, fast women, she realized the men who liked one enjoyed the other. Did quickly bored by same cars entail quickly jaded by same women?

"They all belong to my father's estate, so you might say I'm making up for lost time." He smiled at her. "The one thing I deplored when I left for Europe—parting with the cars. My father never allowed me to drive these beauties, only the one he assigned to me."

Ava's raised eyebrows meant she understood how some guys became car crazed. "Tracy parked her little red Mazda between a Rolls and a Bentley after we drove up last night. Didn't see this one, though."

"This is because the twenty cars the estate owns are parked indoors, back of the house."

They had to talk a little louder, and this curtailed the intimacy she worried might entangle them in such close quarters. The fact she needed to strain to hear him also provided a sound distraction from his leg glued to hers and rubbing up against hers each time he moved his on and off the gas pedal or with the need to change gears.

Staring down at his leg as he lifted his foot to apply the brakes, she toyed with the dream-sensation creeping back into her thoughts, grateful the noisy environment hid the soft moan she couldn't prevent.

Whether her silence intrigued Scott, she who always chatted like a magpie in his presence, he didn't complain. In fact, glancing at him once or twice, her head leaned against the headrest, she encountered a lined forehead and cold eyes, and while she studied the set of his jaw and the squint of his brows, she imagined him toying with thoughts of his own. He didn't seem at all absorbed by the road or getting many thrills from his joy ride.

Thirty minutes later, still silent, Ava craved the coffee Scott made her give up, and now she dealt with hunger and thirst pains. She didn't want to whine like a child—or make the effort to maintain small talk. Why should she be the one anointed with the job?

She spotted signs for the highway and wondered if Scott might drive straight through—in silence. So far, they ambled at a scenic clip down the country roads, terrain she missed in Tracy's haste and confusion to get to the mansion the night before. Maybe, Scott chose a different route, yet not so different she didn't spot the signs for Sunrise Highway.

"Scott, you missed the turn."

"Dinner or breakfast?" He smiled at her eyeing her with resolve.

Seemed he read her mind. "I am hungry and in dire need of caffeine. Something light, though."

"Breakfast it is. There is a lovely Inn, a bed-and-breakfast on Main Street in South Hampton—a little out of our way, but well worth the detour."

She wondered how he remembered the place having been away for so long.

"Liliane brought me to the Inn my first morning back—on the

way to meet Reynard. Quaint and charming, I'm sure you'll love the food. I did."

She agreed in silence, the heart kicking inside her chest from the long, intense gaze he locked her into while removing his glasses, waiting for the light to change.

All too fast he released her, his eyes on the road again. "I figured your silent treatment might be due to lack of nourishment," he said. He chuckled when she couldn't prevent her cheeks from blushing. "Or were you catching up on all the sleep you missed?"

His voice dropped, and the tone caused her to turn and stare at his handsome profile. He turned his head her way but kept his eyes on the road. "I'm surprised you didn't say anything about what kept you awake? I told you why I couldn't sleep."

What Ava refused to handle now—witty banter from the man she loved. Of course, she could not afford to tell Scott how much she loved him. She sighed, the realization dawning on her she was in love with him, but not for better only for worse. "I often experience difficulty sleeping when I'm away from home," she said matter-of-factly, a little lie to save her sanity.

She expected something clever, not a stone silence—a ceasefire she nevertheless welcomed. She hoped Scott's lack of answer did not augur some tactical postponement, the move akin to the ruse of a brilliant chess player allowing his adversary a false move while biding his time, waiting for the poor dilettante to corner her king into a checkmate position.

Well, no time to dwell on impending duels. They reached their destination and Scott did not exaggerate in his description of the place. The bright yellow two-story country house stood nestled with grandeur in the lushness of an English garden brimming with roses.

Scott opened the car door for her. She removed the cap letting her hair down and looked around at the variety of shrubs and plants decorating the front patio. "This is lovely, Scott."

"Wait until you see the gardens around the terrace."

"Am I dressed okay?" Ava dropped the hat on the front seat. "Seems to me I should be wearing something fancier."

"You're all right."

They meandered down a small path well hidden amongst the trees. The footpath led toward the back of the house. At the end of rows of English white daisies, and rambling red rose bushes with their shoots hanging from the top of a white picket fence, a small gate left ajar invited them inside to enjoy an oasis of calm and tranquility.

"God, this garden reads like a brochure," Ava breathed.

They strolled to meet with a pond laced with lilies and English Ivy, and Ava began naming the flowers impressed with their diversity. "Creeping Charlie," she said stopping to admire the arrangement. "Ivy, Creeping baby's breath, and Irish moss—real moss can take decades to grow. Oh, and over by the hydrangeas, the hybrid teas."

She walked over to a bush displaying an array of large blooms of pink roses. "*La France*, the world's first tea rose introduced in 1867. The flower is my favorite."

"You should have seen these trees, all in bloom when Liliane brought me here in May."

She nodded as she glanced at the dark green foliage of surrounding trees. "Cherry trees and apple trees, I can imagine their beauty."

A stout, fair-haired woman wearing a white apron over a blue cotton dress beamed a big smile as she came toward them.

"How do you know so much about flowers? College botany?"

Ava shook her head. "I worked in a flower shop while putting myself through school."

"Good morning, my name is Evy, can I help you?"

"Right. Now I remember." He smiled when Ava cocked her head. "You told me. The night I took you out to dinner."

Ava smiled and turned toward Evy. "Good morning. You own a lovely garden. We were admiring the layout."

Evy smiled. "Thank you. Can I interest you in some breakfast, on the terrace? Much cooler by the fountain." She eyed them with a little tease in her eye. "Also out of the way, private," she added with a conspiratorial smile.

"Sounds perfect." Scott hurried to volunteer so Ava would not refuse.

She wanted to—refuse.

While she sat with Scott at a table for two in front of a lavish breakfast, with no other patrons in sight, and as the babbling roll of the fountain masked the sound of their words, somehow the term privacy became an understated claim more clandestine than secluded.

Perhaps remorse for the pleasure tingling up her spine created the sensation. She did not belong to Scott, Ava reminded herself as she planted her fork in a piece of pineapple.

"Don't you like your omelet?"

She recognized the humor in his tone, yet she refused to be taunted. "I love the food. I am thinking of all the things on my agenda when I get home."

"Stabbing fruit is never a good solution for rearranging your to-do list."

He seemed to be in a mood to tease her or perhaps this morning, he functioned under reduced capacity not having slept all night. She did.

"I'm sorry you had such a terrible night," he told her.

The contrite emotion on his face appeared sincere and seemed to erase any semblance of reserve she clung to. She nodded allowing the warmth in her smile to reach her eyes.

"Here I imagined a feisty, independent girl like you able to sleep wherever she lays her head down."

"Oh, I can. Often slept rolled up in a chair," and checkmate. The ruse she feared reared an ugly head. In one brilliant maneuver, he cornered her with such brio, trying to backtrack would be impossible.

All the while his prying glare took pleasure dancing inside hers, brazen and bold. Scott's stare turned dark and intense, the light in his eyes igniting electric currents running through her lower limbs. She nearly jumped when he placed a hand on hers while her breathing arrested and formed a tight ball in her throat.

"I'm sorry. I didn't mean to upset you." He caressed her hand, but appeared to change his mind and raked his fingers through his hair instead.

She put down her fork and took a sip of her lemonade. She eyed Scott's downturned head careful to hide her love for him. She sensed his gesture might be the preamble to dislodge something stuck in his craw.

His eyes reverted to the kind hazel gold she found so exciting when he next glanced at her. "I suspect your lack of sleep bore the same root cause mine did." He pointed at her and to himself. "You can't deny there's an attraction here, Ava—a strong one."

She bit her lip not to cry out, yes—not to cry out, no.

"Now, since we are going to work together we'll need to ride out the storm."

She cocked her head for an explanation unable to speak.

"As we work together every day, we will begin to breathe familiarity into our relationship. Soon in a few weeks a few months we'll be able to laugh at our predicament at this desire that drives us."

He appeared to be so cavalier about his feelings she wondered how he managed to shelve them as though they didn't exist. Nevertheless, flattered he admitted he wanted her she rallied the guts to retaliate. "How can you just dismiss what we feel for each other? Isn't this dishonest?"

"I don't know what I'm feeling? Can't even figure how to describe this sensation. Do you?"

She did. Of course, she did. She wasn't about to spell her emotions out for Scott even when she sensed part of his tone leaned toward securing a confirmation from her—confirmation of what? Instead, she shook her head, agreeing with his opinion.

"Attraction—a burning, compelling need to hold you in my arms and not let go until you are mine and only mine." He let out a long, shaky breath. "The stubborn idea has been killing me ever since we met. Since the first night at the 21 Club, I thought of nothing else."

"Then how can you say this emotion will just go away?" She whispered the last words not knowing if he heard.

"Experience," he said. He nodded with raised eyebrows when

Ava looked up at him.

"What?"

"Didn't you ever wonder why Sylvia and I weren't married yet? I mean, going out for years then engaged for two. We would be by now had it not been for—let's call them indiscretions."

"She cheated on you?"

"No. No. Me—all me. Frankly, she's a forgiving individual. We'd be done if she weren't."

Ava saw him play with his fork his eyes looking down at the table.

"A few co-workers, a beautiful diplomat even Mathilda once in a drunken stupor."

"Mathilda?"

He nodded. "Sylvia walked in on us—right on cue. She knew about the other indiscretions too. Each time, Sylvia put the episodes behind her and moved on. She forgave me. And each time she did, I wore the big heel tattooed on my forehead and my ravenous hunger for the other woman disappeared—go figure."

He raised his head and looked at her. "Never since. Not since we became engaged. On a few occasions last year I needed to work through my cravings for a beautiful face, and this paid off. I got to know the person better, and longing lost luster. I kept my promise to Sylvia." He smiled. "I guess I'm growing—getting rid of my roving eye." He caressed her face with the sweep of his gaze. "At least, I thought I had."

His soft whisper trickled down to her loins setting them on fire. "Did you ever think maybe your heart is always searching, refusing to settle because you're not in love with Sylvia?"

"Define love. I dare you. Nobody can. Is love an all-consuming need we hold for one person which burns like a bonfire but for a moment? Or is love the sentiment you work on, day in, day out to improve the history you hold with someone, to build a future and become more and more like one another as the years pass?"

"Why can't we enjoy both? People do."

"Good question—although, I never met anybody like this. You?"

She bit her bottom lip. None of the few couples she knew fit the bill.

"Truthfully, Sylvia and I never experienced fiery passion. Still, we share a history, and we strive toward attaining the same goals. We're a good match."

"You make your union sound so clinical. No wonder Sylvia is unhappy."

"Sylvia is not unhappy. She is angry, resentful, and rightfully so."

She noticed his eyes pointing the finger at her. "Because of me?"

He gave her a nod upholding her gaze. "Not all your fault. I suspect she knew about my sentiments for you five minutes after she walked into my office—hell before she even met you. She's so used to my whims by now."

"Great. I won't be able to work with her now." Ava couldn't believe Scott held her accountable for her share in the imbroglio, she did not absolve herself of guilt for lusting after Scott, Sylvia's fiancé. Yet his accusation hurt her.

Scott appeared distant and lost in thought.

"So, I'm the reason you two argued last night."

After a slight hesitation, he agreed. "Sylvia accused me of

sleeping with you. I assured her I didn't. This was when she took a hissy fit."

"She didn't believe you."

"Of course, she did. After everything we've been through, she knows I wouldn't lie about a possible affair." He finished the last piece of ham on his plate. With slow gestures, he picked up his napkin and wiped his mouth his eyes still searching some distant thought.

Ava waited, but he added nothing. She looked down at what remained of her breakfast and found she'd lost her appetite. Furthermore, the worse occurred when she realized this whole conversation did not deter her from being with Scott one iota which only served to prove how big of a fool she happened to be.

He picked up her hand and leaned forward. "This is why I thought we should have this conversation, Ava, clear the air. For what it's worth, I don't intend to cheat on Sylvia no matter what the circumstances. I promised her when we got engaged that I wouldn't and I won't."

She pulled her hand out of his grasp. Scott chastised and humiliated her like some little girl asked to be reasonable—by the big bad wolf no less. How dare he remonstrate to her about proper conduct? "I never cheated on anyone, neither did I ever sleep with a man engaged to someone else. I am not about to start now." She threw her head back. "You flatter yourself if you think I'm trying to get you into bed, Scott."

He wore a sly look on his face as his head dropped. Then he caught their host coming toward them. He signaled for her to bring the check.

He rose inviting her to do the same. "Good. I'm glad we agree.

It'll help. Because I can say with certitude that the root of Sylvia's anger is, she's worried about me."

He smiled as he paid their host and thanked her for a delicious breakfast.

"Wonderful," Ava added putting down her napkin. She rose. "I will definitely recommend your establishment to friends."

"This is what we like to hear. You two lovebirds have a wonderful day."

As they walked out of paradise and into the real world, Ava sensed Scott's hand on her back. For an instant the dizzying sensation left her at a loss: to shake his hand away reminding him of what he just admonished or to enjoy the caress wishing the moment endured.

Instead, she turned to him as he opened the car door for her. "Why does she worry about you? Is she afraid I might seduce you—trap you into breaking your promise?"

His hazel eyes plunged into hers with all the fervor of a gentle lover. Ava took a deep breath and waited for some flippant remark which he seemed to possess in ready supply.

His lips curled almost brushing her own when he whispered. "Well, Sylvia knowing me as well as she does, I believe she worries, this time, my sentiments for you might be more than casual—so much more than I can handle."

He breathed the last part of his sentence in nervous little spurts.

Her back to him with eyes closed she clutched the top of the headrest glad to collapse into the seat. Had the seat not been so close, she would have fallen to her knees so drunk and deprived his words left her. She didn't dare ask him if the last statement might be true. To listen to him deny the idea would wound her more than sensing the hot-and-cold void he'd dug between them.

CHAPTER 17

FINDING A WAY

Ava Spent the entire weekend pacing up and down her small apartment aimlessly going from window to refrigerator to kitchen cupboards and back to the window again. Outside the weather, steaming hot from the sun in glowing form, prodded her to leave the house and celebrate this pristine last weekend of June.

She refused to go anywhere where she risked running into other people. Her state of mind pureed and whipped emitted unsafe doses of morbidity liable to infect any other healthy human.

She never received a call from Tracy, which she thought worked out well. She thought her friend might have spent the weekend with Reynard, and she imagined their relationship would grow from this couple of days in each other's arms. At least, she hoped so for Tracy's sake. Her friend and co-worker did not need another casual fling. Still, this new turn of events elected Tracy as the last person she might confide in—not anything about Scott she realized.

Elaine called twice. Also twice more, the string of calls ending once Ava figured she would own no peace until she picked up. Ava promised to call her Saturday. Elaine worried about her she supposed.

Ava's greeting of, "Stop calling," which resounded at odds with her usual self, brought on Elaine's threat to come over. The prospect of having to share face-to-face time with anyone forced Ava into a more amenable position. Only when Elaine relented on her ultimatum did she regain a sense of peace—at a price, which meant confiding about the Friday outing of course.

An hour later, Ava thanked her lucky stars Elaine had insisted she spill her guts. Of course, the adventure still fresh enough to be part of her system would not dissolve for a long time to come. Still, Friday night's dance and dream, next morning's breakfast, the long, silent and loaded ride home ending with a wrenching, piercing stare and a soft brush of Scott's lips against her cheek could be reviewed with more objectivity. At least, not blaring so much in her head like echoes of a horror show, more like the melancholic sounds of an old movie from which she would in time distance herself and turn off.

"Tell me again how his breath tickled your neck when he opened your door to let you out of the car?" The exception arising from questions like this one, able to crank the horror back up a notch.

"Can we talk about something else? This is not helping."

"Sorry. But your situation is so romantic."

"I don't think so, Elaine. He flat out told me he is going to ignore his emotions for me and wait until they go away like some form of indigestion."

"Hey, this is me you're talking to. I met the man. I've seen the way he looks at you. This is not something he will be able to ignore, trust me."

Ava didn't answer. She didn't want to argue anymore—also, she couldn't afford to hope. Scott remained out of her reach.

"What are you doing tomorrow?"

"I said I might quit my job. Only I don't think I can. Been waiting such a long time for an opportunity like this and when I think about my lot in life, the job is the only thing I own."

"Don't be silly. I'm here for you—so is Tracy."

"Please don't tell Tracy any of this, at least not yet."

"I won't. But if Tracy found out about this, she would march over to Scott and give him a piece of her mind."

Unable to picture Tracy admonishing Scott, Ava remembered she didn't tell Elaine how Scott might become Tracy's brother in law someday. Nevertheless, the image of Tracy flying to her defense served to put things in perspective for her. She'd be okay with support from her friends.

This thought close to her heart, first thing Monday morning, Ava stood at Sylvia's door. She counted to twenty to summon the courage to knock which represented how much she dreaded facing the woman who accused her of sleeping with Scott, although she doubted Sylvia would ever tackle the subject. Still, Ava strapped on her best poker face her eyes schooled not to stare at her.

Ava waited at the door while a faint discussion transpired inside. Unable to make out the voices and since she did not glimpse

Scott at his desk when she first arrived, she figured he and Sylvia were hard at work in her office.

"Come in," Sylvia called.

She turned the doorknob, but the handle wouldn't budge. The door seemed locked.

Mathilda opened the door. "Only Ava," she said tossing her hair toward the other woman seated behind her desk. She gave Ava a twisted smile.

"Come in, please," Sylvia said. She rose and marched toward Ava with hand extended. "You're on the ball this morning," she uttered with a sly snicker. "Mathilda and I were going over figures in another project. Can we postpone our meeting until later this afternoon?"

"Sure," Ava conceded with a little dejection. Having little else to do other than settle and learn the ropes, she tried not to sound like an interloper as she asked. "Can I be of assistance?"

Sylvia chuckled. "That's kind of you, Ava, but work is under control, and this is a private matter. I'd need to obtain Scott's permission first."

Ava acquiesced in silence puzzled about Sylvia's lack of trust. They belonged to the same team. Why would she need to clear anything with Scott?

Glued to the spot Ava tried her best not to stare at her, but she found Sylvia attractive this morning, more rested. She wore contacts as she had in the Hamptons, which brought out the curious gray gaze of her dark-fringed eyes.

Taking a deep breath when Ava witnessed the two turn their backs on her, realization dawned she had to leave. "If you need any help with anything, I'm available," she said grasping how pathetic she sounded. Ava wanted so much to be part of the team. She wondered how long it would take before they allowed her in the game.

Left to her own devices, she ambled down the corridor deciding she would polish up on her research. She'd caught on the news this morning how the government granted a huge chunk of funding to another biotech whiz kid. Young Colby Maddox planned to devote some of his time sequencing large numbers of influenza viruses working with the Human Genome Project and its properties to test different strains of hemorrhagic fever.

In a sense, this became Ava's small part to contribute to world betterment—sell the idea to investors which meant demonstrating the massive profits of a cure, and afterward redirect their dollars so doctors might develop a treatment.

Her mood restored, she hurried to her desk. When she got to her cubicle, her inside line was ringing.

"Hi, Ava, Trevor here. Can you spare me an hour to go over your observations? I need to establish a model on how to implement the legal aspects of your proposal."

"Sure. I'll be right there," Ava said eyeing the folders she needed to bring. At last, someone who needed her and without a doubt the most amenable on Scott's team. Easier even to get along with than Scott. For a man who didn't like to forego his promises, Scott had broken his to her—of not being so irascible—hot and cold, his temperament imitated the antics of a flying yo-yo.

Shelving thoughts of Scott, Ava knocked on the open door to Trevor's office the smallest of the four aside from her little island, of course.

"Hi." Ava smiled at him happy to be on friendly turf.

"Hey." He smiled but didn't get up. Ava noticed he appeared to be hard at work inputting fresh data on the computer spreadsheet "Please, make yourself comfortable," he told her without looking up. "I want to ensure these figures jive with yours."

"I brought some folders with a cast of predictions for you to verify." She dropped them on the corner of the desk and slid the nearby chair a little closer. "You talk about needing figures to legalize the program?"

He nodded. "Number crunching helps me stay focused. I use them to draw probable forecasts, pit potential losses against viable gains, and make sure the variant between them is within acceptable norms. Don't worry about the mumbo-jumbo. Legal, boring stuff—taxes." He handed Ava a copy of the folder he worked with at the moment. "The fact Reynard developed a whole department to handle legalities will lighten the load."

"Interesting. A whole other aspect I never considered," she answered while scanning the data in the folder. "Of course, if stats help I can lend you my forecasts on past and present stocks. I use them to outline specific performances."

"Thanks, Ava. This will help." He picked up the folders she brought with her and skimmed through them. "Just what I needed." He opened his drawer and slipped them in. "I'll ask Cindy to make me copies. I'll send them back by the end of the day."

"Sure." She opened one of the folders he handed her. "Still, taxes—more variables I don't care to juggle. I'll leave this up to you and our team of experts." Ava, considering what Trevor said, added, "You didn't use a tax Firm in Europe?"

He tossed his head side to side. "We did, but we contracted out. However, the legal ramifications were much simpler in Geneva.

How are the ladies treating you?"

The nonchalant tone did not lessen her surprise. In fact, Trevor's question proved to be so unexpected, Ava stared at him nonplus.

"Don't let Sylvia's attitude bum you out. She can be gentle when she lets you witness this side of her. What is unfortunate is Sylvia's insecurity and the fact she is influenced by her cousin Mathilda in a negative way."

A wave of self-consciousness flooded over her. To discuss Sylvia with Trevor whom she hardly knew seemed strange to her, and she wondered if Sylvia confided in him about her suspicions.

He stopped what he was doing and tilted his head an eyeful peering her way. "Don't tell me you didn't notice how short she is with you. The word is, she and Mathilda abandoned you on Saturday night."

She gave him a slight nod albeit reluctantly.

"Mathilda and Victor Danes, Sylvia's father, share a special bond. I'm not sure what that is. Between you and me, I never cared enough to explore their closeness. In any case, what I'm saying is Sylvia was a different young woman before Mathilda came into the picture."

"What does Mathilda do exactly?"

"She's well connected to a slew of influential people all over the world. She's fluent in several languages which make her an excellent public relations expert, and is an all-around people-person—when she chooses to be." He smiled coyly.

"I understand."

"However, like many women with impossible goals to attain—she set them pretty high—Mathilda finds difficult to consider anyone's needs but her own."

Ava nodded wondering where this conversation might be leading and why Trevor displayed this sudden need to confide in her.

"Scott is fond of you." He smiled at Ava. "Be careful to be discreet in Sylvia's presence. She could draw the wrong idea and make life a little hard on you."

"Well, Trevor. Scott may be fond of me, but this is on a professional basis only. I can assure you. Nothing is going on between us. Sylvia has no cause to be jealous of me." Ava's adamancy appeared to calm Trevor's qualms.

"It's none of my business. Yet I know her. We'll get a lot more work done if Sylvia is happy."

"I gather you and Sylvia are good friends?"

He smiled at the inference she made. "Used to be, before she became so fond of Scott. When Scott first talked about launching his firm in Europe, I introduced him to Sylvia at one of the banking functions. I knew Victor Danes possessed the influence and the money to help him get started. Yet, Sylvia and Scott already knew each other, avowed enemies in college, always fighting about something." He released a deep sigh. "A few weeks later, they became lovers. Rest is immaterial. She and I have remained good friends, so I guess you can say I know her well. This is why I'm asking you to be tolerant. Sylvia will come around."

"I will, Trevor—for all our sakes."

A little later, when it came time for her appointment with Sylvia, she kept her promise to Trevor in the foreground. She would deploy all the good will conducive to friendship and hope Sylvia reciprocated.

CHAPTER 18

LUKE PERRY

Two weeks later, down in the first-floor cafeteria, Ava preceded her break with Elaine with much-needed venting—vent or bust. "I don't understand, Elaine. She seemed so civil during our last meeting. I thought I made headway, and we might be friends. Trust me, Elaine seeing someone's winning side and having this same person shun you the next day for no apparent reason is heartbreaking."

"Maybe she's jealous? I caught the way Scott ogles you when he thinks no one's looking. Pretty damning evidence. If Jerry stared at someone else this way, I'd surgically remove his balls."

Ava shook her head giving Elaine a tight grimace. "You imagine this. He's been nothing other than downright proper with me."

"This from the girl who kissed and told." Elaine gave her a mocking grin.

"The kiss happened on day one—long before the scolding he gave me at the bed and breakfast, and I didn't initiate the kiss. He did."

"You're proving my point."

"Lust, nothing more. He admitted to this five minutes after we kissed. To prove *my* point, nothing intimate between Scott and me happened since" Ava glanced up at the ceiling wavering on which event to pick.

Elaine interrupted, "You mean since he took you in his arms and danced you around the floor in a Hampton mansion or since the breakfast of the morning after when he recounted the terrible fight he shared with Sylvia over you?"

Ava's eyes squinted, and her lips tightened—a warning of war on the way.

"Perhaps you dislike Sylvia for a whole different reason?"

"Hey, whose side are you on? You're supposed to be my friend. Now I'm sorry I ever told you about all this."

"Don't kick the messenger. This friend calls things by what they are, and I love you too much, Ava to start mincing words with you."

Ava sighed and knuckled Elaine's arm. "I love you too." She paused and smiled. "Even so, you should be better in tuned to me by now. I don't hate Sylvia, not in any real sense. We could be friends if she let me in."

Elaine finished her coffee. She shrugged nodding as she did. "Yeah. I take back the question. Stupid question. This is you. She'd be feeding you cyanide, and you'd politely tell her, no thank you."

Elaine glanced at her wrist. "I need to get back. Break times are short and shorter." She patted Ava's back. "Sweetie, you can't expect to be friends with this woman, not when you're in love with her fiancé."

"You're right, you're right. From now on I'm going to ignore her foul mood."

Ava ran beside Elaine to catch up to her and laid a hand on her arm as they entered the elevator. "Changing the subject, I promise." She crossed her heart, a solemn gleam in her eyes. "What are you doing this weekend? Want to come to the movies with me?"

"Can't. I'm ovulating. Jerry is spending the better part of Saturday spooning me."

They were in the elevator, and Ava shot her an eyeful when she realized others were listening. "Well," she announced as Ava stepped off the elevator playing seductress with her eyebrows, "May the moment between you rise to the occasion."

Her short-lived reprieve aside, she stepped out of her shoes to run the rest of the way to answer her phone she caught ringing from the hallway. She recognized the intercom line. "Hi, this is Ava." She gulped a little out of breath.

"Ava, please come into my office. Someone here I would like you to meet."

"Sure, be right in." She put her shoes back on her feet and remembered Trevor's advice, what she and Elaine discussed, what she promised herself—to forget about Scott and move on with her life. Tracy managed to hammer the nail on the head. Scott wasn't the man for her.

Ava entered Scott's office and glanced with a ready smile at the pleasant looking young man who stood to gaze at her as she walked in. The diversion became a valid excuse not to allow her eyes to wander over to Scott. These days, she needed to be creative to come up with reasons to direct her gaze elsewhere while in his presence. She detected he didn't seem to mind her aloof reaction or even question the awkwardness some of her evasive maneuvers brought on between them. Perhaps he walked the same path.

A quick scan of the young man in front of Scott's desk confirmed him to be handsome, and the right height for her. She liked curly blond hair and deep blue eyes in a tanned face. Eye candy she thought as she stuck her hand out to shake his.

"Ava Moss, meet Luke Perry the newest arrival in our team." Scott introduced them.

"Ava Moss."

"Luke Perry."

Both said each other's name at the exact same time, and both laughed.

Luke added, "Your name sounds so familiar. Have we met?"

At the same moment, Ava added, "Your name is familiar. Do I know you?"

Again, they shared a laugh.

"You go," Luke said tilting to a big broad smile.

"I don't think we met," Ava rebutted. "I don't ever forget a face." *Not one like yours, that's for sure.*

Scott watched them with his eyebrows anchored high above his eyes. "Well, Ava, Luke will be providing some of the expertise we need for the health module. He studied at Penn State in biochemistry and molecular biology and earned a Masters in biotechnology."

"This is great," Ava nodded impressed and excited by the arrival of this new team member, and she loved the name, Luke.

Memory jolted her with lightning speed. Luke Perry, the name of one of her contenders in the Mate for Life session. The no-picture résumé she left for the end and the no-show she mistook for Scott.

She kept the pasted smile on her face aware of how large her eyes became. Unable to curb her enthusiasm, she turned toward Scott to explain. She encountered a tight jaw and dull eyes—an accusation lurked in those hazel daggers appearing angry all at a once. What could be wrong with him now? Did he think she acted too friendly?

Her impression morphed into sureness when she deciphered deep disapproval written in easy-to-read English all over his face. She prayed to God Luke didn't read any of this.

About to spill her reasons to explain her enthusiasm vis-à-vis Luke, she tossed them back in the pot—served him right she thought. Her personal relationship with Luke Perry did not need Scott's approval, and she didn't intend performing acrobatic handstands to defend her position.

Scott's next words came out abrupt with a slight acerbic tone to their edge. "Well, I'm glad you two will get along."

"I am too," Luke shot still staring at Ava.

"I'm sure you will want to familiarize yourself with the proposal Trevor put together. Can you find your way back to his office?"

Luke glanced at Scott. "No problem. Down the corridor to my left. I'm blessed with a good sense of direction," he added once more staring at Ava.

"Good. He's expecting you."

Luke nodded and turned to leave.

Ava followed not far behind.

"Ava, please stay. I need to run a few ideas by you."

Ava realized Scott's temper bore a lot of resemblance to her own, which made for a volatile situation. She schooled herself to remain calm. "What's up?" She eyed him with the newfound courage she vowed to observe, her smile courteous, her eyes distant.

She wore lower heels these days, so when he came around the desk to stand in front of her, she needed to look up. She wondered about the flinty gaze he ran over her face.

"Listen, Ava. Your personal life is none of my business. So don't take this the wrong way, but I would like you to keep your sentiments for Luke under wraps at least while you're in the office."

Scott's remark, which Ava found left-field and inappropriate in a gross way, appeared so dead on with her interpretation she just stared at him her mouth agape. She shook her head as though water whooshed in her ears.

"Professional etiquette is essential if we're going to measure up as a strong team. I hope you understand this."

"What?" She put up both her hands and stared at the door. She glanced back at Scott her arms dropping by her side. "How can you consider my behavior other than professional? I can't believe you're saying this."

"Oh, come on, Ava." He sat on the corner of his desk. "You can't tell me you weren't flirting just now—evident even to him."

Furious with him she wondered how he dared to accuse her of flirting with a co-worker. Had he gone berserk? "You're nuts if you think I was flirting. You of all people should be familiar with the way I flirt. Ah, this is why, right? Your attitude toward me comes back to the night we met, to the way I tried to snare you into a date and get your phone number. You have branded me easy-Ava ever since, haven't you?"

"Of course not. This does not have anything to do with the way we met."

She had no choice. She needed to tell him the truth. She couldn't keep this information to herself and risk exacerbating an impossible situation. "Well guess what? This does go back to the night at the 21 Club, because of Luke Perry," she started to say as Scott interrupted her.

"Wow, even the way you say his name appears unique. I forgot. You like the name, Luke. I remember you telling me you did."

"This is what I'm trying to say—wait a minute—even the way I say his name sounds unique? What kind of crazy observation are you making?"

He slid off the desk and retreated behind a solid piece of oak avoiding her eyes while fiddling with his pens.

"You talk about being professional—of ignoring feelings in the workplace. And here you are so condescending, caring way too much about what I say and how I say it." Her expression lightened up as she smiled gazing at the top of his head wishing he dug for the courage to show his face. "This is about much more than office politics." She breathed out a treacherous little sigh. "You're jealous."

He looked at his hands resting on the desk and refused to face her as he said, "Not jealous, Ava, disappointed."

He did not move Ava noticed. He kept the desk planted between them like some security barrier. With hesitancy, he added. "A couple of weeks ago at breakfast, I had no doubt you wanted me as much as I wanted you." His eyes were still glued to the desk. "At least, this's what you led me to believe—that day at the inn."

A mere piece of furniture stood between them making Scott

much too close for logic and reason. Worse, she found difficult to put her emotions into words. "You're right about that morning at breakfast. You demanded I ignore my feelings, Scott. You said to put them on a shelf and wait until they pass. You even mentioned you intended to do this, remember?"

Finally, he looked up, and she faced the tortured glare in his eyes. "I recall what I said. No need to throw my words back in my face," he uttered in a gritty voice. "And what about weeks ago in my arms, right here in this office. I admit I initiated the kiss, Ava, but you kissed me back, with passion I might add."

Saving face no longer mattered since refuting the allegations would make her a liar. On the other side of the coin, admitting she was in love with him and lust did not prompt her kiss would not only cause her shame, but the declaration might also jeopardize her career.

"I did want to be with you. I still do. But you're engaged to Sylvia and if you're going to keep your promise to her, well, there's no hope of you and me coming together anytime soon," she whispered.

"So you just gravitate toward Luke as though you and I never happened."

"Nothing ever happened between us, Scott." She stared at the handsome head, at Scott's Adam's apple bobbing up and down in his throat, and hesitated. "Is this your crazy way of asking me to have sex with you?" She muttered the words so quietly, she wondered if he even heard them.

He turned away from his desk to bridge the gap between them and laid gentle hands on her shoulders. "I realize I promised Sylvia. And I meant what I told you on the way home from the Hamptons." He fingered a wisp of her hair, stroked the soft curve of her cheek with the back of his hand. "I'm only human, Ava. Resisting the pull between us might even be harder for me than it is for you. Who can say?"

Ava swallowed the affection welling up inside her. She wanted to scream to his face how much she loved him, how she might be a better fit for him than Sylvia. Her vocal chords remained numb while her heart fluttered in her chest.

He continued, relentless. "All I know is I lie awake at night unable to sleep until dawn creeps in. I sit in a restaurant to enjoy a meal and each time I look up across the table, I expect to gaze into your eyes." He traced her lips with his thumb then he closed his eyes. "So I guess the answer to your question is, yes," he mouthed in a soft whisper.

A soft whisper echoing through her mind like the blast of a gunshot. Dizzy and confused, Ava considered the man of her dreams wanted to have sex with her, asking her to be the other woman.

He did hear her request. She couldn't believe how fast he aimed to capitulate. Tossing all good intentions in the bin, he prepared to renege on his promise to Sylvia and make her an accomplice to his elicit proposition.

Who was she to judge? Perhaps his desperate proposal came packaged as part of the withdrawal he advocated, stare down the precipice every now then and retreat in small steps to avoid the fall.

She swallowed hard. Scott thought she condoned this sort of behavior since he took the trouble to ask. No man would formulate this type of demand knowing there might exist the slightest possibility of suffering a rejection—or did he count on her refusal?

"I do want to have sex with you, Scott. I haven't stopped think-ing about you either." She nodded as she stared into his eyes. "Trouble is well. I realize lying once in your arms will never be enough." Scott backed up a few steps and closed his eyes. "I'd want more of you afterward. Not sure how many times we would need to be together before I was satisfied—you?" She waited, and when he stared at her once more, she caught the intensity in his eyes shut down. "What do we do?"

"Goddamn it!" He turned away rubbing a hand across the back of his neck. He walked back to stand behind the desk averting his eyes. "Of course, you're right. Foolish of us to indulge in a silly whim." He took a deep breath and looked at her his business ex-pression on mighty secure. "Because I agree with you, this is a whim nothing more."

So close to enjoying his arms around her, when he left her alone standing in front of the desk, she almost lost her footing. Yet staring at Scott, Ava caught the hesitant plea in his eyes as though he waited for her to refute the statement. Instead, she bobbed her head. "Very astute of you."

"Good. Now, can you not flaunt your dealings with Luke in front of me or in the office for that matter?"

Kind Ava wanted to alleviate the pain she saw on his face, explain the misunderstanding—about Luke. Street Ava needed to self-preserve. Best for Scott to believe she moved on with her life—give him the peace he needed to keep his promise to Sylvia. "Of course, Scott. I will be discreet."

CHAPTER 19

TRIPPING ON FRAUD

T he next morning, Ava made her way to Luke's office. He wanted to meet with her to understand which biotech companies she wanted to target.

Tired and cranky, which wasn't like her, Ava had spent the night running scenarios in her head wondering how she might be able to live and breathe near Scott without losing her mind.

Around four in the morning, she began to consider leaving her job, the one place where she'd derived a sense of peace these past twelve months. She shrugged, a tad sorry for herself. Over the years, Ava became accustomed to change, leaving people behind and families she loved, something she suffered through countless times in her youth and would need to do again to avoid yelling at this dunce of a man how much she loved him.

Tracy mentioned how Victor Danes loaned Scott the money for

his business venture. She doubted Scott would ever leave Sylvia, not when Sylvia's dad, Victor Danes, supplied Scott the money he needed to start his own firm. The capital forged a partnership between the two men, which almost tied the noose between Sylvia and Scott.

Of course, Ava never mentioned she got the story from Trevor since she supposed Tracy revealed the information to stop her from making a fool of herself. Ever since their first kiss, she'd fallen head-over-heals with little wiggle room to hide the sentiment.

As Ava made her slow robotic amble down the corridor toward Luke's office, a familiar sound coming from one of the offices roused her curiosity. A warm, tingly awareness rushed past her when she recognized the familiar language. Someone in the office she just passed spoke Dutch.

She backed up to better hear the words, not to eavesdrop, but to listen to the language which brought back so many fond memories from her childhood.

At the third foster home she stayed, from age seven to twelve, the happiest years of her life, she lived with an old couple from Holland. They immigrated to America to be closer to their son. Ava took to learning Dutch like a fish to water, even imagining her parents might be Dutch immigrants.

Five years later, the son who sponsored them died in a car accident. Forced to go back, they pleaded with immigration to allow them to take Ava with them. The State, given their age and financial status, refused, and so wrenching and tearful goodbyes followed her pre-teen promises to keep in touch while authorities pulled her out of their arms. All these years, she'd kept up the language, practicing each chance she got in case she ever ran into them again.

The Netherlands' Dutch, complete with all its familiar accents and intonations, and although she found impossible to name who occupied the office, with the door slightly ajar she did recognize Mathilda's voice.

"*Niemand verdenkt.*"

No one suspects. Ava's ears perked at the sound of this conversation.

"*Ja. Mij maak niet ongerust. Niemand Weet, maar het Sylvia gaat akkoord. Wij wachten.*" Ava's ears buzzed so unbelievable were the words she caught.

"Yes, don't worry. No one suspects, but Sylvia agrees. We wait—to be cautious. We will communicate the names of the investors later, but will relay the information on the health package as soon as the data becomes available."

Ava muffled a cry by clamping her hand over her mouth. Mathilda a traitor? Mathilda, and Sylvia both traitors? Shock glued Ava to the spot.

Stunned, Ava refused to accept Scott's fiancée might be a part of the mysterious ghost corporation Scott mentioned stole from them. Some sort of explanation would rationalize this conversation. Besides, Ava couldn't find any valid reason why Sylvia would need to usurp money from Scott. Sylvia possessed wealth in her own right, and these actions meant she stole from herself. Could this be the reason Sylvia's father, Victor, suggested they not report the crime? Might he also be in on the swindle? She thought of Trevor and wondered about his innocence, but figured he might be ignorant of all this. Scott didn't even suspect them.

"*Dank u wel, Tot ziens.*"

Ava realized Mathilda prepared to hang up. She hurried to resume her walk toward Luke's office. As she tapped on Luke's door, she eyed the length of the corridor she'd skimmed.

Mathilda came out of her office and gazed her way as she answered Luke's call to enter.

Ava smiled adding a little hand wave for Mathilda.

Mathilda's eyes twitched for a few seconds. She looked at her door she found open. Ava read the doubt in Mathilda's crossed eyebrows. However, Mathilda smiled returning Ava's little wave before walking off in the opposite direction.

Ava entered Luke's office realizing Mathilda thought her secret safe. How many people in the world spoke and understood Dutch? Not little Miss Moss, whom Mathilda considered too benign a person to matter.

Walking toward the desk she was of two minds. Her first impulse dictated she grab the phone to summon Scott to Luke's office. Of course, she considered Luke beyond reproach.

"Hey, Ava." Luke spotted the worry in her expression. "What's wrong? You look like someone who lost her best friend."

She leaned against his office door, the sense of being trapped hampering her breathing as her mind raced ahead while fidgeting with proof she might provide Scott? It happened to be Mathilda's, word against hers and Mathilda would sway Scott by saying she, Ava, mistook what she said—make up any kind of excuse to discredit her.

"I came across some distressing bit of news. I can't be sure, so I rather not say."

"I'm sorry."

"Don't be silly. The problem is not your fault." At this moment,

Ava came up with a brilliant beyond brilliant idea.

"Luke, would we be able to prepare two presentations with the biotech formula?"

He looked at her at a loss.

"I mean a trial proposal which would not lead anywhere, on which we might scribble equations unsafe to recommend," she slipped in nonchalantly. "And another we would use as our prime target, one Sylvia could present to our group of investors later on as a surprise."

He smiled. He rose and took a seat in front of a small coffee table, legs sprawled fingers steepled. "You are a strange woman, Ava Moss, beautiful but strange." He flicked his hand inviting her to sit with him. "What's this all about?"

"Thank you—I think," she said with a coy smile still weighing his comment of her being strange. She sat down and stared at Luke's relaxed position. She took in his good looks and hesitated whether to confide in him.

She never got the chance to talk to him alone, tell him they were scheduled to meet at the Mate for Life party. She wanted to keep things between them on a professional level despite what she led Scott to believe.

With speed and efficiency, Ava admitted to Luke what she caught at Mathilda's door and how this related to the problems Scott encountered in Europe.

"I agree, those few words do sound suspicious," Luke told her a frown marring his handsome features. "Might be nothing. I think you should tell Scott. He's in a much better position to judge—investigate if he wants to."

Ava shook her head. Thanks to their history together, Ava worried Scott might think she wanted to discredit Sylvia. "He won't believe me, not without proof. This is why if we make two proposals and allow Sylvia to glimpse the real one a few minutes before she presents the product to our investors, we would read the deception from her reaction."

"This won't prove anything, Ava."

"The ruse might force her to admit her guilt and come clean."

He shook his head and leaned toward her rummaging through his papers on the coffee table. "If you're right about Mathilda and Sylvia, they've got their act well in hand. This little stint won't fool them one bit."

Ava thought for a moment. "Mathilda said they would wait to communicate the names of the investors, but give information on the project as soon as this became available?"

"Highly unethical, but not fraudulent. The details on the health package will leak out through different sources once it becomes available—Barclay's Database for one, Morningstar will grab the news I suppose."

"Of course, but we're not talking simple outline and results. We're facing losing the complete project to the highest bidder with all the essential details spelled out. Mathilda mentioned waiting before sending them the list of our clients." She took a deep breath shaking her head faced with the enormity of what she had uncovered.

"This is borderline fraud, I'll grant you this one—if you can prove it." He shrugged. "Stolen clients making money elsewhere become satisfied clients somewhere else."

"What do you mean?"

"I mean stolen clients won't testify against the hand who feeds them. As long as they're making money. If the venture is not illegal, they don't care which firm is making the money for them."

"There's so much more to this, Luke." Ava kept shaking her head. "Let's suppose I'm a client of Extrade and I'm convinced to switch to some other firm promising me more money with the same investment package. I might consider the deal—might even agree to change. Let's say I do. Around the corner come my financial advisers who tell me that for this new firm to be in a position to propose this to me, this new company needed to be in the presence of all my very private and personal documents. Might their recommendation be that I sue Extrade for breach of trust?"

Luke made a face. "Problem."

"Huh huh. I would sue. Think of this. I'd be making tons of money from the health project in someone else's hands, and from the massive lawsuit I would be sure to win."

"More than a problem." Luke's grimace deepened. "Good lawyer might link these activities to Extrade's claim of theft which would mean bad publicity."

"Which brings us to settling out of court meaning little or no damage to me. I mean consider this for a minute. All my information, tax loopholes, money I've earned over the years, past investment records, all out there to be shared with everyone. Nowadays, this sort of information can travel around the world in seconds. What next? Even if Extrade settled out of court which they would, word would get out."

"You're right. The company does hold in trust all investors' private information. Losing control would be a terrible blow." Luke released a long sigh. "You've got my attention."

"I don't even want to think of what might happen," she

breathed.

"What do you propose we do?"

"Well, Scott will want to launch with single digits at first, without fanfare to get proper feedback. Therefore, if Mathilda and Sylvia are smart, they're not going to go for the clients right away. If they did, we would find out in a blink. I suspect this was what Mathilda meant when she said they wanted to wait."

"Makes sense. With just a couple of clients on file at the SEC, we'd discover the compromise right away."

"Yes, which means they intend launching at first with their own few clients to test the waters." She smiled. "Phony presentation is the most practical method."

"This calls for altering biotech projects—streaming the less likely ones to produce and sticking them up front while shoving the more promising ones last." He took and released a deep breath. "This involves a complete reversal of our equations including all the probability factors, along with charts and data configuration."

"You're right. We'd also need to falsify data and figures to explain our choices."

She eyed Luke shaking his head while a reproving smile softened his frown. "I realize you're full of good intentions, Ava, but your plan demands we work around the clock, and this would only leave us with perhaps three to four weeks leeway by which time we would need to put our best presentation in the mill."

"I am aware of this."

"We can't risk this information dropping into one of our investor's ears—not for a second. To steer someone in the wrong direction, even to uncover a scam might very well be construed a fraud in itself."

She smiled. "I understand when you say Mathilda and Sylvia hold a firm grasp of this project. I say faced with the panic of having given wrong information to their investors will make them sweat—big time. By then, they'll realize we're on to them."

"Dangerous little game. Sylvia and Mathilda might choose to report us to the SEC when things go bad as we suspect they will."

"They wouldn't dare—too close to airing the theft."

"Don't see how you can pull this off without Scott knowing about your plan. He's sharp. He'll know something's up when he examines our figures."

"No, he won't because you and I are going to be at our most creative."

"I know he's new here. He told me. If you ask me, I think you are underestimating Scott if you believe we can come up with a presentation able to fool him. From what little I understand of him, he seems to be on the ball and quite a cool customer."

"This means your presentation will need to be intelligent, well-rounded, and forceful enough to fool a quaint, cool customer." She smiled at him.

"Not so fast. I'm not going in this alone. If I jump in the soup, you're coming in with me, Miss Moss." He smiled.

"Of course. This is my plan. Besides, a lot will depend on how fast we can work. We might want to ask for more preparation time."

"Right."

She rubbed her hands together. "I guess we should start on the right model first and backtrack once we are able to produce a hook on the project."

Luke nodded shrugging as though trying to ward off the crazy plan. "Let's get started."

With Ava's knowledge of the various funds and Luke's expertise in biotechnology, they still needed ten days to come up with a scenario they were sure would withstand Scott's scrutiny once the time came to accentuate the proper package.

During such time, Ava and Luke became friends. They lunched together, confided in one another, and Luke found hard to believe they almost dated following the Mate for Life fiasco. Ava omitted to talk about Scott and how the two of them had met or about how she first mistook Scott for him.

She even introduced Luke to Elaine and Tracy. The four of them got along like old friends.

"So we now produced quite a decent package, one which might gather a few kudos," Luke said while eating his salad as the four of them ate lunch on the Friday before the pre-launch.

"Yep," Ava said with enthusiasm.

"I still don't see how this is going to work—good presentation, bad presentation. How are you going to use either to smoke out Sylvia and Mathilda's game?" Elaine tried to catch up as she took a sip of her drink.

"Well," Tracy added. "Supposing Ava understood the language well—and this is a big if." She darted loaded eyes Ava's way.

"I did understand what Mathilda said. How many times do I need to tell you?"

"Ava, you must admit. People are apt to find difficult to believe a woman would steal from the man she's engaged to marry," Elaine argued.

Ava didn't say anything. She figured even though some truth to the saying, hell hath no fury like a woman scorned might exist, she did not wish to betray Scott's secret of cheating on Sylvia—with Mathilda of all people. Perhaps beautiful Mathilda had lured him to her bed just to secure Sylvia's cooperation—a theory she would need to ignore for now.

"As I was saying," Tracy continued. "You're right, Elaine. There is no way to be certain—of anything." Tracy gave Ava an eyeful of reproach. "But, provided all these scenarios pan out," Tracy paused for another eye-roll. "We're hoping by the time we present to our clients, they will have spun enough rope to hang themselves—or at least to help us uncover their duplicity."

"Genius idea." Luke nodded.

Tracy smiled and bobbed her head to accept the compliment. "I also spoke to a couple of buddies at the SEC who said they would snoop around."

"You didn't tell Reynard about this, I hope." Ava cast round eyes on Tracy.

"No, of course not."

Ava breathed a little easier, and as she turned toward Luke and Elaine, she added. "Tracy and I think Victor Danes is a big part of the plot to defraud Scott."

Elaine wiped the corners of her mouth. "Mathilda and Sylvia can always tell their clients they got their facts wrong."

Tracy added, "They can say whatever they like. By then, their game will have unraveled."

"I hear this Saunders fellow is in a hurry," Luke said.

"He'll need to wait like the others," Tracy muttered.

Tracy eyed Ava shaking her head while rolling her eyes, and Ava hated she didn't have more of their trust.

"And why is no one mentioning this to Scott again?" Luke's

side-smile spoke volumes.

Elaine answered him with a peak of her eyebrows toward Ava. "How would you like someone to tell you the woman you're about to marry is stealing from you?"

They all saw Luke's head bob at the answer.

"Since all this brouhaha could very well turn out to be a huge misunderstanding." Elaine tugged on Ava's hair. "You can get why we are reticent to tell Scott."

CHAPTER 20

PRESENTATION

Ava stood in the hall by the elevator clasping her presentation material with sweaty hands and swollen fingers from living through days of unhealthy stress.

She shifted her weight and cursed the new shoes she wore this morning. They pinched her feet, and her big toe tingled with numbness. Vanity did not belong in the boardroom she scolded herself for the nth time. Worse, the pain caused by her vanity did not prevent her from dwelling on how big a fool she might be making of herself and Luke in the next ten minutes, ruining their careers in the process.

She regretted starting this brouhaha behind Scott's back, even when Ava convinced herself he fared better ignoring the problem because she didn't want to hurt his feelings.

She thought of Sylvia, how angry and wounded she must have been each time she caught Scott in a compromising position with another woman. Stealing from him might be her way of cheating on him—getting back at him on her terms.

She thought of Tracy and her newfound love, Reynard Wallace oblivious to what they planned because Tracy didn't believe in her story—well she trusted her a little. She'd gone to a lot of trouble to help her stage this little scenario, all based on her hearsay.

As for Reynard, he demonstrated Tracy a lot of fondness since returning from their weekend in the Hamptons. Well, as much affection as a man like Reynard dared to show in public. Gentle eyes lingering on the curve of Tracy's face, the soft touch of a hand he laid on Tracy's arm. Of course, had Ava not been aware of their tryst she might not be the wiser. Reynard was the epitome of discretion.

Ava turned toward the elevator distracted by the bell indicating someone's arrival.

Luke stepped off and walked toward her. A big smile lit up his face when he spotted her.

She nodded and smiled back recognizing how handsome he appeared in his navy suit. Another person to draw her worries. She'd become well acquainted with him during the last few weeks, and now she was fond of him, and of course, out of the three conspirators Luke stood to lose the most. New to the company he owned no portfolio to speak of with the firm. If their shenanigans hit the fan, Luke would be the first Reynard and Scott would rake over the coals more so when they discovered Luke agreed with a birdbrain like her.

"Hi, Ava. Don't you look smart today—and gorgeous. All fired-up up in a new suit?"

She shook her head. "Bought it on sale last spring. Shoes are new, though—and they're killing my feet." The stretched smile of pain on her face spoke volumes.

He laughed. "New or old, I love the baby blue suede." He stroked the sleeve of her jacket. "What are you doing standing around in the hall? You waiting for someone?"

"You." She confirmed with a head nod. "I'm terrified of going through with this. I need you to tell me everything's going to be okay. I do."

Luke appeared nervous. "Of course, everything is going to be okay. Can't go wrong. I need this job."

"How is this ever going to work? How?"

"Hey, you've gone and grabbed my line. In any case, stop fidgeting or Scott will figure something's up. He'll wonder about mighty Ava Moss flailing about unsure of her moves." He hooked her arm with his. "Come on. Let's get the show on the road."

"I guess you're right." She smiled. His arm around hers surprised her a little, but she didn't mind the squeeze. She only needed to take longer steps to keep up with his stride. "By the way, I couldn't lounge around my desk waiting for the light to turn green. What if Scott wanted to see a preview? Then what?"

"I understand, believe me. These last few days, I worked under a cloak, dodging the question whenever Scott asked me if there appeared to be any loose ends."

"Yes," she almost shouted reclaiming her arm as she rolled her eyes. "Yesterday, I hurried to shove a copy of Addendum A in my drawer seconds after I spotted him coming down the hall. I realize he made this big speech about trusting us well you more than me," she put up her hand to stop his objection. "I'm sure if the proposal had been lying on my desk, he would have insisted I give up the goods."

He gave her a quizzical look. "So, you would have said no, right?"

His comment held so much meaning. Did Ava imagine the loaded question in his eyes? He had to realize how vulnerable she was at this moment. Yet he directed his question toward her feelings for Scott as sure as he stood in front of her wondering whether she would resist Scott's demands.

She smiled sidestepping the taunt with a head-bobbing confirmation. A lie she thought, with lips pinched and eyebrows arched. No way would she ever be able to resist Scott—at least as confirmed to her by a vivid dream one night in the Hamptons—one still haunting her waking moments.

"Another important reason this has to go as planned is I'm afraid I've put you in a tentative position, Luke. You're new to the firm. If Scott or Reynard ever found out about our little dupe—before we can prove we are right of course—you would be …"

"Expendable?"

She nodded. They stood in front of Scott's office, and she waited for his answer before knocking on the door.

"Hey, what's a little risk now and then? The biggest gamble I've lost all year was not showing up at the 21 Club when I had the chance." He took her breath away as he stroked her face with his eyes. "Compared to that, this is a walk in the park."

"You think so?" she asked a little winded.

"I do." He smiled from ear to ear lightening the mood.

As they gazed at each other, the door opened, and Scott stared at them.

Ava turned around. Startled to see Scott glaring at her, she lost her smile.

His eyes hardened, and his tone toughened as he stated, "I hope you'll be conducting the presentation inside rather than in the hallway."

"Of course. I just needed to go over last minute details with Luke."

She watched him walk between them to head down the hall.

"I don't know what you did to him," Luke said. "But he always seems a little resentful toward you."

"You think so?" She shrugged. "He's edgy with everyone. Tracy noticed too."

"How and when do we substitute the right package?"

"Simple. With the extensive portfolio we've drawn, it'll be easy to randomize the order of the playing fields we chose."

"He'll think we're idiots." Luke smiled.

"We'll apologize with lots of excesses when we explain to Scott we wrong-ended our information—no harm done."

He laughed. "You've got everything figured out, don't you?"

"Just pray this works, Luke. We've got to expose those two or there's no telling how much they'll steal before they're through."

"Did you ever consider what might happen should Mathilda and Sylvia find out you're on to them?" He left the rest unsaid.

"There's no way they can find out." She lifted her eyebrows and gave him a big bright smile. "Who's going to tell them, you?"

He laughed and shook his head vigorously. "You, Ava Moss, are a very charming conspirator. I wish you'd go out with me. We were meant to date that night—the terrible night I needed to show up, but never did."

"Tell you what, Luke. Let's finish this deal and I'll give our dating serious thought." She smiled working hard not to appear wistful. Scott happened to be the one she wanted to date.

The same Scott, who once more stood at his office door, staring at Ava while seeming to question her motives she thought. She glanced at Luke and nodded. She took a deep breath, turned, and walked toward Scott. "We're right behind you."

He opened the door and invited her inside with the sweep of his arm. "After you," he said in unctuous tones. Then he filed in behind her leaving Luke to close the party.

"Do you want the door closed, Scott?" Luke asked. "Or are we all headed to the boardroom?"

"We'll do the trial run here—plenty of space." He designated the round conference table to the right of his desk. "Mathilda is at a client's. Trevor and Sylvia are expected in a few minutes."

"What about Reynard?" Ava regretted asking the question when Scott stared at her with a dark expression. Such an innocuous question. What might he be bothered about now?

"I am capable of conducting this meeting on my own, Ava."

"Scott, I didn't mean anything."

"It's quite all right. I understand your concerns—new kid on the block and all."

"Don't be silly."

"To allay your fears," he added interrupting her again. "Reynard has given me carte blanche." He handed them each a file folder. "He trusts us to do a superb job."

Ava clamped down on the giggles threatening to overtake her. Not a laughable matter Scott felt upstaged by big brother with his own project or that he seemed to be venting all his frustrations her way. Yet, the nervousness she harbored around Scott, her fatigue her awareness of Luke knowing all the tricks they intended to play on Scott, wore down her armor.

Sylvia walked in creating a much-needed diversion. Ava found her tall, elegant in a steel-grey pinstriped suit. She also found it easy to understand why Scott loved her as much as he did. Giggles, gone.

"Trevor is right behind me, Scott."

"Good." He turned toward Luke and Ava. "Which one of you will be giving the presentation?"

"Both of us," Ava said. "Luke will start by explaining the science behind the venture, as a reassuring point, then, I'll follow with the profits we can earn. Also, Trevor will add something at the end—legalities he thought would further reassure everyone."

CHAPTER 21

AVA HIDES FROM SCOTT

The presentation lasted sixty minutes allowing for questions and a few alterations.

In the end, Sylvia seemed enthusiastic about the proposal, as did Trevor. He didn't foresee any legal flaws or loopholes. For him, they'd wrapped up the project with brio.

Ava and Luke did most of the talking and pleased with their effort she found no one the wiser as to their choice of portfolios.

Now, all eyes veered on Scott. He seemed pensive and uncommunicative.

Ava worried he didn't like the presentation or perhaps he didn't agree with the way they arranged the material. Did he suspect something? Ava asked with a big tentative smile. "Is this what you envisioned, Scott?"

He dropped the pen he fidgeted with rubbed his face with his hands and stared at her with an intensity that jiggled her nerves.

To Ava the few seconds of Scott's gaze appeared like minutes, his deliberate glare so forceful she figured he did suspect something. She swallowed the nervous lump in her throat.

"Everything is perfect," he answered guardedly. "I think this is the fine edge of a huge market," he added to the smiles and grateful sighs of everyone around him.

"I agree, Scott," Sylvia said as she rose to leave. "I'll rehearse the material with Ava. I've got some calls to return."

"Do you need me?" Trevor asked Scott.

"No. I'm going to go over the material. I'll call you if I do."

As Ava and Luke closed their folders preparing to leave, Scott called out.

"Luke, could you stay? I spotted a few things I'd like to discuss with you."

Luke stood his back to Scott as Ava eyed him with concern. He shooed her away with a surreptitious shake of his head.

"Sure, Scott." He turned to face him. "What can I do you for?"

Scott threw Ava one last glance as she stepped out answering her little hand wave with one of his own. He rose and walked to the front of his desk perching on the edge arms crossed and nodding as he stared at Luke.

He couldn't help wonder how friendly he and Ava had become. "Mind telling me why the proposal I studied and the one you presented here today are different? Almost at opposite ends of the scale, you might say?" Luke seemed shaken, and Scott figured his only options were to bluff or come clean.

"I don't understand."

Scott sighed. He had opted to bluff wishing to avoid an argument.

Luke smiled standing pat favoring the middle of the room. "The proposal you studied?"

"Don't do that. Don't play dumb with me. The one I picked up lying on your desk day before yesterday. We both know this is her idea. She put you up to this betrayal. Why?"

"By her, I suppose you mean Ava." Luke dropped the smile along with the pretense. "I can't believe you helped yourself to information in my office without so much as a word," he whispered. "No wonder Ava won't confide in you." He nodded to lend drama to his last words. "If you think something is wrong, and you suspect Ava, why are you asking me?"

The incriminating answer Scott hoped not to get. Not cleverly disguised, Luke's rebuttal painted him and Ava as tight as thieves. He sighed discouraged and more than disappointed. "How about you tell me, Luke, or did the two of you concoct this to make me look like a fool when the client loses his shirt?"

Luke appeared stunned. "I'm speechless—that you could believe the worst without even knowing."

Scott got up and walked toward him. "Goddamn, it Luke. I hired you because I believed you to be the best for the job. Not the best at getting young, impressionable girls into bed," he muttered in raspy tones his eyes two loaded guns.

"What?" Luke almost laughed. "Ludicrous, man. I admit I'd like nothing better than to *date* Ava. She turned me down saying we need to keep our positions with the firm professional and beyond reproach."

Scott looked down at the floor gently easing an enormous and grateful sigh. Careful not to show Luke the relief he expelled, he added. "I'm sorry. I just thought the two of you had become pretty chummy. How else can I explain this discrepancy and your acceptance of the situation? I understand why she's doing this. I can't for the life of me imagine why you would jeopardize your career over female spite."

Luke seemed puzzled.

"She initially thought she would be presenting her brainchild to the client. I told her Sylvia possessed more experience, and she would be doing the presentation." Scott's tone came out matter-of-factly as though he considered the premise understood and cataloged.

Luke shook his head as though trying to understand better. "You honestly believe Ava would jeopardize both our careers, the client's hard earned money, and the firm's reputation because of spite?" His eyebrows raised a notch. "You're obviously not well acquainted with Ava. She's more the type of person who would risk a lot to go to bat for the firm."

Scott walked over to the chair beside his desk. He invited Luke to do the same. He couldn't figure if Luke, so mesmerized by Ava would defend anything she did, or if the fault lay with him having sorely misjudged and condemned Ava by burying his ethics out of a need to survive the havoc she wreaked inside him. "Suppose you tell me what this is all about?"

Luke walked over to the chair but remained standing. "Ava would be much better at explaining this, Scott. You should ask her," he added.

"I'm much calmer now knowing you can supply me with an explanation." Scott smiled to relieve the tension between them. "I'll also remain calmer hearing this from you." He nodded toward the chair.

After a slight hesitation, Scott spotted Luke straddle the chair and sit down. His expression illustrated he would come clean, own up for the both of them—maybe to save Ava the embarrassment. "Just so you realize, we would never allow Sylvia to present this version to our clients."

"Good. Thank you for telling me."

"Listen, Scott. I didn't sign on to play detective. And I don't care about office politics. But, when Ava told me she discovered the people responsible for the fraud being perpetrated on your company, I went along with her plan."

"She told you about Xfinite?"

Luke nodded. "She overheard a discussion Mathilda held in private, in Dutch." He hesitated briefly. "Sylvia would be in on this too, Ava believes."

Scott got up and began pacing in front of the window. He needed to hide the fact Luke's news stunned him.

"I told Ava she should bring the matter to your attention. She didn't think you would believe her, thought you would need proof. Now, knowing how spiteful you think she is I can't say I blame her."

For the next few minutes, Scott rubbed his forehead with a trembling hand. He couldn't decide on what angered him most, Sylvia daring to plot behind his back or Ava not trusting him enough to confide in him.

Sylvia's treachery would be a huge setback. Scott wondered if Victor sat at the heart of the double-cross. Victor always maintained he didn't need repayment. He preferred getting thirty percent of stock options. Scott negotiated him down to ten percent because he'd acquitted his debt to him a long time ago. Under the circumstances, Scott deemed ten percent a generous offer.

He turned toward Luke, a deep frown marring his forehead. "How certain is she of these allegations?"

"You should ask her," Luke added.

"Goddamn it, Luke I'm asking you. I need you to tell me."

Luke's eyes narrowed to mere slits. "Is something going on between you and Ava? Is this why she's afraid you won't believe her?" He finished with a nod and a cynical smile. "I'm right, aren't I? Sylvia is your fiancée, but you've got the hots for Ava. I can't say I blame you."

"ENOUGH," Scott said. "I don't need a play by play of Ava Moss."

Scott closed his eyes. He took a deep breath desperate to calm down. Livid, Scott still managed to be civil and not throw Luke out of his office. "My feelings, my personal feelings are nobody's business," he hissed. "Stick to the facts. How sure is she?"

Luke's shoulders upped in a show of helplessness. "Ava said she is fluent in Dutch, something about learning the language when she was young with one of the foster couples she lived with."

"Dutch. That's right. Mathilda spoke in Dutch." Scott rambled on to himself.

He collapsed in the chair behind his desk. "Xfinite turned out to be a mere shadow we spotted in our web configuration. At first, we thought the problem might be a sophisticated virus. A few weeks later, an investor blurted out the facts, by accident, confirming the fraud." He eyed Luke warily. "I always wondered how whoever did this were able to get so close without us spotting them."

"You must have suspected an inside job."

Scott stared at him intently. He cocked his head only now realizing, up until this moment, he never considered the breach an internal one unconsciously or otherwise.

He also remembered Victor and Mathilda showing off the love of their Dutch heritage, holding complete discussions in the language right in front of them. Fluent also, Sylvia didn't like to speak the language—often mocked her father's poor origins. Now he wondered if Sylvia played a role for his benefit, a phony show of support.

"What are you going to do?"

Scott shook his head. "Does Ava think Sylvia and Mathilda will give away the investment package to some of their contacts?"

Luke acquiesced. "Truth is more might be at stake here."

Scott figured out what Luke meant. He shook his head pensively.

"You believe her?"

"I'll tell you what I do believe. I believe this is the wrong way to proceed. Sylvia will find out when she gives the presentation, and all hell will break loose. She'll assume Ava did this on purpose to annoy her. A catfight of biblical proportions is liable to ensue. You don't know Sylvia, more so if she already presented this to her clients."

"What happens if Sylvia thinks Ava is aware of their scheme?"

Scott's head bobbed up. He slanted Luke a hard glare. "God, this could be bad," he whispered barely audible.

He rose and stretched his back. He hung his head releasing a long breath. "I will investigate," he breathed out, "without a sound," he stressed when he saw Luke about to argue.

"What do you want me to do?"

"How many people are aware of this?"

"As far as I'm concerned, Ava, Tracy Donovan and Elaine Duffy."

"Geez, all mighty. Why so many people?" When seeing Luke's shoulders drop and remorse dull his eyes, he opted to ignore the infraction. "Take your first proposal and drop the material off on Sylvia's desk. Tell her ... tell her we've been rehashing the material for the past hour, and this is the new way to go. Then leave. If she poses any questions, best she addresses them to me. She can be tricky."

"What about Ava?"

Scott hesitated. He glared at Luke wondering how much of a rival for Ava's affections he might turn out to be. "Send Ava to me," he said with finality.

Luke stood.

Scott and Luke eyed each other, hopefuls for the same woman's affection, the war between them contained for now in the hard look passing from one to the other.

"I'll tell Ava you want to talk to her."

When Luke left Scott, he hurried to his office and scrounged around for the good presentation, his one printed copy. Flinging the cupboard doors open, he picked up the stack of papers and slipped the bundle into a binder. Releasing a shaky breath while stroking the top of the papers, he weighed the last half hour's implications remembering Ava's admonishment.

"Don't you dare print a copy of the real stuff. Someone might find it, then what? We'd both have to kiss our careers goodbye." He made a copy without telling her. They worked so many hours—

made sense to back up their work. The problem arose when he omitted to hide the brief the moment Cindy brought the stack to his office. Now, Ava's dire warning kicked him in the ass.

He closed the cupboard doors and slipped the plastic folder under his arm. He would hurry to Sylvia's office before Ava assailed him with questions about Scott.

He knocked on the door. He waited. Knocked again. Still, no answer. Scott said to leave the presentation and not give explanations. So he tried, but he found the door locked.

Luke thought this strange. He checked his watch and decided he couldn't wait or waste time to search the grounds. His train going upstate left in less than an hour, and no mistakes, Luke planned to be on the train. Busy with so much overtime on the project he hadn't visited his family in weeks. He would leave the presentation on his desk and advise Scott about the change of plans.

Luke looked forward to the few days off. Maybe a step back would help everyone gain a little perspective on this whole mess.

He walked down the corridor to Ava's desk. He wanted to let her know about Scott before he left. She wasn't at her desk. Scott's office door was open so he stuck his head through to give him the material hoping to catch a glimpse of Ava. He found the office empty.

Luke headed toward his office. He would try to call her later. The presentation should have lasted no more than an hour. With all the theatrics afterward, he would need to run the rest of the way.

At the same moment, Ava argued with Tracy. "I'm telling you,

Tracy. I spotted smoke coming out of Scott's ears. He either suspects something or the jig's up by now."

"Don't worry. Why would Scott suspect anything? Where are
you and why are you whispering?"

"I'm on my cell phone. I just got to Luke's office ducking along
the corridors. Now I'm hiding behind his door. I want to talk to
Luke before Scott tries to wring my neck."

Tracy laughed. "You are so melodramatic, Ava. Scott is a gentleman—an edgy and often filled with angst gentleman—but I bet
you the man wouldn't say shit if his mouth happened to be full
of it. I still don't get why you didn't want to tell him about your
suspicions."

"After our history, he's bound to think I made up the whole
thing. Sylvia would cover her ass, and meanwhile, I'd find mine
in a sling."

Again Tracy laughed. "Don't tell me. This is another one of
your spy development. Are you sure you didn't imagine this entire
story, baby?"

"Someone's coming," Ava whispered even lower. "It's Scott. I
think I heard him call my name. He's looking for me," she finished
in a terrified little voice.

Ava overheard him pass by Luke's office. The slit in the door-
jamb she thought, peeking through. Too late to catch a glimpse of
the stranger, she sensed him stop and come inside. Her heart beat
so fast, she didn't realize her cell phone was still on in her hand.
A mimic of pain stretched across her face as she ended the call
praying he didn't catch their conversation.

She waited a few minutes counting the loud beats of her anxious heart. *Please let Scott walk away.* She heard him drop some-

thing on the desk. *Please, please let him walk away. Oh God, I would be so mortified if he found me here.*

CHAPTER 22

MYSTERY DEEPENS

Ava squeezed out of her small hiding space. She tiptoed to the open door peeked on both sides and breathed a little easier.

Her wristwatch read four thirty. Luke did not return which meant either he ran an errand or left.

She readjusted the collar of her suede jacket as she walked out of the office and reached for the side flap to slide her phone back into the pocket. Looking up, she ran headlong into Scott.

"Oh, my God, Scott. You scared me." She put a hand over her heart when she stared at the menacing little smile playing over his features. Somehow she sensed she wouldn't be going home anytime soon. "Looking for me?" she asked without guile. "I thought I overheard you call my name."

"What were you doing in Luke's office with the lights off?"

"I went into his office twenty minutes ago—to take a break. My little cubicle at the end of the hall doesn't afford me much privacy. I guess I fell asleep waiting for Luke." She hated lying to Scott, too ashamed to tell him she'd been hiding from him.

"So you haven't seen Luke?"

She shook her head unable to tear away from those mesmerizing eyes.

"Strange. Luke left me a message saying he'd dropped off the material on his desk before leaving."

She bit her bottom lip, realizing Luke happened to be the one who entered the office while she hid. "Missed him, I guess."

He tilted his head. "Okay, follow me. I need to talk to you."

She followed Scott wishing she'd worn her highest heels today. She resented the weakness in her limbs each time she needed to raise her head to stare at him, and something in his tone shouted he resented her. She would need to haul out the heavy artillery.

When they got to his office, he moved aside to let her enter and closed the door behind them.

Ava turned when her ears detected the sound of the bolt he flicked to lock the door—something she never thought Scott would do. She stared at him her forehead puckered.

"I don't want to be interrupted by anyone," he mentioned with a calm that frightened her.

He indicated she should sit with him on the settee also something he never did. "I think we'll be more comfortable over here," he added.

She sat on the edge of the sofa at the far end hoping he'd sit at the other.

He didn't. He sat right beside her his arm draped over the back of the cushions. He twisted and shifted his body to stare at her.

Ava smoothed the blue skirt she wore wishing the edge draped over her knees and ignored his eyes roving over her.

"Ava, please look at me."

She did, with visible reluctance. She found Scott's eyes guarded yet kind while not angry in any way. "What's this all about?" she said releasing a shaky breath.

"I need you to explain something to me."

"Sure." She smiled her heart somersaulting in her chest from the warmth on his handsome expression.

"I want you to tell me how can you trust a stranger with an office dilemma yet be too scared to come to me?"

"What?"

"Please," he interrupted her. "No more lies. I admit I first thought you'd pulled the portfolio trick out of spite and for this, I apologize."

Ava's heart sank. He knew. Either Luke told him, or he guessed. She lowered her head unable to support his eyes.

"Ava, look at me." He waited until she did. "How could you not trust me? You know how I feel about you."

Her head acquiesced before she gave him a rueful expression. "I guess I do. You made them your feelings clear weeks ago."

Scott breathed out, his head negating his frustration. He smiled as he tugged on the silky strands of her hair. "Don't pretend you don't know."

She turned toward him his words surprising her. Did he mean deeper sentiments than sex? Both their knees touched, and she shied away a few inches.

"Now she's afraid of me," he muttered loud enough for her to understand. "Forget about my goddamn need to have sex with you. I'm talking about friendship, trust. I thought I'd proven this when I chose you to be on my team."

Oh, that! She nodded her eyes downcast.

He slipped a hand under her chin. "Can you show me the same consideration?"

For the next few seconds, she stared at him. She loved him with all her heart and all her mind. Love did not exist without faith.

"You're right. I should have trusted you. I'm sorry."

"Good." He smiled wistfully, replacing his hand on the cushions behind her. "How sure are you of your findings?"

"I kept wanting to be wrong, Scott. Maybe I am. Might all be a huge misunderstanding. I guess I wanted to be certain before I told you. I don't want to be the one to accuse the person you love of stealing. That's not what a friend does."

"*U bent een warme, en gevende jonge vrouw.*"

Ava blushed at the compliment. Scott called her a warm and caring young woman. "You speak Dutch."

He smiled. "Enough to get by, but not enough to matter. I guess there's no doubt you heard correctly?"

"No doubt."

"Do you remember the exact words?"

She nodded. She repeated in Dutch what she'd understood from Mathilda. "So much more than simple words, Scott. I read stealth in Mathilda's behavior. The way she eyeballed me when she came out of her office and caught me standing in front of Luke's door—damning evidence."

"I guess Mathilda never figured you'd be fluent in Dutch of all things. And Mathilda mentioned Sylvia, you're sure?"

She nodded. "I'm so sorry, Scott. You should talk to her about this. Might be something else, and we're making a big fuss over nothing."

Scott leaned forward resting his elbows on his knees and pulling his face into his hands. A loud sigh escaped him as he rubbed his forehead.

Ava hesitated. He seemed to forget about her. She placed a delicate hand on his back. "Is there anything I can do to help?" She caught his shiver.

He stood and walked away. "Nothing you can do. I need to work this out somehow. Please do not attempt to play amateur detective. This would only bring you grief," he answered without looking at her.

After what seemed like a long pause, Ava sensed he wanted her to leave. She got up and walked toward the door. A quick turn to stare at him while her hand twisted the lock on the knob. A half-hour ago, she did everything to avoid this confrontation. Now, she didn't want to leave.

He still had his back to her his palms spread out on the desk supporting his deflated bearing. She realized how devastated he must be. "I'm going home, Scott, but I'm still available if you need to talk."

***

Scott came within a hair of pleading with Ava not to leave. Her hand down his back came close to shredding him to pieces. Ava's touch sent a sharp current running through his whole being—his first impulse to hold her, caress her, feel the warmth of her body tremble against his.

Sitting on the edge of his office chair, he didn't remember ever experiencing any such euphoria for Sylvia, or for anyone else.

Betrayed and disappointed by her duplicity, he pondered she could not be ecstatic about their relationship either, not if she appropriated herself of his hard earned labor and dispensed it around as though the results were hers to do so. He sighed toying with the need to confront her, to demand an explanation hoping she would supply one.

He hesitated as he drummed his fingers on the handset on his desk rehearsing in his mind the best way to broach the subject. Together for five years, Scott wondered if he knew Sylvia, shocked she could abuse his trust this way.

Then visions of the times she caught him in a lie flashed before him. Each time, Sylvia's eyes mirrored hurt and deception. Over the years, things changed between them. Subtle little changes he never quite grasped at first, yet intimacy between them vanished in a gradual manner, even difficult to come by during sex.

He got up to pace in front of his desk. For a long time, he believed the distance Sylvia put between them was due to a grudge— her rancor against his womanizing. Now, he wondered if her duplicity shared some responsibility in feeding the remoteness between them.

He stopped pacing long enough to pick up the phone. Scott supposed all things considered part of their work's profits belonged to Sylvia. In truth, he didn't mind Sylvia's need to be independent and make an income outside his circle of investors.

Stroking the handset, Scott stopped short of making the call to Sylvia. He would ask her for an explanation. However, the situation might no longer be a private affair. At the moment Sylvia and Mathilda planned to plow through his brother's contacts attempting to usurp Reynard's and their family's longtime clients. He needed to talk to Reynard.

Scott tried to picture what Reynard might do, what big brother would say. And because he needed a clear-headed impartial view of all this, he made the call. "Hi, Carole. Has my brother gone home yet?"

"Hi, Scott. He's still around here somewhere. I'll page him for you."

"Thanks, Carole. It's important, please make sure you locate him."

He got up and stared at the traffic below his window. He'd chosen the corner office because of the double-sided view of manmade scrapers stretching their steel structures to pierce the clouds. As far as his eyes roamed, the city's financial jungle lived and breathed to the sway of tall blades of concrete propagated by man's ambition—human drives which sometimes committed people to make stupid decisions.

A knock made Scott jump. He turned and realized Ava closed the door on her way out.

"Come in."

Sylvia walked in with a smile on her lips. Yet, the smile didn't quite reach her eyes. He wondered why. He considered perhaps those eyes had not sparkled in a long time, only he hadn't noticed.

"Surprised to find you alone," she said. "Happy with the presentation?"

He answered guardedly. "Luke and I spent the last hour going over it, ironed out some of the kinks, changed some of the perspective buyers for a better fit."

"Is Luke around? Trevor told me he wanted to meet with me—something about a revision—probably along the lines of what you just mentioned."

He nodded. "This will keep. Luke has gone home for the weekend." He walked toward her and sensed his nerve slip. He realized once he discussed the matter with her nothing would ever be the same between them. "How about I take you out to dinner? We've had a long couple of weeks settling in."

She slinked toward him the rest of the way. "How about we enjoy dinner at home just the two of us. We can ask Ramsey to whip up your favorite, slow cooked sablefish with butternut squash." She smiled as she gently pressed up against him. "Perhaps a little caviar beforehand and a couple of bottles of Chardonnay?" She kissed his ear lobe.

He resisted taking her in his arms part of him wondering why she was so aggressively sexual. When she fingered his bottom lip to fasten her mouth to his, the phone rang.

He pushed her away in a gentle manner. "Hello, a moment please." He turned toward Sylvia. "It's Reynard. Do you mind?"

"You want me to leave?" The shock in her round eyes and tight smile was evident.

"Big brother stuff. I'll discuss this with you later when I get home."

"Well." He spotted she seemed hurt. "Give him my regards." She turned and walked away. "See you at home," she finished closing the door behind her.

CHAPTER 23

SYLVIA ON ALERT

O ut in the hall using her right arm against the wall to steady her bearing, Sylvia took a deep, quivering breath. What might Scott discuss with his brother that he could not do so in front of her? She flexed her left finger to stare at her engagement ring and found her hand shook. Both hands did.

Gathering all her courage, she marched back to her office to pick up her purse and briefcase. She worried about what Mathilda and her father dearest might ask her to do. Most of all, her deepest concern veered around Scott discovering their little game. He would hand her marching papers for sure if he did, and she would scratch and claw rather than lose him. What would people think? To cultivate and grow a relationship like theirs turned out to be difficult all these years. Nevertheless, she enjoyed the envy of all her friends. Now, for her engagement to collapse at her own hand, she didn't want to think about this alternative.

On her way back to her office, Sylvia passed Luke's office and found the door open. She peeked inside and called out, but no one answered. She walked in and surveyed his desk. She picked up the presentation Scott mentioned. She wondered if this happened to be the one on which they made all the changes.

Checking the hallway, Sylvia realized she disposed of no time to examine the proposal on the spot. She picked up the papers under her arm and took a beeline to her office. Checking behind her to confirm no one followed her she closed and locked the door.

***

Scott understood how dumbfounded and shocked Reynard appeared to be from the information he handed to him on the phone. He practically ran to his office hoping to disprove the theory somehow. Now, big brother sat on the edge of the sofa going through a series of awkward gestures. Flexing and rubbing his knuckles he said his tone laced with dejection, "I'm not sure what to do." He coughed a little seeming as uncomfortable as he was perturbed. "Is there any way of discovering if they've transmitted our information to whomever? Perhaps through our computers?"

Scott shrugged. "First thing I checked all the access codes into our client database. Sylvia and Mathilda's codes were not among the entries, not since we arrived. This doesn't mean they didn't use someone else's code."

Reynard rose and picked up the telephone. "Carole, I hate to ask you this on a Friday evening, but this is paramount." A few seconds passed as Reynard remained silent.

"Ok. Enjoy your evening. Sorry to disturb you." Reynard hung up the receiver pensive and worried.

"She can't stay?"

Reynard shook his head.

"Hey, why not try Tracy Donovan. Someone told me she knows about the situation."

"Tracy is aware of this?" More shock registered on Reynard's pale face. "Strange how she never mentioned a word to me." He eyed Scott with this new concern since Scott knew about his recent closeness to Tracy.

"Don't know what to tell you, Reynard. You'll need to ask her."

Reynard dialed Tracy's number and put the communication on speaker for Scott to follow.

Scott read his brother's relief to find Tracy at the office.

"Still at work on a Friday night." He tried to keep a light voice glancing at Scott to make sure he listened. "I need your help with the log entries into our clients' personal information. You mentioned once you were adept at this sort of technology."

Scott heard Tracy catch her breath. "You found out?"

"Yes, I did. Frankly, I'm surprised you never said anything."

"I wasn't sure—all conjecture." She stopped. "Useless to go into this now, Reynard. I'll be there in minutes."

"I'm down in Scott's office."

When Tracy got there, she dispensed with the pleasantries at once. "First thing you do is call your programmer and have him revoke all the codes except your own."

"Why didn't I think of that?" Scott barked as he picked up the phone. "They're going to need to talk to you, Reynard."

Reynard gave Scott the number to Etco Security Systems. "Ask to speak to Paul Digby. He is the rep in charge of our system."

Paul had left for the day, but his assistant would try to locate him. "You don't understand, Miss. This is a matter of utmost security," Scott stressed into the phone.

"I'll give you his cellular phone number."

Scott called the number and breathed a little easier when Paul greeted him at the other end. Scott gave him a quick recap.

"I won't be able to revoke all your codes, not within the next couple of minutes. Even with me being at the office, you're looking at a couple of hours' before our system processes. I can implement a better security backup plan. You're going to need to go to the administrator's computer in Reynard's office. I'll need to talk Reynard through the procedure. Meanwhile, I'm going to look for somewhere to park. Call me back in twenty minutes or so."

***

Having combed through the new version of the presentation, Sylvia picked up her cell not wanting to chance someone hearing her. "We've got problems."

"What kind of problems? You're not letting your imagination run away with you again, are you?"

"The presentation Ava and Luke gave us changed from start to finish. Despite my poor knowledge of the subject, I can read how the investors and biotech firms are at opposite ends of what they were during the presentation. No way is this accidental."

"Didn't you say Trevor told you Luke needed to fill you in on changes he and Scott worked on?"

"Yes—changes. These are not mere changes, Mathilda. They are complete and absolute do-overs. The only way to explain this metamorphosis is if they found out about us and want to preserve the integrity of their system."

"Impossible."

"I was just in Scott's office. He asked me to leave while he spoke to his brother." Sylvia rigidly pronounced every word of that last sentence. She fought a bad case of nerves. "How certain are you the office snoop, Ava Moss, didn't listen at your door when you discussed this a few weeks ago?"

"Sylvia, relax. I spoke Dutch. Ava is a little chit who's never traveled, never been anywhere. What makes you think she might suspect us? Besides, Scott would never suspect you. Even if he did, you guys are as good as married. Half of what's his is yours." Mathilda chuckled.

"Not on this continent."

"Will be when you two are married," Mathilda sang into the phone.

"I told you I didn't want to pursue this over here. I wanted out of this merry-go-round for months," Sylvia breathed with angry snorts. "You promised me Scott would never find out, now goddamn it, Mathilda. I don't want to lose him," she whined.

"Well he'll never learn this from me, sweetheart, but if you continue to act like a scared rabbit, he's going to know something's up. As for dropping this project, tell this to your formidable father. Me I don't give a damn one way or the other."

Sylvia fumed, and she sensed something was on the verge of exploding, but she couldn't put her finger on the problem. Worse, she couldn't convince Mathilda. "Where are you?"

"I'm almost home. Why?"

"Never mind. I'll talk to you later."

She hung up and hesitated before dialing her next number. She no longer had a choice. She wrung her hands with disgust, yet the thought of losing Scott prompted her to make the call.

"Hi, it's me. I think Scott's on to your little game."

"My little game?"

Sylvia heard the person snicker at the other end.

"He's on to Mathilda and me which would lead to you in a heartbeat. So don't be so cocky," she scolded. "What do we do?"

"Stay calm is the first thing you do. Scott has no proof. We've talked about this contingency. There are no documents, no paperwork, no one to testify. He can suspect all he wants. Short of throwing you out of his life, he can't save his investors or his projects."

"I've told you time and time again. I don't want any part of this, and I don't want to be thrown out of Scott's life."

"Stop whimpering. Doesn't suit you. What can you download for now?"

"Nothing. Too soon to start Xeroxing the name of his investors for God's sake. We only got here a few weeks ago."

"They're on the computer, and you have access, right?"

"Yes, I do."

"So, open your computer and proceed with the download. We'll take all you can send at this end."

"No way am I doing this now. I told you I wanted out. These names don't belong to Scott."

"Forget about your damned ethics. If you don't do as I say, I can guarantee you Scott will find out."

A long pause occurred. Sylvia continued with a nervous catch in her voice. "I can't, daddy dearest. All computer entries into the company's files are logged with time and specific codes. For this to work, I would need to use someone else's code at an hour when many people are working at their computer."

"Nonsense. You do this now, more so if you think Reynard and Scott suspect something's not right. Who cares what both of them think? Proceed with the download and get out while you still can. They'll never prosecute—too much bad publicity."

Sylvia fudged. She'd called her father for advice, now she wasn't sure she liked his brand of help oneself's philosophy. "No. No way will I betray Scott's trust anymore."

"Fine," Victor Danes answered annoyance marking his tone. "I'll get Mathilda to do it. Meanwhile, you pack your things and get out of the building."

Sylvia ended the conversation. With a quick look around, she searched the place to gather the few mementos she cared about and her laptop computer. She needed to sit down and talk to Scott, beg for his forgiveness. The game ended here for her.

She thought of Mathilda, how she'd need to double back and return to the office to do her father's bidding which would put her cousin in real danger. She ignored the nagging little thought and left locking her office door.

CHAPTER 24

LIFE BY A THREAD

S itting downstairs in the building's central atrium, Ava fidgeted watching the gold needles on the huge clock over the securities' desk ticking in slow motion, so slow the hands appeared stuck. Checking her own watch to make sure the darn clock worked, she blew out an impatient little sigh as she waited for Tracy. She tried her at the office and on her cell, but no answer. Tracy promised her a ride home when Ava told her how awful her meeting with Scott ended, how he discovered about her suspicions from the presentation. Of course, Tracy had brought her car to work should she need to execute a quick getaway from Reynard. "Once he finds out you briefed me about this, and I didn't tell him, there'll be hell to pay."

"I will take full responsibility," Ava avowed. "He'll understand. Don't worry."

The big building emptied with gradual speed. Except for the

on-duty security guards and a few diehard enthusiasts, everyone scurried home for the weekend. She wondered why Luke didn't return any of her calls. Might be on the train, she thought, with no reception in some areas.

Well, either Tracy decided to work late, or she forgot about her. Fastening her purse strap across her shoulders, she rose and walked along the wide hallway to the front doors. She turned left, right, and right again to head to the front of the building. Tracy might be waiting for her parked by the curb.

She looked around but couldn't spot the red Mazda anywhere. She did catch Mathilda getting out of a cab.

Ava hurried to hide behind one of the columns when she glimpsed Mathilda running up to the front entrance. She ran through the swinging doors showing the security guard her pass before she moved in the direction of the elevators.

Ava wondered what she might do this late in the afternoon that couldn't be done during the day. Might be nothing she thought. Perhaps Mathilda forgot something. Still, she decided to follow her up to the third floor. Keeping her distance Ava took the next elevator.

When Ava got out, the sound of Mathilda's footsteps hurrying toward her office alerted her to what direction to take.

Removing her shoes, she hurried to follow Mathilda. She posted herself on the other side of the door, stepping into her shoes while trying to listen to what she said on the phone. Nothing. She couldn't understand a word. Ava thought of the empty office adjoining Mathilda's, and thanked her lucky stars the door stood ajar. She tiptoed inside and posted herself at the edge of the connecting door. Her luck. Mathilda's office door stood ajar, enough for her to listen.

She spoke Dutch laughing and saying she would use Sylvia's code since Sylvia refused to download the files herself.

Ava reeled at the thought. Mathilda would need a blink to download the firm's years of hard work.

***

Reynard called Paul back on his cell to find out how to prevent any weekend saboteurs from stealing his lifelong work.

"Go into your network administrator's field. Type in your password."

Reynard answered the request. "Done."

"Now, click on the box with a bomb."

"Done."

"A little clown will pop up. Double click on the icon and a long box will appear at the clown's feet."

"Ok. Now, what?"

"Enter the following sequence of numbers and letters. When I give you a string of four digits, you need to make a space between the next series of numbers. Do you understand?"

"Think so. What's this for?"

"It's a sophisticated virus. If someone downloads anything from your computer to theirs, once this clown's activated, upon reaching destination your files will gallop back to your corral bringing with them all the saboteur's files as well—empty out this other person's life without leaving a trace."

Reynard had put Paul on speakerphone. He stared at Scott and Tracy with concern in his eyes. "This method seems quite dire—

and I'm almost certain this procedure is against the law."

"You're not planning any activity over the weekend, are you?"

"No."

"This is only a precaution until I can revoke and change your access codes. I'll admit it's a little drastic, but your kind of game warrants this. If anyone acquires your information, Reynard, no matter how much you complain, all your material will be gone for good. No amount of suing, no court order large enough, no semblance at any kind of agreement will bring back your clients."

Reynard's eyebrows rose. He nodded.

"Plus," Scott added to convince him further. "If word gets out the confidential information we hold on these clients is now public domain because of a fault in our system, they can sue us for everything we've got."

"Go ahead," Reynard agreed. As he began typing, he missed a few spaces. Big brother had to restart the sequence twice—his nerves shot.

"Here let me try," Scott told him taking his place at the desk. "Start again, Paul. I think I figured out the sequence now. By the way, what happens if someone sends an FTP folder so they can drop the files right into their server?"

"Similar process. Once the crooks try to open as little as one file, an error message will pop up. When it does, all the material on the thieves' hard drive will be swept and copied. A click on a second file will again produce an error message while the motion will rally the material copied from the thief's hard drive. The third click on any file will bring all your files home to Papa—along with all the bad guy's history."

***

Glued to the door next to Mathilda's office, Ava realized she couldn't let her download their files. She also considered once she emptied the computers, they were in breach of trust with a significant number of clients.

She jumped in uncaring of the circumstances. "Oh, no you don't, you traitor. You're not going to download anything. I'll call security before I allow you to steal Extrade clients. You'll never leave the building."

"Well, well. Miss Muffet herself," Mathilda spat as she pounced on Ava with a small automatic revolver. "Come to sit on her tuffet." Mathilda grabbed Ava's left arm she swung behind her back. Keeping her arm pinned, Mathilda pushed her toward the desk. "Sit on the chair next to mine. You'll enjoy a bird's eye view of everything I'm doing." Mathilda laughed.

Once she shoved Ava on the chair keeping the gun's barrel lodged between her shoulder blades, Mathilda pulled modem cable from the bottom drawer. She tied Ava's hands around the chair's high back, keeping the gun pointed at her ribs she then secured her legs together and bound them to the chair legs.

"Along came a spider," she hissed out of breath, "the spider is me of course," Mathilda pointed to herself. "Who sat down beside her and frightened Miss Muffet to death." Mathilda brandished the gun in her face as she yelled boo showing her how fast she cocked the weapon.

"You wouldn't shoot me over data files. This is crazy," Ava said in a trembling voice unable to tear her eyes away from the weapon's barrel. She couldn't believe Mathilda held a gun to her head.

First time Ava set her eyes on any sort of weapon up close. The simple shiny steel contraption would kill her in a matter of seconds.

"You've made me waste so much time I'd be in by now. I may shoot you after I'm done to teach you some manners."

Ava worried Mathilda might be insane if she thought she could get away with this. Uncaring the cable appeared to be tight and cutting off circulation in her legs, she shrunk into her chair loneliness enveloping her. No one realized she was here, in this office, in the building.

Mathilda answered her phone. She put the cell on speaker to continue to work.

"What's taking you so long?" Ava didn't recognize the male voice.

"An unexpected visitor. Don't worry. I neutralized the threat. I'm loading now waiting for my login page."

"Don't forget. Use the download server I'm sending you. The particular server is big enough to take a large number of gigs."

"Yeah, only don't expect this to be done in a flash. A lot of files here."

"Do what you can under an hour. I want you out of the building by six fifteen."

"Why six fifteen?"

"Sylvia mentioned a guard goes around each office to make sure everything is secure. He does his rounds at six thirty every night."

"Ok. I'm inside the hard drive and into the client database. The code still works which is most convenient." Mathilda lassoed what seemed like a high number of files and pasted them into the server.

"Send me a test run. I can't wait to take a peek at these."

"Here they come." Mathilda pushed enter to upload so the other party might study the material at his end.

***

In Reynard's office, the situation became a waiting game. "How do you know the crazy clown is active?" Scott asked Paul Digby.

"He whistled and laughed, didn't he?"

"Yeah, he did."

"Good. Now, let the clown do his work. Trust me. He's deadly."

"I hope you created an antidote for this poisonous little fellow," Tracy thought to ask.

"I did. The clown's homegrown. Created him myself. I would never grease the fire if I didn't understand how to douse the flames."

Tracy thought aloud. "God, I promised Ava I would drive her home. I forgot all about her." She picked up her phone and tried to contact her. "She's not answering her cell. This is odd."

"By now, she figured you stayed to work late and left," Reynard attempted.

Tracy shook her head. "Not Ava. She's liable to be out there looking for me wondering where I am. Even if she decided to go home, Reynard, she would be answering her cell phone."

"Don't worry, Tracy. She may be underground in the metro. Well, we owe Ava Moss a debt of gratitude," Reynard added. "She is one alert young woman."

"We are still not certain any of this is true yet," Scott told Reynard. "These are precautionary tactics, drastic but tentative."

"I'm leaving," Reynard said. "Can I give you a lift, Scott?"

Scott shook his head. "I'm staying. I need to face Sylvia, and I don't know what to tell her. I'm going to try to come up with a plan in the next hour, I hope."

As Reynard prepared to leave, the little clown began to swear. "Now what?" Reynard asked his patience running thin knowing he would need to stay behind.

"I'll stay also," Tracy rubbed Reynard's sleeve staring up at him anxious eyes betraying the fear she hid so well.

Scott phoned Paul.

***

In Mathilda's office, she'd uploaded another bunch of files. "What are you seeing, Victor? Anything interesting?"

"Your first two files popped up with an error message. Are you sure you're doing this correctly?"

"I'm not an idiot. How many ways do you think there are of uploading files? Try one from the last batch I just uploaded."

"The same." Ava caught a loud swear word on the speaker phone. "Hold everything. This is a virus. Bloody bastards. They've activated an upload virus," Victor yelled at the other end. "The shit thing is sweeping my entire system," he continued screaming. "Get out, leave now. Leave. They are on to you, and they set you up."

"What are you talking about, old man? Wait a minute. I've got double, triple the number of folders I uploaded to you. What the hell is going on?"

"Leave. The virus will warn Ex-trade you're in their files."

"Great," Mathilda grabbed her bag. "I can't leave Muffet here. I need to silence her. She can identify me."

"Don't be crazy, Mathilda. They'll overlook the repercussion of stealing a few files. For murder, they'll put you away for life."

"I hate the little creep." Mathilda eyed Ava, who worked hard to contain herself from smiling and alienating Mathilda more.

Mathilda gritted her teeth and kicked over the chair beside hers making Ava fall to the ground hard.

Ava tried not to let her head hit the floor too hard, but she couldn't manage her body from taking the full brunt. Ava sensed the painful bash on her arm and shoulder spread as her weight exacerbated the bruise. Still, grateful to be alive Ava remained silent while Mathilda grabbed her purse and ran toward the exit.

Before leaving Mathilda stared at Ava tilting her head to leer at her face-to-face. "Hope they don't find you until Monday morning. Wouldn't that be a hoot?" Mathilda closed the door and locked it.

Ava tried not to panic. A guard would be along she realized this from previous encounters. She needed to bide her time and scream for help when the time came.

Ava waited for the elevator bell, but when no sound came, she figured Mathilda ran down the stairwell to avoid detection.

However, as soon as Paul Digby confirmed a hacker penetrated the system, Scott called security to advise them of Mathilda and Sylvia's description and to tell them one or both of them were fleeing the scene of a crime.

"I'm going to go to their office and see who's at the helm. Maybe they're still on the premises," Scott announced running toward the direction of their offices.

When he reached Mathilda's office, he jiggled the handle and found the door locked. He caught a cry for help inside.

He tried to ram the door, but Ava shouted for him to enter the office next door.

When Scott reached Ava and saw her tied to a chair, lying on the floor, a few unfriendly epithets flew out of his mouth as he hurried to her rescue. "God all mighty, Ava," he grunted in a trembling voice. "What the hell happened here?" Scott cursed through his teeth as he hurried to redress her seat with a delicate hand so as not to hurt her.

Scott caught Ava's painful moan when he stabilized the chair on all fours. "Be careful, Scott—my arm."

"You're going to be okay," he added his hands shaking as he untied the cable binding her arms and legs. "Stay put," he cautioned as he examined her head for bruises. "What are you doing on the floor? Who did this to you?" he demanded his face grim.

Scott's whole body shook with Ava's recount of what had taken place. "I can't believe Mathilda threatened you with a gun." His voice broke when he knelt and encircled her in his arms to steady his nerves and to stop her from shaking. To feel her heart beating next to his meant, she would be all right. When he squeezed too tight, she complained about the pain.

"Hurts quite a bit," she said grabbing her left arm. I think I bruised my shoulder when I fell."

Scott kept his left arm roped around her waist to help Ava to her feet, and she swung her right arm around his back, clutching a fistful of his shirt.

Once he held Ava on her feet, Scott released her, but as soon as he did, her knees buckled. Both her legs went weak from tingles and numbness. "Damn Mathilda," Scott exclaimed. "Red welts all over your legs," he whispered. Scooping Ava up, he steadied her against him. Scott carried her over to the sofa.

"I needed to do something," she sniffed her face muffled against his jacket. "I waited for Tracy downstairs when I spotted Mathilda racing back. I thought she might be up to no good so I tried to stop her, but she wielded her gun around like some sort of toy."

"Crazy Mathilda," he exclaimed. He released her putting her down in the soft leather cushions. He stared into her eyes. "What you did was stupid, Ava, goddamned irresponsible."

With delicate fingers, Scott undid her jacket's top button, and with her help eased the garment off. Scott also undid her shirt's buttons and tugged with a gentle hand at the collar to open the blouse. He slipped the silk material off her shoulders to check her arm. "God, this is going to turn into a hell of a nasty bruise," he whispered as his fingers softly delineated the big red welt on her arm.

He shook his head faced with her weepy expression. "Nevertheless, Ava, you bought us the extra minutes we needed to upload the virus into our computer."

"You did that?" Wiping the few renegade tears rolling down her cheeks she smiled at him.

His nod adamant, he explained, "Our programmer did. He helped us perform the upload in the nick of time thanks to you." He placed a kiss on her forehead. "We not only recuperated all our files we are saddled with most of theirs." He brought the blouse back on her shoulders. "Do you need my help with this?"

She shook her head while tying the buttons to her blouse. "I'll be fine." She pulled on his jacket's sleeve. "I'm sorry about Sylvia," she whispered.

He lowered his head exhaling the last few hours of pent up frustration. "Until now, I guess I didn't want to believe it." He waited until she slipped her jacket back on. "Can you stand?"

She nodded as she propped herself against the divan's armrest, but fell back into the cushions. "Don't worry about me. My legs will be functional in a few more minutes."

Scott bent on one knee and began rubbing Ava's limbs to get the circulation going again. "Is this a little better?" he asked reaching under her skirt to massage her thighs.

A beep on his cell phone grabbed his attention. He rose and unclipped the cell from his belt. "Scott," he answered while hitting the speaker button.

"Mr. Wallace, this is security. We apprehended a young woman fitting your description, sir. She verified her name as Mathilda Redding. The police are on their way. Do you wish to come down and corroborate, sir?"

"I'll be right down."

He turned toward Ava. "I'm not leaving you here alone. Call Tracy on her cell phone. She's worried about you. She's in Reynard's office. I'll wait until she gets here."

"The call is urgent, Scott."

"I can wait, Ava."

"No. Go. I'll be okay. Tracy will be here in minutes. You need to take care of Mathilda," she added her eyes angry rather than sad.

He nodded. "Okay." He left. As he reached the door, he turned to look at her. "Please find some other place to go to for the next couple of days. If you want to stay at a hotel, the company will pay for everything, including meals or anything else you might need. I don't want you staying alone in your apartment." He hesitated faced with her raised eyebrows. "We are not quite sure how this will play out. Precautions are for your safety."

She nodded as she watched him leave. Where would she go? Who would take care of Oscar?

CHAPTER 25

SCOTT FACES SYLVIA

S cott got downstairs as two police officers entered the building. He sprinted from the elevators to the security office at the back of the corridor, behind the guard's desk. He wanted to be the first to talk to Mathilda before chaos broke out.

He caught her standing beside the chief's desk a cheeky smirk on her face. The thought she played a game popped in his mind, and he wondered if she realized how much trouble she'd caused.

When she looked up and spotted him, she laughed. "Look who's here, Sir Galahad and his twisted sense of ethics." She stared at the guard sitting at the desk and told him, "This is all a bunch of hooey—this false detention. Truth is, his new flame is jealous of his old flame, so he's trying to find a way to be rid of me." She sniffed as though waylaying tears. "What's a girl to do, I ask you?"

Scott shook his head in disbelief stumped by Mathilda's attitude. No doubt, Mathilda was a beautiful woman, and her blatant attempt at manipulation weaved its magic on the guard in charge.

Scott noticed him looking from one to the other with hesitant eyes not hiding the fact he wondered if he acted too fast on Scott's call for help.

At this moment, Scott realized he would need to keep his personal feelings out of the mix and be nothing other than factual, or Mathilda would dance circles around him and make them all look like fools. He realized the improbability of discussing anything with her now. In fact, Scott believed she waited for an argument from him which would give her free rein to muddle the events even more. He decided to wait for police to take his statement.

When they entered the office, the guard quickly gave the officers his version of why he called them. By now, Mathilda whimpered and dabbed at her nose with a tissue.

"Mr. Wallace, I'm Officer Blouin, and this is my partner, Officer Lewis." He turned toward the guard. "We need to take statements. Can we use the other office?"

"Yes, of course." The guard unlocked the door and allowed them through.

"So, what seems to be the trouble? And please understand, Mr. Wallace, calling the law to settle an argument for your own personal gain is a serious offense."

"Is this what the idiot guard whispered to you?"

"Just state the facts, please."

Scott recounted how they thwarted the attempted theft, and how Mathilda tried to run once they discovered her double-cross.

"Are there any other witnesses, Mr. Wallace?"

"Yes. I just rescued one young woman whose life Miss Redding threatened at gunpoint. By the time I got on the premises, Miss Redding had tied her to a chair with such force, the cable she used left red welts all over her legs. Miss Redding kicked the chair to the floor and abandoned the woman uncaring if anyone ever found her."

The officers exchanged a blank look. "Thank you," Blouin said. "We'll verify your statement."

When they reentered the outer office, Mathilda stared at the younger officer. "Please don't let him fill your head with hogwash. The man is vindictive, mean, and trying to destroy my career. I'm counting on your help."

Scott couldn't believe Mathilda's gall, despite how well he knew her. The only thing he pondered was she didn't know he'd found Ava. She argued about the theft damn certain nothing would be traced to her.

"Miss Redding, before we take your statement, I would ask that you, please empty the content of your purse on the desk."

Mathilda's eyes narrowed when she gave Scott a dirty look. She lost her weepy eyes and Raggedy Ann expression. Her remoteness grew as her chin spiked inches higher. "I don't have to."

"No, you don't. But since we suspect a serious crime has been committed, you leave us no choice but to take you in. When we arrive, you will have to check the content of your purse. You're only delaying the inevitable, Miss Redding."

"I refuse to say anything else until I speak to my lawyer."

Scott watched Lewis lead Mathilda outside through the door at the back and felt a twinge of sadness invade him. A bright, beautiful, and ambitious young woman with a brilliant career ahead of her slipped, slipped badly. She committed a crime, but not just any crime, one involving a permanent record. He wondered if jealousy of his relationship with Sylvia or of his feelings for Ava trig-

gered her reaction? He remembered the contempt in her expression when she eyed him. Had their affair meant more to her than
he realized? Perhaps she followed Victor's orders playing a game
which deteriorated to the point of landing her in jail.

One thing certain, he hoped Victor would not abandon her.
The real villain in all this, Victor should be the one they hauled
away. Scott thought of Sylvia at the hotel waiting for him. The one
phone call her cousin would make would not be to her, although
Mathilda might call Victor, who would warn his daughter.

The thought kicked Scott into gear. He needed to reach Sylvia
before she fled, frightened and ashamed of her role in this affair.
Sitting down and asking Sylvia for the reason behind her behavior might help shed some new light on their relationship, perhaps
even help unfortunate Mathilda get her bearings.

"May I leave?" Scott asked Blouin.

He hesitated. "If you have any urgent business, do it now. We'll
need you at the precinct in the next couple of hours to file a more
detailed report."

"Of course. I'm at your disposal." Scott pulled a business card
out of his pocket. "You can always reach me on my cell." He took
his leave and ran out.

Across town, handing his car keys to the valet, he looked up
at the prestigious building called The London. He remembered
being filled with pride on the day he rented the space while Sylvia
worked to vacate their lodgings in Geneva. He wanted to surprise
her with lavish surroundings. Disappointed when he accepted his
brother's offer, Sylvia fixated on the West Coast as a place to begin
a new life since most of her friends and family resided in the Bay
Area.

He pushed through the revolving doors nodding at the uniformed attendant, irony whispering how the expensive, luxurious suite witnessed nothing but the contempt and disillusionment they lavished on each other.

Upstairs Scott found the door unlocked. Then he remembered giving his keys to Sylvia earlier in the day since she had forgotten hers.

Putting down his briefcase by the door, he searched the place for signs of her yet only sweet aromas greeted him. Scott liked the fact the place didn't smell like a hotel—of floral deodorizer and industrial carpet cleaner. Instead, the spicy scent of rosemary and cilantro lingered from the meal they seasoned the previous evening, paired with the robust aroma of orange slices and brandy sniffers left overnight on the living room coffee table. The place should be shouting, *welcome home*, but the cold emptiness made him shiver.

"Sylvia?" he called out dreading the meeting ahead. With habitual reflects, he scanned through the mail on the marble table while straining to hear movement upstairs. However, the only sound came from the soft peal of *Ode to Joy* pouring from the Hermle grandfather clock in the corner of the room, a lavish gift from one of his Geneva clients. He often counted on the chimes to soothe his soul.

He walked toward the panoramic view of immense bay windows and glanced at the stunning Manhattan skyline. He liked the horizon best late evening when muted neon streamers warmed the darkest hour. At this time, the sun still dangled over Manhattan, but the gold sphere would soon take a dip in the Hudson sinking with silence in a splash of colors to disappear while leaving darkness to single the end of another day. He wondered if this day would be about endings and he found himself wishing it were tomorrow.

A sound distracted him, and he turned to gaze at Sylvia. She'd kicked off her shoes and made her way toward him without a sound, slinking like a cat on the prowl he thought. Dressed in a bathrobe she left open, the slight part in the middle revealed she wore nothing underneath.

"I wondered what kept you," she cooed as she wrapped her arms around his neck pressing her whole body against his. "What do you say we meet in the Jacuzzi room? Massage each other with oils before we soak in the tub?" She kissed his earlobe pushing her tongue deep inside his ear the way he liked it. "I'll do the thing you love so much."

He closed his eyes hating the involuntary moan escaping his throat. This hour would be their decisive moment. Long overdue, nothing would delay him anymore.

"Scott?" she whispered backing up only enough to search his eyes. "Anything wrong?"

He took a deep breath but felt his head negate her question. He tightened his fists by his side. He would not weasel his way out of the situation, not this time. His inaction had caused enough misery to last both of them a lifetime. Here and now his inertia stopped.

"I ordered dinner from Ramsay," she spoke in soft tones. "So we have one hour to play. Interested?"

Who wouldn't be interested? He placed both hands on her shoulders and gently pushed her away. "First, we need to talk."

The ominous tone of his voice seemed to push her back more.

She watched him, her gray eyes narrowing to mere slits. Her cheeks colored as she wrapped the robe around herself securing it with a swift knot of the belt.

The phone rang. Scott reached for the receiver. He listened, and he smiled. A few seconds later, he said, "Call back later. Sylvia's getting dressed." He hung up and punched a code into the phone so they wouldn't be disturbed again.

"Caller for me?" she asked her demeanor cool and composed.

"Victor, your father."

"Why didn't you," she began irritated by his remote behavior, he thought.

"Don't worry. He'll call back. For now, I suggest you get dressed. We need to talk."

CHAPTER 26

TRACY'S GUEST

Several hours later once Reynard had worked with Paul to restore the computers and their programs to their original setting, Tracy bid farewell to the man becoming a fixture in her life. "Call me later? You might need help in setting up a dummy trail leading away from what happened," Tracy said to Reynard. "So the papers don't get a whiff of this."

"I understand. I appreciate the effort. For now, I think Scott's the one who needs my help."

"You will need to call me before anything goes down with the media."

"I will." He hesitated. "I'm sorry about the weekend."

"We'll do the outing some other time," Tracy answered looking around at Ava. Shyly she leaned in and kissed Reynard's lips. "Ava won't tell," she said with a smile. "And I can't leave without, well, call me."

He agreed to call her locking the office door behind him. As Tracy drove home, Ava sat in the passenger seat with her face glued to the car window. Tears poured out of her silent and bitter. She felt Tracy's occasional glance on her as she drove out of the building's garage her usual serene expression marred with a painful frown. "It'll be ok, Tracy. Don't worry," she cooed.

"I'm not worried, sweetie. You'll bounce back from this. By the way, we'll stop off at your apartment. You can pick up some clothes, anything you need, and we'll scoot over to my place."

Ava didn't say a word. She couldn't.

"Oh, and of course you can bring Oscar. It's only for a little while. Would you be more comfortable in a hotel?"

Ava tossed her shoulder. She didn't know what she wanted. She hated living like Oscar everyone staring at her and commiserating on her problems. She also knew she couldn't afford to be alone. She needed noise around her other than the echo of Mathilda's gun cocking in her ears. "Maybe I would be better at a hotel, Tracy. I hate to put you out, you and your three kids. I'd only be crazy Ava disrupting everyone's routine. I heard Reynard when he said he'd stay at the club." She turned to gaze at her friend. "You invited him to stay with you, didn't you?"

"Yes. But you're not the reason Reynard is staying at the club. He'll be out most of the evening helping Scott. Ava, a lot needs to be done to square this mess. Pulling the right strings to keep this situation out of the papers for one, which is my job, and the responsibility is not a pretty one. On top of this, Victor Danes is threatening to go to the media if Scott and Reynard don't plead for Mathilda's immediate release. So don't worry about you being any trouble. You're the reason the Wallaces still own a company."

"Does this mean I still have a job?"

"Of course, you do. I happen to be aware Reynard will want

to meet with you, Trevor, and Luke in a couple of days to stream-line the new projects you've begun. He'll likely be taking over for a while, at least until Scott returns."

"If he ever does," Ava whispered loud enough for Tracy to catch.

"Of course, he'll be back. He is juggling a lot at the moment which is understandable, but he's committed to continuing the projects Saunders and others are waiting to implement—anxious-ly I might add."

Ava nodded. "I'm sorry I'm such a baby. I don't mean to upset you." She put a trembling hand on Tracy's arm. "Thanks for ev-erything."

"Hey, you're not a baby. You might have been seriously hurt. oh, and I think the nasty bruise on your arm needs to be exam-ined."

"Not to worry. My arm will heal. I'll need to wear long sleeves for a while." Her arm would heal fast enough. A broken heart, however, would take a long time to mend.

The last comment Ava overheard before leaving with Tracy was they'd booked Mathilda on charges of assault with a deadly weap-on, although Scott didn't think he wanted to press theft charges.

"Did Scott talk to Sylvia yet? Is Sylvia aware Mathilda's in cus-tody?"

Tracy nodded. "Think so. Reynard said Scott went to talk to her to give her the benefit of explaining why she did this. He men-tioned Scott might consider giving Sylvia a second chance—should she want one. He says Scott's a pretty forgiving guy."

True love, thought Ava. She sighed with finality. Nothing like drama to bring two people closer together, stir things up a bit, perhaps what Scott and Sylvia had needed all these years—a single moment of blaring truth.

Tracy arrived in front of Ava's building. She parked the car in the first spot she found along the narrow street. Keys in hand, Tracy turned in her seat to stare at Ava waiting for her to decide what she wanted to do.

"Come on, Ava," she coaxed rubbing her hand. "I'll go up with you. We'll make this quick and painless, you'll see."

Ava did not respond. Instead, she grabbed the door handle.

"Ava," Tracy stopped her motion. "He's out there Ava, the guy for you." She nodded with a tentative smile.

"Meaning I should stop thinking about Scott."

"Meaning you deserve to be happy. Scott is a mistake, sweetie. I mean, he has a history with Sylvia—no matter what she did. Plus, Scott and his fiancé hold similar interests." She took a deep breath as though hesitant to say more. "Listen, sweetie? Scott might be enamored with you now. Something tells me he is, but would this last?"

Ava shrugged.

"On the plus side, Luke's been calling everyone trying to find you. Elaine said he called her several times. He's worried about you. He even got a hold of my cell phone number—don't ask me how—twice."

"I didn't notice," she droned. "I'll call Luke."

"He's a catch, Ava, and he likes you. Plus, you like the name, Luke."

Ava gazed at Tracy. No malice lurked in the phrase, only good intentions. Ava smiled. "True. All this started because of the name Luke."

"Of course. By the way, you're staying with me. The girls are with Kevin this weekend. So we can vege, watch old movies, stuff our faces with greasy takeout, and talk about all the things we would change to make the world a better place. Deal?"

Ava nodded and smiled. "Won't you be busy stomping out fires?"

She winked at Ava. "We'll cross that bridge when we need to."

***

During the following days, Tracy happened to be a bigger help than Ava might have anticipated. Her stay became therapeutic for Ava, to be with someone like Tracy who anticipated her every thought—someone who tolerated her swinging moods veering from sadness to hope back to misery again in the space of mere hours. She would be forever grateful for the companionship, and her friend's acceptance of the distress enveloping her.

Reynard never called on Tracy to help with the mess at police headquarters or to deal with the glare of potential media frenzy. Instead, he threw thousands of dollars at a hush team of professionals used to leaving no scent for newshounds to grab, curbing all information about the case apt to provide media with a trail in which to sink their teeth.

Come Monday morning, rested and wearing her best suit of business resolve, Ava packed up her stuff and headed to the office with Tracy.

She gravitated to the fifth floor hoping to find Elaine and a cup of coffee before the meeting with Reynard.

"Hey, what's with the fish on my desk?" Elaine joked, pretending surprise when she got off the elevator.

"Sorry. Poor little Oscar." Ava pinched her lips. "He's like me bent out of shape and a little out of his element."

"Out of his element?"

"Yes, abandoned and all by his lonesome."

"Huh," Elaine protested. "Oscar—what a weird name for a fish—is a whole lot braver than you are," Elaine eyed her straight and forward.

Sitting on the desk, Ava wore a rueful half smile on her face. "Ok, Missy. Throw me your best curve. I'm ready for you."

"Well, this is not a curve, I speak the truth, and the truth is you should follow the example of your fish. Look at Oscar in his little bowl blinking and happily blowing bubbles, content to swim round and round whereas you, my friend, are busy drowning in your own goo."

A short giggle escaped Ava. Elaine could always cheer her up. "I'm not drowning." She knuckled Elaine's arm. "Thanks to the help of my BFFs."

"Yeah. Sorry, I wasn't there for you on Friday, and to think I needed to hear about the Ava-runs-to-the-rescue chapter from Luke, of all people. I'm glad he reached me, though. Did you ever return his calls? You didn't return mine."

"I apologize, Elaine. As of this morning, I'm back with the living. And no, I didn't return anybody's calls. That's why I stopped in to see you."

Elaine poured herself and Ava some coffee. After handing Ava a cup, she sat down at her desk removing her glasses. "Now what? Any news from Scott?"

Ava shook her head. "None. He didn't even call to see if I am all right." Ava bit back on tears she'd sworn she would preempt from leaving salty little traces on her cheeks, at least in public.

"He's been a little busy. Besides, I'm sure Reynard reassured him on the subject. He'll call. Don't worry."

"I don't think he will—I mean he should. If only to say, hey I'm all right or fill the space between us with courteous platitudes. I'd even be grateful for banalities—just to hear his voice."

Conscious Elaine waited for her to air out her dark thoughts and let loose the boogeyman, Ava continued, "I hear bits and pieces from Tracy. And I'm sure Reynard will mention a few words. But you know as much as I do listening to the tone of his voice or the sound of emotion behind his words is ten times better than overhearing some banal conversation about him."

Elaine nodded. "True."

Elaine's surprising lack of rebuttal encouraged Ava to go down the dark route she had vowed not to follow. "Only one reason can prompt his absence. Scott and Sylvia made up."

"Oh, come on. Impossible, Mathilda only made bail this morning. DA refuses to drop the assault charges. How do you think this will sit with Scott—or with Reynard of all people?"

"They'll say good riddance. Mathilda is the problem, not Sylvia. In my mind, Scott doesn't seem like the sort of man who would abandon a loved one because of a bad judgment call."

"Meaning you think he's going to patch things up with Sylvia?" Elaine shook her head. "He doesn't seem the type to be turned on by a double-crossing Mata Hari."

Ava swallowed a nervous giggle. "If I stole from you, and I *begged* for your forgiveness, would you turn me down?"

"This is not a fair question." Elaine hid inside her coffee cup sipping the hot brew slowly. "I would forgive you just about any-thing, Ava," she mumbled inside the cup.

Ava slid off the desk and dropped a kiss on top of Elaine's head. "I would too by the way." She smiled at Elaine who acknowledged the sweet gesture with a smile. Ava swung the other chair around and dropped into the sturdy structure. "What Scott is also capable of doing, he has a big heart."

Elaine nodded refraining from speaking.

Knowing Elaine, Ava figured she didn't want to shove foot number two into her mouth not to mention silence could always confirm what words could not.

The silence became loud during Reynard's meeting when Ava did nothing other than nod as Reynard asked the trio in atten-dance for their participation.

Trevor looked at each one of them and seemed to notice the un-ease around the room. Perhaps Trevor imagined the little group's silence occurred because of him since he appeared to need to dis-pel the awkwardness. He cleared his throat to attract everyone's attention. "I thought you might like to know. I'm truly sorry for all that's happened."

"We understand," Reynard interrupted him. "Sylvia exonerat-ed you. She assured us you had nothing to do with the theft."

"I guess it's no secret," he shrugged meekly. "I'm still fond of Sylvia. I believe extenuating circumstances led to her actions, and I'm sure she and Scott will work it out, with a little help from you, Reynard."

"Well," Reynard interjected somewhat non-committal. "We'll iron all this out when the time comes."

He glanced at the presentation on his desk. "For now, with your help, we are going to get these projects underway. Investors who heard about what the three of you are brewing here are awaiting your formal presentation with great trepidation. You whetted their appetites," he smiled toward Ava.

Ava smiled back. She couldn't help noticing how Reynard's polite personality differed from Scott's dynamic presence. She fancied Reynard missed the bowler hat to complete the picture.

"The thing is, Reynard." Ava thought she should own up. "Scott doesn't think I am ready to present to clients. He seems to think I need more practice, and I agree with him."

Reynard paused his eyes in the distance. Then he turned toward her. "How about we hire someone from Tracy Donovan's department for a while, someone to assist you in honing your presentation skills?" Reynard supplied.

Ava raised both shoulders. "Yes, this might work."

"Good. Leave this with me. I'll find the right person." He hesitated. "Ava ... by the way, it's good of you to bring this up." Reynard smiled. "Good teamwork."

In the corridor after the meeting, Luke insisted Ava talk to him if only to give him her version of the facts.

"I'm sorry, Luke I didn't return your calls." She gave him a sheepish look. "You can't believe how many times I've had to apologize today, to everyone. I needed time to myself."

"I'm glad you're not hurt." He touched her arm.

"Ooh," she winced from the pain of his touch. "Careful," she pulled her arm away. "Not your fault." She addressed the concern on his brow. "I fell on my arm. Bruise hurts like a sprain."

"Maybe you should go to the emergency. Check out if the bone is chipped."

She nodded to avoid an argument. "Want to go over our proposal? I'll ask Trevor to bring you up on the weather project."

"On one condition," he grinned. "You have lunch with me and tell me what happened Friday night after I left."

"Deal," she smiled. "You inviting?"

He smiled a tad on the coy side. "Yeah, I'll buy."

Monday night, Tracy gave Ava a lift back to her apartment her luggage in the back seat while little Oscar swam back and forth at Olympic levels in the small bowl resting on Ava's lap.

"Oscar seems so anxious and worried," Ava said about her little fish.

"Ava, he's all right. He is a fish." Tracy chuckled as she pulled one bag out of the car. "You'd think you were gone a week with the stuff we hauled out."

Jeff, always the faithful attendant with Ava's wellness in mind, spotted them from his window and ran out to help with their bags. On hot days like today, he would sit inside to keep an eye on the building's entrance.

"Thank you, Jeff," Ava mentioned with a big smile. "I'll trade you. Oscar for this bag," she said as she caught Jeff's nerves when he swung Oscar's bowl side to side.

Jeff's help was appreciated as neither of them would need to make a second trip. In the elevator, Jeff painted a sad face as he announced: "Too bad about Mrs. Chapel. She wondered where you'd gone the day before she passed."

Ava almost dropped Oscar's bowl on the floor, and when the elevator stopped, Jeff stuck a bag in front of the doors to prevent them from closing right away. "What do you mean she passed?

She died?"

He leaned his head to the right as though too shy to be the bearer of such bad news. "Sunday night, in her sleep." Her daughter Mary-Ann found her on Monday morning. She was due to spend the week here with her."

"Oh my God! Ava followed Jeff to her place while Tracy took the rear. Ava handed him the keys her hands shaking too badly, and he unlocked her door. "I'm sorry you had to find out this way. She really liked you, Ava." Jeff opened the door and invited Tracy inside placing Ava's bag as close to the door as possible.

"I did too," Ava whispered. Penny's best friend and now they were both gone.

"Are you going to be all right, Ava?" Tracy asked.

She nodded yet only managed to pull off a tight smile since Tracy offered to stay. Ava saluted Jeff with a little wave, and once he closed the door, she faced Tracy. "I'll be fine, Tracy. You go home to those gorgeous girls of yours. Please don't worry about me."

Once Tracy left, the death of Elspeth Chapel became the proverbial drop that filled Ava's cup of sorrow. So many things took place in the last few days. This last one brought home such loneliness. When she observed tears rippling the water in Oscar's bowl, she placed her fish and his home on the old wooden coffee table in front of her and collapsed on the sofa sobs overtaking her. Curled up in a little ball, she fell asleep while little sighs interrupted those first few gulps of peace.

CHAPTER 27

AVA DINES WITH LUKE

Two weeks into their project with Reynard, Ava and Luke picked up their friendship from where they'd left off, almost intact. Ava tried not to think about Scott, although the man occupied her mind, and instead of fading away, her need to be with him grew with each passing day.

A tacit agreement existed between her and Tracy not to discuss the gaping hole left by Scott's absence—a hole Reynard worked hard to fill needing to pull three people from other departments to help shoulder the load.

Fill away, Ava rued. She still sensed Scott's presence everywhere on the floor, in the building, stamped on the project in which they'd poured their heart and soul. In some ways, the toils of love were worse than the toils of war. She couldn't mourn and pick up the scattered pieces of her life, couldn't even rebuild—not when every little thing in her vicinity reminded her of Scott living and breathing with someone else.

Scott's presence also took over some of her thoughts when they presented the finished product to Maxwell Saunders and his associates. She imagined how proud he'd be with a presentation that glided without a hitch and grabbed everyone's imagination at the meeting.

"I think the demonstration went well, super well, don't you?" Luke coaxed Ava out of her thoughts with a bright smile.

Ava stared at Luke injecting amusement into her expression. Pleased with his performance, Luke owned the right to be happy, he played an excellent role. Plus, three people including Ava and a seasoned speaker worked hard to seduce the investors.

Luke checked his watch. "I say we celebrate. We go home early and I take you out to dinner this evening."

Ava nodded at the prospect. Friday night and she would be glad to skip her yoga class for once.

"Wonderful, Ava. How about I pick you up around seven in front of your place?"

"Hum, hum. Sounds great. I'll be ready," Ava added as she hailed the first cab she spotted.

"Wait. What's your address?"

"I'm in the book, hotshot." She grinned as she swung the cab door open. "Two colleagues having a celebratory bite to eat. That's all."

"Of course," he added with a broad grin.

Later that evening, after picking her up at her apartment, Luke would not tell Ava where he wanted to take her. "It's a surprise. For once you'll need to be patient, Ava Moss."

Ava glanced at him her eyes narrow and appearing a tad suspicious. He wore a fancy suit, a tie, and a slight dab of cologne. This soirée depicted all the trimmings of a date. "I thought we decided this would be a victory dinner and nothing more," she fudged with half a smile puckered on her lips.

He grinned like the Cheshire cat of the famed fable. "We'll soon find out, won't we?"

"Hum, answering a question with a question and not a fair one."

He glanced her way. He could not stop smiling. "A sexy dress," he gestured toward the cleavage of the low-cut black sheath she wore. "A lovely hairdo, gorgeous face. You sure this is all you want—a pleasant evening with a colleague?"

"Another unfair question—I needed to dress fancy. You wouldn't tell me where we were going."

He laughed. Then he slowed to pull up by the curb in front of the 21 Club and waited for her reaction.

She recognized the busy area where she first encountered Scott. The memory tugged at her heart for a few seconds which made her turn toward him more willful than she intended to be. "Are you crazy? Do you know how expensive this restaurant is?"

"Hey, since when does a date object to how elegant a restaurant is?"

"Ah ha! This *is* a date. I knew it," she blared. She waved a finger at him. "Luke Perry, if I wasn't so ... hungry, I'd turn around and take a cab home." She burst out laughing wanting to wipe the concern off his face. "Come on. Let's share the Mate for Life rendezvous we never did."

He exhaled relieved and appeased. He stepped out handed his

keys to the valet and opened Ava's door. "Allow me to escort you in." He tipped his head and extended his arm. "By the way, I may have been your number six that night, but you were my number one," he grinned as they entered the restaurant.

"Well, if this dinner is supposed to make up for your no-show, you're going to need to eat quite fast. All a *mater*'s allowed is twenty minutes." Her turn to flash a bright smile.

"Okay, I give up," he said. "Truce, I beg you. I'm sorry I never showed up at the 21 Club. I'm sorry I'm late. Most of all I'm sorry I never told you tonight was a bona fide date. Satisfied?"

"Yes." she tugged on his arm as the waiter brought them to their table. Ava realized with a pinch on her heart she needed to reveal to Luke her sentiments about Scott. Luke's comportment was evident to her. He was marking his territory here, and she wasn't his to keep—on loan, pure and simple at least until she banished Scott out of her heart.

Ava wondered how much time a heart in love might need to recuperate, for the resident to vacate the premises once the lease was broken. Never having been in this situation, she had no idea how many weeks or months she would need before she could house someone inside the occupied region again. As a technicality, a lease between Scott and her never existed other than in her imagination, only the passionate and brief commitment of a kiss.

After a signal from their waiter, Luke led Ava to a secluded booth at the back of the Upstairs room and squeezed in beside her. Ava admitted she loved the area, the perfect condiment to go with her main dish of a delicious entrée of heaven.

"I'll be right back," Luke glanced at his phone. "I'm sorry. I have to take this call." He excused himself and left.

The waiter came and brought them water and menus. "Would you like to hear this evening's specials?"

"I'll just browse. My partner will be back momentarily."

"As you wish."

When the waiter moved aside, Ava spotted another couple entering the room. All at once, a wild beat drummed in her chest. Her heart had foretold before her head did the new arrival happened to be Scott. The sight of the woman beside him, Sylvia, smiling with her arm comfortably looped around Scott's arm caught her breath and felled her legs.

She closed her eyes willing the burning constriction in her throat not to make her cry. They were back together. They had kissed and made up and were blissfully strolling across the restaurant area, arm in arm as happy as clams and oblivious to everyone around them.

Ava didn't even have the presence of mind to hide behind her menu so shocked Scott could pick up his life from where he'd left off. Men hated change, she knew this, but this brought the need for tedium to new heights. Perhaps Scott and Sylvia's love rekindled, now stood the test of time and drama to become the sort not to be denied.

She didn't have the chance to dwell on the last question. Scott looked up and stared at her. His first impulse produced a smile from ear to ear. Then he tilted his head inviting her to do the same.

She couldn't, too floored to extend the slightest courtesy.

She spotted him turn toward Sylvia and whisper in her ear.

Sylvia turned in her direction and smiled adding a short wave to her gesture.

Ava nodded. She couldn't believe the woman acted as though

nothing had happened between them.

Ava's mortification took a turn for the worse. She watched Sylvia follow the waiter while she shuddered to see Scott walk toward her.

She picked up the menu and raised it up to her face pretending to read the content.

She noticed Scott pulling a chair from the next table to sit beside her. "Ava, I know you saw me. Please," he added quietly.

She put down the menu. "What are you doing here?" happened to be all she could say while she really wanted to ask what he was doing here with Sylvia?

"Same as you," he smiled. Then Ava caught him losing the smile. "Or are you here on another Mate for Life excursion? This is where the group usually meets, isn't it?" She thought she noticed bitterness color his eyes. "Still searching for the perfect mate, I see."

"Still rubbing my nose in it." She stared into his eyes. His tired, drawn expression did nothing to assuage the rage coursing through her at the sight of Sylvia and him together. "You know me, Scott. I'm not looking for love, just a good time."

Her slap in the face wiped the semblance of a smile lingering on his lips. He got up, looked down at her and gave her a polite nod as the warmth in his eyes turned to ice.

At the precise moment as though to break the bondage of screams and shrieks billowing in silence between them, Luke walked up to the table. "Sorry, I took so long. My sister had an emergency," he paused thrown by the look on Ava's face. He turned and spotted Scott standing at the table glaring at her.

"Scott? What are you doing here?" Surprise drew Luke's eyebrows higher. "Is there something wrong with work?" He turned toward Ava. Scott didn't seem in any mood to answer.

After tearing the tie between her and Scott, she turned and smiled at Luke. "Not at all, Luke. Scott is here with Sylvia. He came over to say hello." She raised her eyebrows toward Scott indicating he should leave.

Scott turned to shake Luke's hand. "Nice to see you, Luke. I heard you did a great job with the presentation to Max Saunders."

Luke shook Scott's hand a little puzzled. "Well, we made this a team effort. Ava is fantastic." He no longer had Scott's attention.

Scott veered toward his table and nodded absentmindedly. "Well, I'll see you all soon. Goodnight."

The meal between Luke and Ava became stilted. Ava figured Luke to be intelligent enough to realize he'd rubbed elbows against high voltage electricity—yet too much the gentleman to probe the subject. At the most, he appeared resentful gaiety no longer colored their date.

Halfway through the main course, Ava put down her fork took a long sip of her water, and followed the interruption with a deep breath. One of her hands placed on Luke's arm she decided to let him in on the strange way she and Scott met, also recounting with punctured brevity the circumstances that followed.

"I think somewhere I already sensed this, not because it's obvious to everyone," he hurried to add. "To a guy who's interested, indications do tend to show."

"I'm sorry. I guess seeing Scott again I didn't realize how bothered I still am by all this, Luke." She squeezed his hand not knowing if she might ever think of him as more than a friend. "I'll need time to recover."

"Of course," he added his eyes upholding hers. "Don't apologize—unnecessary."

"I don't know how much time I'll need, or if I'm even going to continue working at Extrade."

"You can't leave your job, Ava. You're too good at what you do."

"Thank you. Your praise means a lot." She turned to ask the waiter for more water. "In a way, I'm glad Scott hasn't returned to work yet."

"In a way you wish he had, right?"

She shrugged unwilling to hurt him, unsure of how she would resist if she did have to run across Scott every day.

"Hey, you'll get over this." He smiled. "And I told you, I'm a very determined fellow."

Ava smiled to show him she understood. Yet for the rest of the evening, she sensed Scott's eyes branded on her from across the room. Ava applauded the fact she brought a wrap to drape around her shoulders—great to ward off ice-cold stares.

CHAPTER 28

CENTRAL PARK

Ava spent a good part of Saturday morning fuming as she paced miles up and down her small apartment and furious with her lack of strength to deal with her own despair. She thrived on being resourceful and in control of her emotions.

Last night, Luke drove her home and behaved like the perfect friend. And although she realized Luke might be knighted as a women's best suitor, he would never become her knight. Ava had never enjoyed a brother's love, but she imagined her fondness for Luke might well represent the love a sister might have for her brother.

Ava spent the entire night crying over Scott bawling without control. The last time depression hit her this hard she ran away from a foster home where a young man spent weeks harassing her while she planned her escape.

By nightfall, Ava decided she would talk to Tracy and Reynard and ask to transfer to Tracy's department. This would be considered a step-down, but she couldn't afford to work with Scott whether Sylvia returned to the office or not. She loved him with all her heart. The only way to forget him meant trying to avoid bumping into him as much as possible.

Ava crawled into bed with the same book she'd started eight weeks prior—not a bad book, only her life happened to convey more drama than any book on her shelf.

The phone rang, and she raised her eyes heavenward. These days, whenever she claimed a little rest, the phone rang. "Hello?"

"Hey, a little birdie told me you ran into Scott and Sylvia last night," Elaine said yanking the cap off the frag threatening to shatter what little peace she clung to.

Ava couldn't believe Elaine blurted this out as though she would do for some juicy piece of gossip. She counted to ten not to lose her temper, fought not to let tears overtake her and asked "Which little birdie are you referring to? No. Don't tell me."

Ava figured Luke called Elaine and expressed concern, perhaps one of the callers who'd rung her earlier. She didn't bother picking up for anyone today—and she regretted answering now. "Elaine, if you don't mind, I don't want to talk about this," she delivered with annoyance prominent in her tone of voice.

"Fine. This is not why I called. Jerry is away tomorrow, and I thought you and me might hang around Central Park and laze around the Bethesda Fountain for a while."

A pity summons Ava realized. "No thank you, Elaine. I have lots to do tomorrow," she fudged.

Silence prevailed on the other end of the phone.

"Elaine?"

"Fine. I didn't want to tell you over the phone. It's so stupendous."

Another dramatic silence followed prompting Ava to ask again. "What?"

"I'm pregnant."

"Oh, my God," she breathed. Ava heard Elaine's uncharacteristic little giggles on the line. "I'm so happy for you, Elaine." In an instant, Ava forgot about her troubles. Elaine and Jerry had been living together for six years trying to conceive for five of those years. The stork remembered where they lived at last. "How far along are you? Did you see a doctor yet?"

"I did consult a doctor. I didn't want to say anything until the tests came back. I'm six weeks along."

"So wonderful. What did Jerry say?"

"He's calling all our friends and family and passing around blue taped cigars."

"You can't tell this early—can you?"

"Of course not. He's being Jerry, the big dick. I'm hoping for a girl." Another awkward pause followed, and Elaine added, "I thought we might get together, share some girl talk," Elaine said with excitement. "Please, Ava. I need to talk about this or I'll bust."

"Sure," Ava capitulated. "What time do you want to get together?"

"I'll be down in the Park around 11:00."

"One condition, Elaine."

"What?"

"We do not talk about Scott or Sylvia or Luke or anything connected to my life. Promise?"

"Of course. Not everything is about you, Ava."

Ava stared at the receiver in her hand a probing expression in her eyes. She couldn't swear on any Bible Elaine's invitation did not constitute some lame attempt to draw her out, but she decided to believe her without a doubt. "See you tomorrow," she murmured.

Next morning rose a gorgeous day, the rarest of days when the sky overhead mimics a glowing blue dome, cloudless and unperturbed. The temperature not too cold, not too hot, offered a slight breeze which hovered around the park allowing the young-at-heart to perform aerodynamic feats with their kites.

Sitting by the fountain, Ava spotted Elaine from a distance. Her petite frame in a fast jog unmistakable, no matter the distance. Ava spotted her talking to herself motioning with arms and hands and nodding as though Elaine practiced a speech of some kind. Rehearsing something she intended saying to her? She hoped not. She refused to glean advice of any sort. She'd agreed to come to ease out of her life for a couple hours, and she hoped Elaine would respect her wishes.

As soon as Elaine came within earshot, Ava couldn't resist asking, "Hey, Elaine, are you all right?" Ava walked up and gave her a hug. "What were you mumbling about? I caught you talking to yourself all the way here. Is this about Jerry? Is he not happy about the baby?" People tended to change their minds about starting a family sometimes, more so men.

Elaine shook her head while a guarded look lurked in her eyes. She stepped aside and glanced behind her. Ava followed Elaine's glance and came face to face with Scott stepping out from behind a group of people. No smile to warm his expression. He appeared tense and nervous, his hands deep in his pockets almost as though he didn't know what to do with them.

Ava glared at Elaine. "What is going on?"

Elaine looked at her shoes and raised a pair of helpless shoulders. "I'm sorry, Ava. He followed me here."

Scott's first words when he reached them, "Don't blame Elaine. I phoned her about your whereabouts. When she wouldn't tell me where she was meeting you, I waited outside her door and followed her here. I need to talk to you, Ava."

"He followed you here?" Stunned, Ava considered Scott to be the last person in the world she needed to bump into now.

Elaine nodded a little embarrassed. "Listen, Ava. I don't want to get involved in this mess. I'm sorry. I never meant for this to happen." She stared at Scott with all the scorn she could muster. "Call me later, Ava. I'll be home."

Took mere seconds for Ava to realize Elaine left her alone with Scott. Ava turned and started walking in the opposite direction picking up the pace when she heard him pleading with her to stop.

"Ava, please. I need to talk to you."

"Go away. I don't want to speak to you. You're a lousy human being," she threw at him hoping to discourage him from pursuing her.

Scott only ran faster. He grabbed her arm the minute he caught up to her.

Ava turned to face him with a menacing look in narrow, angry eyes. "Let go of my arm or I'll call for help. The park is crawling with cops."

"Okay. I'll go. First give me two minutes to hear me out. After if you still want me to leave I will."

She yanked her arm out of his grasp and hesitated. He seemed different out of his suit, wearing a T-shirt and beige slacks, taller since she wore flats this morning yet more relaxed, less formidable. She gave him little bobs in agreement.

"Thank you." He indicated the bench nearby.

Ava preceded him there. She sat on the edge of the bench poised to run while she kept her back straight and her head high.

Scott sat with his shoulders slumped as though searching for the right words. "I'm sorry I didn't call you these last few weeks. I'm not going to make excuses telling you I've been through hell and back. I didn't realize you lived your own sort of hell."

"My feelings are not your business, Scott, not anymore—in fact, they never were." Ava rose and began walking away.

"Wait," Scott walked behind her. "Please, this is not what I meant to say. Hear me out."

She stopped but stayed pat refusing to look at him.

"I thought you knew Sylvia, and I called off our engagement. I thought everyone did."

She turned to look at him. "And how am I supposed to know that? You didn't even take the time to pay me a courtesy call."

He shook his head a rueful look in his eyes. With a nervous hand, he rubbed the back of his neck. "The rumor mill is usually rife with this sort of details. I had no idea how closemouthed my brother Reynard could be."

"Don't blame your brother for your shortcomings. No one can explain your version of the truth but you," she argued. For the first time, Ava noticed how haggard he appeared to be.

"You're right. I guess I felt sorry for myself."

A sentiment Ava could relate to without any difficulty.

"As for the courtesy call, I did go to your place on the following Saturday morning. Stupid me, I forgot I'd asked you to leave your apartment and go elsewhere. No one told me you spent the weekend at Tracy's place."

"Again, your brother didn't mention anything? I'm surprised since my staying with Tracy ruined their weekend. He had to make plans to stay at the Club."

"This is Reynard for you. I did bump into Mrs. Chapel when I went to see you. She sat in the lobby waiting for Jeff to walk her upstairs. I volunteered." He looked at Ava with a slight smile on his face. "She is quite an interesting lady. In fact, she kept me there for an hour, very talkative that morning."

The thought of Mrs. Chapel brought back sadness to the forefront. Ava searched behind her and sat on the first bench she found. "She passed away."

"When?"

"During the weekend I spent at Tracy's. Jeff said she died in her sleep."

"I'm so sorry. She expected a week-long visit from her daughter."

"She's the one who found her Monday morning." She looked up at Scott wiping the tears in her eyes. "Where were you staying all this time?"

I moved out of the hotel the night of the theft. I've been staying at Reynard's club since my return from California where I helped Sylvia start her new life."

"What?" She breathed unwilling and unable to believe the last phrase.

Towering over her, he asked permission to sit beside her.

She agreed and twisted her body toward him ready to listen.

He gazed at her face for a few minutes, silent, a slight smile dawning on his tired expression. "You are beautiful, no makeup, no frills of any kind." He took a deep breath.

"You said something about Sylvia's new life?"

He nodded glancing at his shoes. Then eyeing her squarely, he admitted. "I couldn't just leave her and walk away. God knows we both did a ton of mistakes in our relationship. I needed to help her, and the separation of five years of assets complicated the situation a great deal. Then she needed help to find a new job."

"Reynard wouldn't."

He shook his head to negate the idea. "Can't say I blame him. Her presence at the firm would have made us all uncomfortable." He ran a hand through his hair. "She has friends in California. Her mother and a couple of cousins are down there. So I introduced her to the President of an investment firm in San Francisco—a man who owes me a couple of favors. They hired her on the spot." Scott hesitated and continued. "Of course, she promised me she would not use any of the information she learned from us to help her new company. I believe her."

"Well, at least Sylvia has a new life," she answered unable to erase all the reproach out of her eyes. "Why didn't you pick up a phone, Scott, if only to explain." She stopped unsure of what he might say. "Anyway, I'm glad Sylvia got a nice send-off," she added a little of her jealousy edging through.

"I told you, I moved out the night of the theft. In California, I stayed with friends. Truthfully," he added eyeing her with hesitancy. "Sylvia and I have not been a couple since she came back from Europe."

"What?" Shocked, Ava put her face into her hands as though trying to rub Scott's last words out of her mind. Looking at him, she added, "Do you realize the terrible position you put me in?"

"I'm sorry. The truth is I fell in love with you, Ava, that night at the 21 Club. Took me a while to recognize the sentiment. I never experienced anything like this—my whole life consumed by thoughts of one person."

She shook her head. She couldn't believe his last words. "That's not what you said in your office or at breakfast in the Hamptons," she reminded him. "You made me feel so small, so insignificant that morning."

"I wanted to tell you. I did. I made up my mind to do so during the sleepless night after Sylvia and I fought like two dimwits. I thought you and I belonged together. Then you became so distant on the ride home, refusing to talk or look at me or even answer my question on why you'd spent the night tossing and turning. Remember?"

She bit her bottom lip and nodded looking down at the bench.

"Hell, you seemed so uncomfortable around me." Ava sensed Scott's hand reach for hers. "But it's not your fault." He caressed her fingers until she looked up at him. "My fault. I lost my nerve, talked about some platitude or other, anything to allow me to preserve what friendship we shared."

"I should have said something. I lost my courage too.

"Please don't blame yourself. All me. I refused to accept how much I needed you. The damn sentiment made me weak, vulnerable. I would've done anything to shake the emotion from my system including sleeping with you."

She lowered her head. "This is not love, Scott," she whispered.

"It's love all right. I became so exposed, so raw. The experience left me bitter and more than a bit crazy around you." He smiled while his eyes remained soulful and sad. "Sometimes it's difficult to come to terms with the changes life deals you, the hard choices you realize need to be made. Sylvia and I had been together a long time. Truth was when she pleaded with me to forgive her about the theft, I did."

Ava nodded staring into his eyes. "I thought you might." In a sense, Scott's gallant gesture filled Ava with pride. "I'm glad you're not holding a grudge." She hesitated. "D.A.'s office called me day before yesterday. They're willing to file Mathilda's actions as a misdemeanor provided I give my consent. I received a handwritten apology from her. She sounded sincere. I agreed to their formal recommendation she gets probation and treatment instead of a record."

He shook his head stroking her cheek with the back of his hand. "That's good. You did a good thing. You and Reynard both own big hearts."

"Reynard?"

"Yes. He and Tracy sorted out the accounts we own from those belonging to Victor and his company. Took them two days of hard work to do so. They asked Victor for an FTP folder in which they could drop these accounts. Sylvia mentioned her dad cried on the phone when he told her about this."

"Wow. Very generous of Reynard, especially when you consider Victor might not have done the same thing."

"Not without exacting a round little sum."

"What ever convinced Sylvia you weren't angry with her anymore?"

"Tricky." He took a deep breath. "She'd wanted to tell me about her father's shenanigans for a long time, torn between his wishes and the fear I might leave her if I found out. So I needed to convince Sylvia my reason for wanting to leave her had nothing to do with her betrayal."

"How?"

"I told Sylvia I love you. I told her I needed you and couldn't wait to make our love official."

"You two seemed pretty chummy Friday night." Ava couldn't drop the subject.

"Having a bite to eat before her flight to California." His expression changed at once. "And you're a fine one to talk about Friday night. Jealousy grabbed me by the ... when I thought you went to the restaurant looking for a date," he stressed the words. "These past few weeks, I guess I didn't think about us, refused to entertain the thought you might be enamored with someone else." He gave her rueful eyes. "Like a fool, I dared hope you waited at home for me to clean up my act. I didn't want to discuss my emotions over the phone or in an e-mail." He rubbed his forehead with a weary hand. "Stupid decision. I realize this now." He exhaled a long breath. "What is it they say about hindsight?" He coined her with a sharp glare. "When I saw Luke cozying up to you, I thought I'd lost you."

"Luke and I are friends," she answered a tad defensive.

"Hey, you're the one who brought up Friday night. All I can say is when I called you on Saturday—five times—I thought you'd spent the night at his place. I came within inches of showing up on your doorstep and wringing your neck."

Her heart beat so fast Ava doubted she'd be able to breathe to say what she needed to say. "You called Elaine. You're the little birdie who told her about meeting me at the 21 Club," she spoke under her breath realizing now the situation Elaine tried to bring to her attention.

He nodded. "Desperation made me do strange things. I thought perhaps you'd confided in Elaine."

"Go on."

"I phoned her again this morning. When I told her I intended going to your place, she said not to. Elaine informed me you and she were meeting today. She refused to say where."

"You're going to need to smooth things with her. She's my best friend."

"I will." He brushed a mesh of hair out of her eyes. "Now, you know."

She shook her head. "No. I don't," she whispered.

He picked up her hand in his and caressed her fingers with a gentle, sensuous motion. "I love you, Ava. I want to spend the rest of my life with you. My biggest mistake was I told Sylvia before I told you."

She nodded trying not to cry. "You said you'd stopped being a couple."

He exhaled a deep breath. He hesitated, his eyes resting on Ava's hands. She sensed his shiver when their eyes met. "I couldn't bear to make love to her. I'd work late into the night, tell her I was exhausted."

Sadness invaded Ava. "No wonder she hated my guts. On some level, I'm sure she knew. Well, most women *usually* do," she finished in a soft whisper.

He nodded. "Pretty drastic. You don't need to tell me. I just couldn't pretend anymore. I think I'd been complacent for a long time. Having no reason to rock the boat, to change the status quo, I didn't. Then I met you."

"The worst humiliation came from you—the morning we shared breakfast. I was prepared to leave the company. Didn't know how I would ever be able to work with you again."

He lowered his eyes. "Well, if it's any consolation, you couldn't hate me more than I hated myself." Ava caught him wipe the bridge of his nose with his thumb and forefinger.

"I didn't hate you. I could never hate you," she whispered. Ava thought of all the love she'd harbored for him—a sentiment she'd kept quiet for too long. She tugged at his sleeve stroking the little strand of hair jutting over his forehead. "I guess we're going to need to grow up and work on our communication skills. I love you so much it hurts." She stopped as tears began rolling down her cheeks.

"Ava," he groaned as he gathered her in his arms.

She leaned into him, and for a long time, he held her nuzzling hungry little kisses in her neck. "I've waited a long time to gather Ava Moss in my arms?" He smiled as he caressed her back with impatient hands.

She plopped her palms against his chest. She needed to gaze into his eyes. "Is Reynard aware?"

"Yes, he is. He is the second person I told. Everyone knew except for the one person who mattered."

"Tracy?"

"No. I told you. My brother's discreet behavior surprised the hell out of me since I'm sure he's itching to tell Tracy. I think Tracy and Reynard are becoming an item."

"Fantastic." Ava laid her head in the nook of his arm. "I happened to be as big a coward as you are—worse. I told all my friends I loved you. I even told Luke Friday night. I'm sorry I didn't mention this sooner."

"Shh," he whispered as he flicked her chin up to gaze into her eyes. Bending his head he kissed her lips. "We'll have the rest of our lives to discuss our crazy beginning. For now, all I want to do is enjoy the moment." His lips parted, he almost kissed her again. Then his eyes stared at all the kids gamboling in the park and at the other couples sitting on benches nearby. He added, "To enjoy this moment, I think you and need to leave."

Ava looked up and allowed her eyes to sweep the area. "Gosh, I forgot we were at the park." Turning to him again, she added, "My place is forty-five minutes away."

"Not by car." He smiled. "As of a few weeks ago, I am homeless. So I'm thinking your place or this park bench and providing these good folks with an entertaining afternoon." His smile tugged at her heartstrings.

Nevertheless, she thought of her humble apartment with all its flaws, with the fact she hadn't put away the dishes, sorted out her clean laundry still sitting in a basket on the bed, and Ava bit her bottom lip feeling a slight blush sweeping her cheeks. "I'm afraid my little apartment is not very romantic. I doubt you'll be impressed with it."

"Ava, I understand your place cannot be representative of who you are. I don't care, sweetheart. I need to be with you, please."

Her loins stirred from the appeal in his eyes, and the fact she felt the exact same urge gave her the courage to nod. "I do too."

He smiled, got up, and held out his hand for her to grasp. Once she stood beside him, he roped an arm around her waist and led the way.

"Where's your car?"

"Two streets down." He chuckled as he added, "In front of Elaine's apartment."

"You know Elaine happened to be right about you all along." Ava looked up at him while butterflies tickled her stomach when he crunched her against him.

"How?"

"She said you were in love with me. She said she could see it whenever you stared at me."

"I like her. I really do, and sometimes I think we should pay more attention to our friends," he whispered in her ear.

CHAPTER 29

A WALK IN THE PARK

They got to Scott's convertible, and he went around the car to open the door for her, but never had the chance to do so. They both turned as someone called out, "Ava, wait up."

Ava looked up and caught Elaine's head floating out of the second-story window, a big smile on her face. "I'm coming down. I want to talk to you."

Ava glanced at Scott, who nodded patience etched in his smile.

Once out the door, Elaine bounced lightly down the stairs, and Ava visualized her friend as a child bounding with joy with free rein on needing to satisfy her insatiable curiosity—as she did now. Elaine appeared to want to quench her nosiness about Ava and Scott, an interest seeming bigger than her promise not to meddle.

"So," she panted a little out of breath. "I guess this means you guys made up?"

Difficult for Ava to be angry at her looking as she did, with her hair in pigtails and her cheeks pink in a face rounded by a big smile.

Scott stared down at Ava's upturned face and acquiesced they had indeed made up. Ava pecked his lips a gesture she found liberating since she no longer needed to hold back.

"You guys are so cute. Where are you going?"

Scott turned toward Elaine and changed the subject. "I apologize for the dupe, earlier. I needed to talk to Ava."

"I understand—try telling this one, though," she answered tilting her head toward Ava. "So, where are you going? Want to come in?"

Ava peeked at Scott as shyness crept in. She hoped he might answer for the both of them.

"We're going for a drive," he said with a smile opening the car door.

Ava hesitated. "You had something to tell me?"

Elaine nodded. Sliding one hand out of her pocket she removed her glasses slipping them on top of her head her dark eyes very round. "Tracy was looking for you," Elaine said her eyebrows traveling up and down. "She wants to tell you something," she added with pinched lips.

As Elaine's signals began to take effect, Ava asked, "Her and Reynard?"

"You didn't find this out from me," Elaine answered her expression dipped in a kooky smile.

Ava's face changed from surprise to joy. Laughing she looked at Scott wondering aloud, "Oh, my gosh, did you know about this?" When it became evident he did, Ava knuckled him on the arm. "Why didn't you say anything? Talk about your brother being closemouthed."

"I believe Tracy wanted to surprise you," he said with a snicker. "Besides, it's not my news to tell." He gave Elaine a raise of his brows.

"Well, I didn't tell." Elaine took on her most offended expression. "Ava guessed." She giggled. "You'll need to pretend to be surprised when Tracy tells you. But that's not what I wanted to say," she pursed her lips trying to get Ava excited—her version of a drum roll.

Ava glanced at Scott worried he might be anxious to leave He hadn't signed on for unbridled girl talk, and she wondered if he was even used to grown women acting so silly. "What?" Ava smiled filled with a warm sense of friendship. Elaine happened to be her best friend. She deserved her full attention at the moment. "What did you want to tell me?"

Elaine took her right hand out of her pocket and stuck it in front of her friend's face so she might admire the giant rock decorating her ring finger.

Ava's jaw dropped, and she broke into the biggest grin, one she could not hold back had she tried. "Oh, my God," she exclaimed laughing and shedding a tear at the same time. "I can't believe this," she said grabbing Elaine's hand. "This is a beauty." Ava turned the ring to reflect different angles of the light making the diamond sparkle. "This had to cost him a fortune."

"He's been saving up long enough."

Ava turned to Scott. He smiled, and Ava couldn't help read affection in his eyes as he stared at her. "Six years Jerry's been dodging his commitment finding all sorts of reasons to avoid marriage." Dropping Elaine's hand, she asked. "What finally did it?"

She hoisted one shoulder. "Well, I'm pregnant. Jerry said he didn't want his little child to be born from unwed parents. Who knew the oaf was a big marshmallow?"

"Congratulations, sweetie." Ava gave Elaine a big hug and held on to her a little while longer. Elaine looked at them both and added, "Happy times, happy times. And," she stared at Scott as she said this, "I'm hoping for a girl. Cause I already picked out a name." She stroked Ava's arm. "I'm going to call her Ava, after the bravest, nicest person I know."

Ava pressed her lips together. She didn't want to cry in front of Scott. She wiped a few renegade tears peeking out of the corners of her eyes. "You're so sweet." She laid a gentle hand on Elaine's stomach. "I have to go. But you take care of my little namesake."

"I will. Have fun, you two," Elaine added her tone laced with innuendoes, and Ava spotted Elaine standing by the curve until they disappeared from view. Emma glanced at Scott while shyness poked its nose again. He appeared relaxed and free of tension, and as though reading her thoughts, he turned and smiled at her. He reached for her hand resting on her lap toying with her fingers. His eyes were kind, and a cheerful glint shone in the hazel depths, yet passion lurked there with the same intensity she'd witnessed when swept her off her feet in the Hamptons—Scott waltzing her around the room for the last dance.

The light turned green, and he placed both hands on the wheel again to negotiate a turn. "You're quiet," he cooed. "Anything wrong?"

She tried to answer, but nothing came out louder than a thwarted whisper so she shook her head for emphasis, clearing her throat.

"Would you like to go for lunch?"

She shook her head berating her little-girl tension. What was wrong with her? The man she loved had just begged her to sleep with him. She stared at the bridge in the distance. Soon, they'd be seeking passage and traveling toward her little street. What if he changed his mind once they wallowed in each other's arms? What if she couldn't satisfy his passion—the need he built up for so long? 'Sylvia and I haven't been a couple since her return from Europe,' he'd said. This laid a lot of expectation on the line.

She turned to stare at him to gather strength from the love she sensed each time she looked at him. "I'm a little nervous, I guess." She reached to cover some of the space between them, laying caressing fingers on his thigh.

Scott gathered her hand with an urgency Ava found surprising, and kissed her fingertips one by one his eyes glued to the bridge up ahead. "Don't caress my lap," he warned. "This car can stop on a dime—and there's a nice shady spot up ahead." He released a long breath and smiled at her. "Don't worry," he chuckled. "I've managed to avoid devouring you since I first saw you this morning. I can wait. More to the point," he added his eyes back on the road, "I'm in love with you, Ava. I'm planning our first encounter to be gentle, and slow—very slow." He grinned as he let go of her hand. "As if I would ever get enough of you."

She relaxed in her seat. "I might not be all you expected," she said as if to reassure herself.

He chuckled. "That'd be like the puppet master telling the puppet he's worried about which strings to pull." He laughed again. "You own me, Ava."

Their eyes met a few seconds, and she shivered the burn in her loins returning full force. Nerves were gone as anticipation took hold of her senses.

He pulled up in front of her building and backed the car up a few hundred feet behind the hydrant. "Parking ought to be good for a while," he mumbled to himself.

He took her hand to help her out of the car and kept her strapped to him. He pecked her lips in a slow, deliberate kiss.

Ava trembled in his arms. "Yes," she whispered. "I see what you mean about everything disappearing and surroundings no longer making a difference." She too could have made love to him right here, and now.

"Glad to hear we're on the same page," he breathed taking her hand to lead her toward the door.

Eyes glued together, they entered the building, and Jeff became the one who broke the spell. "Good afternoon, Miss Moss." He gawked at them with a big goofy smile on his face.

"Hello, Jeff."

"You had a visitor, Miss Moss. She left a message for you."

Ava took the slip of paper and noticed the first printed line, *from the desk of Tracy Donovan.* "Tracy's news," she indicated to Scott a wistful smile tugging at her lips as she tucked the small envelope in her pocket. "I'll read it later."

He nodded his arm wrapped around her waist giving her a squeeze. With his free hand, he slipped a little salute to Jeff as they walked to the elevator.

Once on Ava's floor, they came face to face with Mrs. Chapel's daughter, Mary-Ann who'd stayed in New York to clean out her mother's apartment. "Nice to see you, Ava," the older woman said.

Aside from the fact she didn't wear blue hair or a blue dress, Mary-Ann Chapel did not resemble her mother. Tall and well built, her imposing stature commanded respect. "My mother left this envelope for you with her attorney. Laurence Harvey gave it to me yesterday since I'm the executor of her will. Apparently, he told me her stipulations were I hand you this letter personally. He also mentioned his firm would be getting in touch with you sometime next week."

"Why?"

"Well, Penelope Arden and my mother shared the same attorney—a little unorthodox, I realize, especially since Penelope chose my mom to be the executor of her will. My mother kept this letter for years." Mary-Ann gave Ava the envelope.

"Thank you," Ava murmured unsure as to what Elspeth needed to give to her in writing.

"Don't worry, Laurence Harvey penned you into his appointment schedule and will explain everything when he sees you." Mary-Ann grabbed the handles to the cases she carried. "Well, I'm done here." She brushed a tear from her eye. "I pleaded with my mother so many times to move in with us. She wouldn't leave this place. She said it held too many memories for her—of late, the ones she could recall."

"I'm so sorry for your loss," Ava answered squeezing her arm as she weighed the small envelope in her hand. There was more than one sheet of paper in it. "I was very fond of her."

"Is this your young man?" Mary-Ann asked.

Startled Ava realized the question sounded as though it came from Elspeth.

Ava peeked at Scott not knowing what to say.

"I'm only asking because when my mother and I spoke on the phone Saturday night, she was all excited about a chat she'd had with Ava's young man."

Scott stepped up. "Yes, Mary-Ann. I am Ava's young man." He added looking into Ava's eyes, "The only young man she'll ever need."

"Well, best of luck to you both." She walked off rolling a couple of suitcases behind her.

Ava unlocked her door and allowed Scott to go first. She watched as he walked around her living area surveying the room with a smile. "Charming and deliciously sweet," he breathed. He stopped in front of the kitchen counter. "Aren't you going to introduce me?" He designated Oscar swimming in his little bowl.

"You're silly," she giggled as she closed the door behind her.

"Silly? In the Hamptons, you didn't want to stay the night because of your obligations to Oscar. You don't know what silly means until you've played second fiddle to a fish."

Ava laughed knowing by the big grin on his face he enjoyed teasing her. Putting her purse down, she walked to him. Shyly she put her arms around his neck. "Oscar, meet the new man in my life. The love of my life," she finished with a little catch in her voice.

He wrapped his arms around her waist. "Glad you're wearing flats for once. Allows me to be the grownup." He bent his head and kissed her gently at first, but then unable to resist his kiss deepened causing the heated embrace to fuse their bodies together.

Ava's inhibitions melted away. She wriggled passionately in his arms in a desperate attempt to remove any space between them. Then Scott interrupted their growing passion.

"Sweetheart," he breathed with difficulty. "Unless you care to open the envelope scratching the back of my neck I suggest you put it down somewhere." He looked around and then added. "Anywhere you want."

Hanging on his lips, she dropped the envelope on the floor with a soft moan of surrender as she waited for a deeper kiss.

"Ava." He tugged at her arms still wound tightly at the back of his neck. "I can wait for you at least for the next few minutes." He smiled. "I love you so much. What's a lifetime compared to mere moments?"

"Why?"

"I believe you should settle this envelope business first. From the few garbled messages I got from Elspeth on Saturday night this might be important to you."

"More important than you and I coming together?"

"Rather more urgent than more important."

She backed up slightly and bent to reach for the envelope on the floor. "You already know what's in this, don't you?"

"To a small extent. Elspeth tried to relate some story about you and your real family. Only she was not clear, and I had other things on my mind at the time."

"My birth family? Oh my God." Ava collapsed on the settee staring at the envelope as though it might explode were she to slit the flap open.

Scott sat down beside her and looped his arm around her shoulders to give her courage. "She started to tell me about your family, where you came from. Only her mind kept wandering, and I didn't know what to believe although I understood enough that we might be able to hire a good detective to do some snooping around."

"You hired a detective?" Ava could not hide the disappointment in her eyes. Did she need roots to satisfy his notion of her?"

"No. I didn't. I merely said we might be able to do so. I believe this decision is one we both need to make."

She took a deep breath relieved by his answer and proceeded to open the envelope. "What is all this?" She handed the papers over to Scott.

Scott perused the first legal form. "This is an affidavit. Elspeth D. Chapel is the person sworn in on the legal document as providing the information. Elspeth writes on this first sheet that having been the executor of Penelope Aarden's will and testament she is letting you know Penelope bequeathed the remainder of her fortune to Ava Moss." He paused to show her the document.

"Aarden, written with two a's." She stared at Scott. "My God. Says here, three and a half million dollars?" she breathed as she attempted to stop her hands from trembling. "How can this be possible?" She read on. "Mine to receive when I turn thirty-five."

"Not for a couple of years yet," he squeezed her against him. "Why not read the handwritten page at the back. Might make more sense."

She agreed to flip to the neatly written pages in bold square letters.

She mumbled through the first paragraph where Elspeth Chapel declared being of sound mind and that she obtained this information first hand as told by Penelope Aarden while Elspeth acted as her nurse, and confirmed to her when she became the executor of her will. "I knew these two were more than friends. Elspeth often appeared more effusive toward Penny than Penny was toward her which probably came from years of Penny accepting Elspeth as a subordinate—someone who worked for her."

She stared at Scott her eyes round with surprise. "Says here Penny is my actual grandmother, and my mother's name is Myriam. I can't believe I have a family." Ava took a deep breath and accepted Scott's offer of a tissue to wipe her tears. She stopped and glanced at Scott. "What Elspeth meant when she said I looked like Myriam."

"What else is on there?"

After a few more paragraphs Ava said, "Penelope was a famous concert pianist. Played all over the world. Myriam was the product of a one-night affair with a younger man who disappeared when Penny told him she was pregnant. She raised Myriam on her own, but later this put a crimp on her career, which stopped altogether when Myriam became a teenager. Elspeth writes that they fought all the time, and Myriam finally ran away from home with a young man making his way to California. Penelope heard from her two years later when she arrived on her doorstep with a baby." She eyed Scott and took deep breaths to stop the tears from flowing. "Me. Elspeth continues to say too much resentment in Penelope prevented her from hugging the daughter she missed so much, and rather than hear her mother's speech, Myriam left in a huff with the child." For the next few seconds, Ava remained silent picturing the drama unfolding in front of her eyes. She brushed away at tears to read more. "Penny regretted her comportment immediately and hired many detectives to try and find her daughter and her granddaughter, but to no avail."

Staring up at Scott, Ava asked. "Do you suppose this was when Myriam dropped me off at the Church?"

"Could well be."

"I wonder what happened to my mother."

"We'll find out—if you wish," he added.

Ava stirred. "A.M on my blanket—Aarden Myriam." She continued reading. "Letter says this was why Penny fainted in the subway when she faced me on the day we met. All the time we spent together, and she never told me."

"Most likely embarrassed about the way she treated your mother. Thought you might resent her, I suppose."

"Yeah, not to mention I recounted the awful ways some of the foster families treated me. I'm sure this did not prompt her to tell me the truth. Hey, the name Aarden. It's Dutch. Isn't it?

"Yes, I believe it might be." Scott smiled remembering her love of the Dutch language.

"I knew I had Dutch heritage. I took to the language with such ease." She put the papers down.

"Is that it?"

"More details about Elspeth's friendship with Penelope."

"We can be grateful Elspeth Chapel took the time and trouble to write this down. She must have guessed Penelope would not find the courage to tell you."

"You're right. She would have needed to write this letter after I met Penelope, and while her memories remained intact."

Scott picked up the letter from Ava's lap. "Elspeth writes she didn't agree with Penelope's decision not to let you know about the money until you turned thirty-five. Yet she still respected her wishes and left the information tucked away when Penelope died."

"She left me some money when she passed away—six years ago. Enough for the day to day running of this condo and I used the rest to put myself through college. I guess she feared I would pull a Myriam and follow some guy somewhere or blow the money unwisely."

"In her misguided ways, Penelope Aarden tried to protect you."

"Yes, she did. Except had I not needed to support myself with so many odd jobs, I would have received my diploma much earli-er." Ava lost her smile and worried aloud. "Does this mean I have to change my name?"

She heard him groan as he buried his head in her hair his lips traveling along the base of her neck. "No, silly. Ava Moss is the entity Elspeth mentions. Besides, Mary-Ann confirmed Laurence Harvey would be contacting you next week—you as in, Ava Moss. Therefore, you can keep your name—a lovely name. Although I would rather you take mine as well," he muttered. "Ava Moss Wallace." He pulled back to look into her eyes. "This ring finger's mine by the way," he breathed while caressing her hand.

She nodded. "Ava Moss Wallace. Suits me." Unable to endure being apart even by a few inches she clung to him her breath fanning his cheek as she ran her lips against the moistness of his clean-shaven face. She'd dreamt of a real home all her life never sure where she might find one. Who would have thought home would be on an island—in the little island of Scott's loving arms. The sweet, irresistible discovery filled her with anticipation. Nibbling his ear, a soft moan escaped her parted lips. "So, this is home."

Please be so kind:

If you enjoyed this book, please be helpful and leave a review.
Thank you for your diligence.
Reviews are very important to an author.
Also by the same author:

I Can See You (Emma Willis Book 1)

Mirror Deep

Exhale and Reboot, A Novel

Ava Moss, coming out in a couple of weeks.

The sequel to Emma Willis Book II (I Can Find You) should be
published soon.

Having you as a reader is the start of a beautiful friendship.